"Snappy and full of sass, Briana Kaleigh fields the punches in The Belvedere Club, the evocative debut by Nicola Trwst. A girl with attitude who you want on your side when it comes to murder. I loved it."

—*Cara Black, author of the Aimée Leduc Investigations, set in Paris.*

The Belvedere Club
By
Nicola Trwst

NgH Press
San Francisco, CA

The Belvedere Club
Copyright ©2012 by Nicola Trwst
All rights reserved

Discover more of Nicola Trwst's work at
www.nicolatrwst.com

Published May 2012 by NgH Press
978-0-9855208-1-6

Publisher's Note:
This is a work of fiction. Names, characters, businesses,
places, events and incidents are either the products of the
author's imagination or used in a fictitious manner. Any
resemblance to actual persons, living or dead, or actual
events is purely coincidental.

Many people are to thank for helping me bring *The Belvedere Club* to press.

For sharing their professional knowledge:
Marin County Coroner: Kenneth Holmes
Marin County Sheriff's Department: Sergeant Crain & Sergeant Fruy
Belvedere Police Department: Lylene Phillips & Ryan Smith
Dr. Charles Palmigiano

For sharing their critiques, ideas, and patience:
Margaret Lucke, Bette and J.J. Lamb, Shelley Singer, Judith Yamamoto, Diana Orgain,
Cynthia Greenberg, Vicki Dobbs Beck, Stanton Close, Jill Cagan, Frances Palmigiano & Katherine Forrest

Many Thanks to you all.

CONTENTS

The Date

I hadn't had sex in two years. But the winds of change were whipping around like a tornado on roller skates. I called him Jamie for the James P. Quinn printed on his business card. As I fumbled for my keys, his warm breath on my neck kicked my libido from recharge mode to fully operational. Now, if I could only get the blessed door open.

We both toiled for a daily out of Washington D.C., the *District Dispatch*. For the last year I had worked as a photojournalist for the *Dispatch* and before that as a crime reporter for the Metro Desk, but that's another story for another time.

I jangled the key ring. "Found them." *It wouldn't be long now.*

Jamie, the new Sports Desk editor, had bought me coffee twice within the last month. This generosity, I figured, was his way of guaranteeing an extra photographer whenever he needed one. Haylee Macklin, my best friend, colleague, and partner in numerous unmentionable crimes saw the situation differently. She thought Jamie's sandy hair, blue eyes, and soft jaw would mix well with my classic Celtic genes, creating highly photogenic offspring.

Jamie squeezed between me and the door, and then closer. His spicy smell, an enticing blend of nectars, drew me in. His embrace was sure. His lips, curious and playful, shattered any doubt about what was to come. I had never swooned, but two years was an awful long time.

When the second lock gave way, we stumbled over each other into the apartment, lip suction holding us together like Chinese handcuffs. My handbag crashed to the floor. I flung off my overcoat. We broke apart for Jamie to rip off his parka, and we were back in each other's arms, groping and breathing heavily.

"What's that noise?" he asked between nibbles.

All I heard was the snare drum beating of my heart, but I pushed back from his chest to see if I was missing something important. A low pulsing sound cut the room's darkness. A soft red light flashed. My answering machine. I had turned off my cell phone during the concert and had forgotten to turn it back on.

"Oh, I better check." I dropped my arms. "It might be the paper."

"They can wait," he said, pulling me back against him.

He tasted like the cigarette and coffee we'd shared at the concert hall. His lips tugged at me, but the beckoning machine held my concentration at bay. "Sorry." I broke away. "Let me get this. Afterwards, I'm all yours. Promise."

My fingers found a wall switch. Glaring light flooded the bare walls and Salvation Army sofa and ottoman. Jamie headed back to the door, and after withdrawing my keys and tossing them on the empty bookcase, he closed it and threw the top bolt. *Oh, yeah.*

A red number three lit the LED readout on the machine. Haylee's voice fired fast. "Briana, call me." Messages two and three were the same but with an added four-letter exclamation. I hit "Erase," and sauntered to the worn sofa where Jamie slouched, one foot slung across his knee.

"She probably wants me to research something. She can wait. How about you? Can I get you a drink? Coffee? Water? I don't have any alcohol." I wished I did. I really, really, wished I did. I wasn't sure that I'd ever had sex without floating on an alcoholic life preserver.

Two years. *You can do this...sober.*

Jamie crooked his index finger, summoning me. For an

instant, I thought of playing coy. *Yeah, right. Who was I fooling?*

The phone rang.

"No," Jamie said, giving my hand a gentle tug as my brain took over and I turned toward the sound.

Nice to be wanted. "No one but Haylee or the paper would call this late. Let me take care of her, then we can have some peace."

I grabbed the handset ready with a clever remark, but Haylee never gave me the chance.

"I need you out here now." Her voice squeezed passion into each monosyllable.

"Jamie's here and we were about to test your theory. When can I call you back?"

"Get rid of him. This can't wait."

"Let me repeat myself or is this a bad connection?" I hung up.

Before my hand left the phone, the second ring came. *Love that speed dial.*

"Hang up on me again and I'll have your cable cancelled."

I shuffled to where my back faced Jamie. "If you call back in another hour, I might not need cable anymore."

A burst of static came across the line, and then Haylee. "Hey sweetheart, I'm glad the glacier is thawing, but now is not the time. I need you out here, pronto."

I glanced over my shoulder at Jamie. I lowered my voice. "Okay, I'll forgo quality. Call back in thirty…no, twenty-five minutes."

"No can do, Madame de Pompadour."

Always with the comebacks. "Compassion, please. Back here, it's after eleven." Haylee was on the other side of the country where the sun still shone.

But curiosity pricked the base of my brain; I'd be lying to say otherwise. I was familiar with the series she was

working, had read her opening piece and some of the
material she'd sent back to have fact checked. When it came
to the old joke that said the world was tilted and all the fruits
and nuts rolled to California, Marin County was the pine nut,
the most expensive.

Ten days ago, Haylee had flown to Marin to write a series
on the Belvedere Club and its affluent membership. She'd
balked at the assignment, thought of it as a fluff piece, until
now.

"Bring plenty of film. We'll need visuals, proof. No one's
going to believe this without pictures," she said before
another blast of static came through the line.

Haylee was a scroll in an electronic-reader world. A
Luddite in a business that was becoming more and more
computer-centric.

I didn't use film. I had a digital Nikon, a detail I kept to
myself because Haylee was too idea-centric to care about the
technical process. "Hey ace, can you hear me? Check the
clock. I can't get a flight before morning. Besides, I have to
clear it with Terrance."

Terrance was our editor and my current nemesis. He'd
prefer to fire me, but I had too many contacts in too many
places so the best he'd managed was to demote me.

Jamie had uncrossed his legs and was sitting up, listening
like a pit bull on the offensive. Rebellion wrinkled his
forehead, but his bravado was looking a bit shaky. I half
hoped he would leap off the sofa, rip the phone away from
me, and toss it out the window. Afterwards we'd ride into the
moonlight, hand-in-hand.

"Terrance is a go and there's a redeye from National
leaving at twelve-ten with your name on the passenger list.
Get moving. I can hear you, you're not moving," Haylee
said.

I slumped against the side table. "The last time you did

this to me, I spent the night in lockup."

"We've never done a story like this. Trust me Briana, it's big. It's...Pulitzer."

Pulitzer? That was our code word. It didn't actually refer to winning the coveted prize (although one can hope). More likely, it was a story that would raise questions and cause chaos within the status quo. My favorite kind, and oddly, as rare as an honest newscaster.

Cradling the handset between my chin and shoulder, I unplugged my laptop and grabbed my camera bag all while jotting Haylee's instructions on an electric bill envelope. My flight would arrive at San Francisco Airport around three something in the morning. I was to take a taxi directly to the Belvedere Club in Marin County where she would meet me. She said I should bring a flash. *Ooooh, Haylee.*

I hung up and turned to Jamie, who was on his feet and headed towards me. Palms out, I threw my hands up in surrender. "Sorry. The job. You know how it is."

He wrapped his arms around my shoulders and the zipper of my dress started a cold path down my back. I ducked under his embrace and twisted away. "Now Ja—"

He slapped the top of his thighs, hard and loudly. A mixture of anger and frustration washed over his face. He was going to blow or pout, but I hadn't the time to talk him out of either.

"There's a plane at National. It's not the end of the... We'll hook up next week," I said, my eyes on him, but my thoughts already shifting through clothes in my closet. Skirt set, pant set, what kind of weather?

Reminding me of my four-year-old nephew throwing a tantrum, Jamie stomped across the room, his dull rubber heels thumping the worn hardwood. "Next week my wif—" He plucked his parka from the floor.

Electricity singed my veins. Now, he had my attention.

"You're married?"

He glanced down, fingering the collar of the coat. He pulled a thread and let it drift to the floor. "I, uh, I told you."

"Really? When exactly? Was it that time you joined me in the cafeteria and told me how you loved red-heads, or perhaps, when you asked me to go hear the jazz ensemble tonight? No, maybe you told Haylee, when you asked her if I was involved with anyone."

"Come on, I'm not married, married. I'm here, she's there. We have an understanding." He took a few steps in my direction, the parka's zipper dragging the floor. His pearly whites flashed through a killer smile and his lids drew down giving him that lazy, easy-going look that was hard to resist. Apparently, he thought that was all it took.

I clutched the answering machine, lifting it in the air. "Understand this, in about three seconds you're going to be picking this out of your teeth. One…two…"

The door slammed shut.

The Club

For ninety minutes, my plane sat on the tarmac at National while a snowstorm delayed our take off. I phoned Haylee to tell her the bad news, but reached her voicemail instead.

"Forgot to ask, should I bring a bathing suit? I'm delayed. Winter's making one last pass, but I'm told by a steward with a Cheshire smile that we'll be off the ground soon."

I used the time to pull up Haylee's initial article on my laptop.

The Club That Moxie Built
By Haylee Macklin, District Dispatch Staff Writer
March 25

MARIN, Ca—High above San Francisco Bay, with a magnificent panorama, The Belvedere Club holds court. This exclusive women's club makes Augusta National Golf Club look like a community center. That isn't to say men aren't allowed; plenty of men worked the kitchen.
Belvedere Island, once considered the summer playground of affluent San Franciscans, boasts some of the oldest and most expensive real estate in Marin County, the century-old club included. Designed by William Caldecott, the Belvedere Club's unique architecture was inspired by a popular comic book drawing. Caldecott adapted the design to the precipitous piece of land owned by Amanda Weathersby, creating the first modern architecture on the island. Mrs. Weathersby, San Francisco's famed philanthropist who single-handedly revived high society after the 1906

earthquake, ignored objections by homeowners who were less than pleased with her vision.

The Belvedere Club opened its doors May 10, 1904 to a membership of nineteen women. Mrs. Weathersby held the office of President. Their first order of business was to create the bylaws, which banned male memberships and created a policy for the female lineage.

Immediately, the Belvedere Club went to war with the newly created Homeowners Association, the Belvedere City Council, and many of the members' husbands who objected to the "women only" regulation. Back before women won the vote, before women won the right to their own bodies, these women won the right to assemble in a club of their own creation.

For over a hundred years the women of the Belvedere Club have been giving back to their community through the charities they support, the events they organize, and the politicians they believe in. All this, they have done without male membership, yet once again, the battle lines are drawn. Their bylaws are under attack from the Politically Correct movement that has pervaded our society. Groups within the state such as the National Organization for Women are pushing for legislation that would ban clubs from refusing membership based on sex.

"We're not worried," said Charlotte Warren, the Belvedere Club's acting president. "We're descendants of warriors." Many of the Belvedere Club's members mirror her sentiment.

We, in Washington, can only wait and see what California voters will do if such legislation reaches the ballot this November. Next week's column will visit inside the exclusive Belvedere Club and its current elite group of women.

The article included a black-and-white photo of the club,

shot from below emphasizing the word *Belvedere*—a rooftop pavilion, offering an excellent view. Built into a hillside, a huge compass window of ten tall panes jutted forward adding a wagon wheel effect to the otherwise rectangular building. The roof, a simple A-frame, looked tacked on like an afterthought, most likely an addition to the original design.

Nothing in the article hinted as to why Haylee needed a photographer or why she needed one tonight.

By two-twenty, we were airborne and by six-thirty, from the rear of a taxi, I watched the sun debut over the San Francisco Bay, one of the Seven Wonders of the World. The temperature was pushing seventy-five degrees and I was sweating like a wrestler in my cashmere overcoat.

Belvedere Island, attached to Tiburon by two two-lane roads, was blooming with crabapples and dogwoods, with emerald lawns and budding gardenia hedges. The dew-drenched flora surrounded me like a comforting embrace.

The scent of lavender and jasmine wafted through the taxi, sweet spring blossoms perfuming the dawn and leaving me about as peaceful as one can be without sex. *And I should know.*

Over the bay, the sun streaked its magic into gentle waves of turquoise and yellow-gold. Paradise. I realized that I was happy to be away from the city, the snow, and sports editors who needed their jockstraps tightened.

As if to rebel against my newly found tranquility, the taxi's engine downshifted into second, halting nature's music with a dull painful grind while jerking me forward in my seat. I couldn't wait to tell Haylee about Jamie's wife. She'd help me devise the perfect revenge. My schemes leaned toward the painful, but Haylee was more of a psychological warrior.

I dug into my camera case and pulled out a pack of Silva Thins. After placing one between my lips, I reached for my lighter.

The Asian driver wagged a bony index finger in my direction. "No smoking, not here." He pointed over my shoulder.

At first I didn't see anything, but when I leaned back, there, glued to the side window, were the words "No Smoking" in white letters. Transparent white on transparent glass, it might as well have been Braille. I threw the Silva and lighter back in my camera case.

"This California. No smoking in California," the driver said with a heavy accent.

"Outside."

"No. Not outside." He shook his finger at me again. "Not in California."

I didn't argue, but as far as I knew, the great outdoors had yet to be regulated (I would soon learn otherwise). Within a block, the scenery changed. The road grew steeper, darker, and the air more fragrant with an odor I remembered from childhood. Vicks Vaporub.

Towering, like giants from another galaxy, Eucalyptus trees bowed over us—their massive trunks stately, their fingerlike leaves fluttering—shutting off the morning light and sheltering extravagant homes behind high-gated drives. Every so often, an architectural marvel, hidden within the hillside, peeked into view.

At one time or another, Marin County had been home to some of the nation's most famous: Carlos Santana, Barbara Boxer, Robin Williams, Isabel Allende, and to some of the most infamous: John Walker Lindh, Charles Manson, and more recently, Scott Peterson. Here, multi-million dollar homes shared breathtaking views of the San Francisco skyline to the south, and to the north, the more sobering view of San Quentin prison.

Where the road peaked, the taxi pulled right into a narrow

parking lot overhanging a straight drop into the glassy bay below. The driver pointed left to the other side of the street and the asphalt drive that inclined up to the Belvedere Club. Two Sheriff's cars, green and white, blocked the entrance in an inverted "V" behind which, lining the drive, was a Belvedere police car, two black-and-white highway patrol cars, a Tiburon paramedics van, an ambulance, and a gray evidence van.

Oh no! I'd missed the action. Haylee, and subsequently, Terrance, were going to be furious. I might just get fired this time.

"Stop here," I said and threw four twenties over the front seat. I snatched my camera bag and knapsack and hit the pavement sprinting.

A female deputy, wearing dark green slacks and a taupe shirt with the Marin County insignia sewn on the left sleeve, snatched me by the elbow and swung me to a stop. "Where do you think you're going?"

I slammed my bags to the pavement, slung off the cashmere coat, and wrestled the camera strap over my head. My press pass was somewhere among the jumble, but I had no idea where and I was in no mood to search for it.

"I'm meeting Haylee Macklin. Where is she? She broke the story and she's waiting for me." I tore free from the woman's grasp, but as soon as I did, she clutched my other arm.

"I need to see Haylee. She'll tell you who I am."

"I'm afraid—" The deputy tightened her grip, bruising the muscle beneath, while waiting for me to stop struggling.

I held up a palm. "I'm good."

She released me. "Thanks," she said without the slightest sign of gratitude. "Now, I need a little more information. Your name again?"

Her inane calm was irritating. "Briana Kaleigh, *District*

Dispatch, Washington, D.C. Here to see Haylee Macklin, colleague."

She pointed at me with her left hand while removing a walky-talky from her belt with her right. "Let me call up and see if you have clearance."

"Of course, I do. I just flew three thousand—"

The pointed hand went rigid.

"Get Haylee, she'll tell you. And make it quick. Please." I reached for my camera, showing her I planned to obey.

She repeated my name into the walky-talky as I snapped her picture using the emergency vehicles as backdrop. Through the lens, I caught a shift in the deputy's demeanor. She stiffened and cut her gaze to me, listening to whoever was giving her orders. She stared at me without moving. Was Haylee putting her in her place for keeping me waiting? Good. Haylee wasn't afraid of anyone, least of all cops. She'd wrangled statements from the worst D.C. had to offer: politicians, police commissioners, lobbyists—lowdown scoundrels all.

The deputy nodded toward the club, "Okay, go on up."

I hoofed up the drive too fast and had to stop near the top to catch my breath. As I bent to wheeze in some oxygen, two attendants wheeled out a stretcher with a body bag on top. Nikon in hand, I zoomed the lens and started shooting. Never lose an opportunity. A body. The story had veered in a direction I'd never imagined. Haylee was good. Although most people dusted her off as another pretty face, she was amazing. She always found the story beneath the story. Her talents were wasted at the *Dispatch*; she deserved a bigger venue, a daily like the *Washington Post*.

Farther up, I shot several more photos of the front of the Belvedere Club. Until I knew what angle Haylee was writing from, she'd want me to record as much as possible.

The club certainly lived up to its namesake. The

foundation, or perhaps basement, was built into the hillside and painted a moss green to blend with surrounding shrubbery. A flagstone, jonquil-lined path snaked around to the right, leading to the main level's side entrance. This level stretched horizontally across the hillside, sporting the impressive compass window. A rectangular balcony for sunning or outdoor dining was built on the far side. Inside or out guaranteed a San Francisco Bay view. Gray stones covered the façade of the main level with plate-glass windows trimmed in red—Williamsburg Red as we call it on the East Coast. I've often wondered if the rest of the country called it Rotten Tomato Red.

A lot of love—and greenbacks—had gone into the design of the various gardens scattered down the hillside. By the entrance, bamboo palms and calla lilies in white and pink framed a terraced garden with tulips and butterfly bush. Filled with various police and medical personnel, the patch had abandoned its feminine charm to the testosterone-toting crowd. I scanned the group for Haylee, usually the center of such attention.

With each flagstone step I climbed, the masculine group drew together, forming a voluntary barrier across the entrance. The wisecracks and laughter died away, leaving me feeling as I was supposed to—like an outsider. I snapped a shot of the boys in uniform, which back East might have gotten me smacked, or at the very least, a beautiful exposure of someone's hand. But these guys struck a pose and smiled into the lens. In California, everyone's a star.

The tallest man broke from the others and hiked down the last remaining steps to greet me. Dressed in jeans and a Forty-Niners' tee shirt, he wore open-toed sandals with leather straps twisted around his ankles. His clean shaven scalp was beginning to re-sprout blond roots and a Glock was mounted on his right hip. Imagine my surprise when he introduced himself as Lieutenant Arkansas from the Marin County Sheriff's Office. Where I came from, sheriffs wore uniforms.

"You're the one with the *District Dispatch*?" He shifted the beige windbreaker draped over his right arm to his left and held out his hand. "Have we met before?"

We shook. "No, we haven't."

"You look very familiar. I'm sure I've seen you somewhere before."

"I get that all the time, it's the hair." I whipped a few copper strands over my shoulder. But if another person told me I look like Julianne Moore, I might have to shave my head as close as his. No one noticed that my hair was longer, almost to my waist.

"I know, you look like that actress, what's-her-name." He studied me like I was a rare blossom. "It's uncanny. Has anyone told you that before?"

"Not really. My nose is sharper and…" I pointed to my chin. "I have a dimple."

"She doesn't have a dimple?"

"Not that I know of." My butt was bigger too, but I saw no need to announce the obvious. "Can I go up? Haylee's waiting and she's one lady who doesn't like to wait."

Lieutenant Arkansas shuffled around, his gaze finding the entrance. Without answering, he headed for the side door. I trotted after him, hoping Haylee wasn't too pissed.

The other officers watched us approach, but something was off. This was all too easy. I'd never had an officer lead me into a crime scene; they were always so silly about forensic evidence. But hey, you know what they say about California. *Mellow Yellow.*

When we reached the doorway, the uniforms broke apart, clearing our way. All eyes were locked on me as if I were purple with four arms and six eyes. My fingers tightened around the Nikon—my security blanket.

Inside, the floors were polished rosewood. Sunlight, streaming in from the circular windows, made the floorboards shine. To the right was a coat check area, empty hangers evenly spaced against a cedar backdrop. To the left, a faux-marble painted wall partially blocked our view of the main room. Framed photographs hung on the wall, photographs of the Belvedere Club's past presidents, dating back to Mrs. Weathersby, the founder. All hard-jawed women with a striking resemblance except for the last one, Charlotte Warren, who was listed as acting president by a brass plate beneath her picture. Her face was puffy and round, but with the same piercing regard as the other women.

We continued along the wall until a sun-filled dining room opened to the left. Linen-clad tables circled a larger rectangular table, the focal point of the room. Between the larger table and where we stood were chalk markers delineating a human form. The body was gone, but a rust colored stain radiated from an area between the shoulders and head defining the upper torso. I'd seen such markers many times, even full outlines drawn on concrete, but something compelled me forward. I stopped at the stain.

From the width of the shoulders, I could tell the person had been slight, a woman or teenager. The height, somewhere between five-six and five-nine. About the same as...

I turned to the lieutenant. "Where's Haylee?"

For an instant, our eyes locked, during which time all sound ceased. He glanced downward.

I tried to swallow, but my throat, my whole body seemed to be collapsing in on itself. I dropped to my knees. My camera thudded against the floorboards. My hand reached for what would have been her head had she been before me, hovering over what would have been her corpse. "What happened?"

"The chef found her, this morning."

"I need to call Terrance," I heard myself say, but my mind was numb, my heart dead. "Has anyone…um…called her parents?"

"What are you doing?" Lieutenant Arkansas asked. "What are you doing!"

His shadow fell over me as I curled up inside the chalk markers and closed my eyes.

The Sheriff's Office

Funny, how the brain protects itself from implosion when it can't handle any more emotional pounding. One night while sleeping, my five-month-old daughter flew away with the angels and my brain shutdown for weeks.

So when I became aware that I was sitting in the Marin County Sheriff's Office, I wasn't surprised that I had no memory of getting here. I was like a barnyard chicken that gets decapitated and keeps on running.

The office was an ultra modern space clogged with built-in oak cubicles. The colors were earthy, the voice levels respectable, and my butt rested in an upholstered chair, not plastic, not wooden or the cold metallic most police stations offer, but a soft, comfy chair. As far as the eye could see, nothing looked government-issued or administrative except for the few uniforms that strolled passed. With government offices this nice, it was no surprise that California was bankrupt.

A clamping sensation in my left arm drew my gaze to a chubby, middle-aged man wearing a white lab coat. He stood over me, pumping a blood pressure cuff wrapped around my arm. Bowed, he held the cold end of a stethoscope to the crook of my arm, but I felt nothing because the cuff had cut off all circulation. I stared into the smooth sheen of his perspiring forehead and had the irrational desire to rip his head off. I'm not usually given to angry outbursts (okay, I'm Irish, outbursts are as normal to us as our daily constitutional), but I'm also a professional so, in silence, I gnawed down my irritation until well digested.

"She hasn't said a word since," Lieutenant Arkansas said.

"She'll be all right," the doc replied. "Shock, but she's in good physical condition." He removed the cuff and dropped it and the stethoscope into a dark medical bag.

"To be safe, should we take her over to the emergency room?" Arkansas asked.

"No," I said, perturbed that they were talking about me, but not to me.

Arkansas drew up next to the doc and both peered down at me as if I were alien wreckage. "Ms. Kaleigh?"

"Lieutenant Arkansas?" My voice sounded raw and flat.

His six-two stature squatted, knees popping like a crackling fire. He looked me straight in the eyes. "Call me Dusty. We brought you back here because you were walking on your own, but perhaps you should go to the emergency room."

Dusty. Arkansas. I started giggling. *Dusty Arkansas.* Absurd. I pictured the desolate Dust Bowl of the Depression and the man before me standing with the dry winds whipping around him. Was there a metaphor here? Then, I was laughing. Whether from nerves or emotional overload, it was as if I'd heard the funniest joke of my life. And I couldn't stop. My hand flew to my mouth in an effort to quell the silliness, but I couldn't stop. Heads popped up over dividers, coworkers stopped to stare and still, I couldn't stop. Several other chuckles joined in, building an awkward chorus. Not Dusty Arkansas. He stood, hanging over me like a gavel about to strike.

I tucked my chin and bit the tip of my tongue, an old trick I used whenever my editor launched into his diatribe on "honesty in reporting."

Straightening, Dusty glanced over his shoulder. "We've all heard it before," he said without humor.

With a smile twitching at his lips, the doc picked up his case and left me with the brunt of the reprimand. The deputies and office staff drifted back to what they'd been doing before my gigglefest, while beneath my hand, my cheeks felt wet. Suddenly, I no longer remembered why I'd been laughing, or why I had reason to be. I rolled forward over my knees, curling into myself, and let the tears flow.

During my freshman year at Boston University, Haylee had been my Big Sister, the title administration gave sophomores assigned to incoming female students. She was the most beautiful girl I'd ever seen. Five-eight, a choppy blond hairstyle, and polished Tickle Pink nails. She was everything I wasn't. Beautiful, sophisticated, and feminine in every way. Having been raised, along with six brothers, by an Irish cop, I might as well have been a boy for all anyone knew. Giving life to Mel, my youngest brother, my mother had hopped aboard a heaven-bound chariot, taking the secrets of womanhood with her. I grew up thinking tweezing was an IRA torture tactic and mascara was a Jewish appetizer.

At first, I tried to emulate Haylee in every way, but I was a poor study, my movements too awkward, my patience too expendable. But rather than be annoyed, Haylee picked up on my desire to learn the feminine mystique and volunteered to become my teacher. She taught me about clothes and how to dress my boyish figure, about waxing and lipstick, about nylons and nails, but mostly she taught me how to be a woman and to desire the respect a woman requires. The competitive tomboy in me learned that my femininity could be as strong and effective as the masculinity of the men I'd grown up trying to beat in everything from stickball to basketball to football. The games were different, the strategies, the same.

I switched from law to journalism because Haylee taught me how journalists made a difference. Later, she'd introduced me to Conor, my soon-to-be ex-husband. When I grew bored back in Massachusetts, photographing regattas for the *Plymouth Review*, she'd gotten me the journalist job with the *District Dispatch* in Washington. We shared enough history that a piece of me was lying beside her in the morgue, the piece missing from the gaping hole in my heart.

I pulled myself up and tipped my wet face to Dusty who looked like he wanted to be anywhere but next to a weeping female. "Do you need an identification?"

He uncrossed his arms, let them fall, and patted out a quick rhythm on his thighs. "We found plenty of ID photos in a leather handbag, driver's license, press pass, gym card. The body matches. Her mother's flying in and—" He checked his wristwatch. "She might be at the mortuary by now."

"Tell me what happened," I said, using my sleeve to dab at what I imaged to be runny mascara eyes.

"Ah, how about I get you something to drink or eat."

I stood and shook my head. "Tell me about Haylee, please."

He glanced over his shoulder as if he was expecting someone. "Let's move to my office."

* * *

We walked through a set of heavy wooden security doors which cut off the personal offices from the public ones. Back here, it was quieter and less populated. Each side of the corridor was lined with glass-fronted offices, the outer ones with exterior views allowing sunlight to filter in.

The contrast of natural wood and glass was quite soothing. "Nice place you have here."

"It's an architectural shrine; design by Frank Lloyd Wright."

"No kidding?"

"No kidding," he repeated without mirth

We stopped before an interior office and the lieutenant gestured for me to enter first. An eight-inch bronze Buddha, sitting on the desktop's edge, caught my eye. Several one and two-inch Buddhas sat around the base. Buddhas worshipping Buddha.

Lieutenant Arkansas took a seat behind the desk that split the room in half. I sat opposite. Behind him on the wall hung a framed, signed photo of the current Dalai Lama and a poster of a Buddhist temple filled with praying monks, the orange of their robes blending together like floor tiles.

He picked up a Bic pen and twirled it between his thumb and pinky. "Like I said, Ms. Macklin's death has been declared a homicide." He paused as if he'd forgotten something, or remembered something, or maybe had just changed his mind. He tapped the desktop twice with the pen, paused again, and then he continued. "The chef, Tony Amato, found the victim at about five-fifteen this morning when he went to the Belvedere Club to pick up the fish cooler. Today's Thursday, the members have a weekly luncheon. You sure you want to hear this?"

No. I nodded.

He hesitated, glancing at the Buddhas as if they might reassure him. "Her throat was cut." He looked back at me. "Several puncture wounds and lacerations on the forearms and hands suggest she put up a fight. Listen, your editor told me to give you the details, but you don't look so good."

"Please, go on."

"The coroner puts the ETD, ah, Estimated Time of Death, at around four a.m.. There was no rigor, I mean—"

"I know what rigor mortis is," I said. "Cut from left to right, right to left, from the back, from the front? How was her throat cut?"

He tapped the pen on the desktop, rhythmically, while studying me in a way that made me uncomfortable.

I looked at the Buddhas, the larger one's shiny eyes drawing a bead on me. Maybe I should cross myself and say a prayer to St. Michael for protection. "My dad was a cop. I work the crime beat for the *Dispatch*. I'm not a virgin."

His head tilted sideways and the corner of his lips curled. My fist tightened as I waited for an inappropriate remark. To his credit, he kept his mouth shut.

"Hyperbole," I said.

He continued. "The cut wasn't completely across the throat. It was from here to here." He motioned with his index finger to an area on the right side of his throat.

"The carotid artery. That's what I'd aim for. What about a weapon?"

"Nothing found at the scene. We'll know more after the autopsy." He checked his watch again.

His obvious discomfort made me think of something I didn't want to think about. "Was she…um, were there signs of…." I grabbed my hair, pulled it over my shoulder, and twisted it, searching for the words I wouldn't let myself imagine.

Dusty, a little slow on the draw, tapped his pen twice more and relieved me of my stuttering. "Oh, no. No evidence of sexual, ah, activity." He put the pen down and clasped his hands on the desktop. "What can you tell me about Ms. Macklin?"

"She's my best friend." My voice cracked, betraying my professionalism. My feet suddenly became the center of my world as I glanced down at the knapsack and camera case lying beside them. "Was…was my best friend."

"I'm sorry. What I meant, well, do you have any idea why she was at the Belvedere Club at that hour? I understand from Mr. Port that she was working on a story and she was excited about a new development." From his windbreaker he removed a small ringed notepad and flipped through a couple of pages.

I thought about my last conversation with Haylee and her reference to a Pulitzer. Her voice was still alive in my head.

"After her scathing exposé on men's golf clubs last year, she'd been assigned to do a series of stories on women's clubs around the country. The Belvedere Club was her first. Other than that, you'll have to ask Terrance. Ah, do you mind if I smoke?" I was already digging through my camera bag for my cigarettes.

"Not at all. Terrance is…?"

I shoved the Silva that I'd discarded in the cab between my lips and lit it. "Mr. Port. Our editor." I exhaled toward the ceiling, my shoulders so tense that the stretch sent pain shooting down my spine.

A younger man with a fresh face and a sweater vest stopped in the corridor, backed up three steps, and leaned into the office. "I'm sorry, but this is a nonsmoking building."

"Get lost, Evans."

"But Lieutenant—"

"Her best friend was just murdered," Dusty said and turned back to me. "Sorry. You said 'our editor,' I thought you were a photographer."

"Photojournalist. But I used to be an investigative reporter like Haylee."

His eyelids opened a little wider at this revelation. "Demoted?"

"Long story." My glance fell on the larger Buddha's bulging belly and the jeweled belly button.

"Give me the twitter version."

"Why?" But Terrance would tell him, relish doing so. "I'm not a suspect. I loved Haylee. I was on an airplane when she was killed." I reached into my coat pocket, pulled out my boarding pass stub and launched it across the desk. "Check for yourself."

He ignored the stub. "Why did she need a photographer?"

"If I had known it was going to be our last conversation,

you can bet I would have asked her." I picked at my nails, flaking polish into my lap. "Sorry. She was in a hurry...that much I remember."

"Okay." He drew in a breath. "After the autopsy, I'll speak with her mother. Next, I'll head over to her hotel room to go through her notes, her computer. Maybe you could help me understand the way she worked."

"For one thing, she didn't have a computer."

He looked at me as if I were speaking Cantonese. "How did she write her stories?"

"Long hand, then faxed them to the office, and some assistant typed them in. That's how she worked on the road. At the office, she had a computer, but she never traveled with one."

His gaze locked on me. Did he think I was lying?

"A BlackBerry, an iPhone, a tablet of some kind?" he asked.

The thought of Haylee using an iPhone brought a smile to my lips. "She was a people person, Lieutenant, anti-tech. Did you find her notebook?"

"All we found was her handbag with wallet, cell phone, and the keys to her rental car."

"Haylee didn't go anywhere without a notebook. She's more likely to forget her handbag and has on a few occasions."

"What does this notebook look like?" he asked.

"The covers are always glossy stock and usually with a reproduction of a well-known painting." I closed my eyes, trying to bring to mind the evening she'd packed. She'd been ranting about how demeaning her assignment was, that because she'd broken a story in her series on men's clubs, Terrance automatically assumed there was a story to be found in women's clubs. "Women aren't that stupid," she'd said.

"I believe the most recent one had a burgundy background and a winged angel on the cover, that's it." I opened my eyes. "That's the one she took with her. I remember now. Deep red cover, winged angel."

"Bound or spiral?"

"Bound. She only used bound. She wanted the notes to be there years later."

"Hope they were acid free," he said, no longer looking at me, but through me and probably back to the crime scene. His stare was frozen in time.

I, too, pictured the crime scene, what little I remembered, the flowers, the gardens…. How had she gotten inside? "Were the doors normally locked?"

"Yes. No signs of forced entry. Was it possible…" He pointed the pen at me. "Do you know…could Ms. Macklin have entered on her own?"

Sometimes in the newspaper business we didn't play by the rules. It's a small detail often overlooked by the law enforcement community because it's a way for us to help them obtain evidence they legally wouldn't have access to.

"Depends on the lock." I'd taught Haylee a few breaking-and-entering tricks that I learned from the boys in the old neighborhood back in Boston, but she'd never mastered anything other than simple warded locks. For everything else, she depended on me.

Lieutenant Arkansas, Dusty, checked his watch again, this time more discreetly. "I need to go over to the mortuary for the autopsy. How about I have someone drive you back to the Belvedere Club and you take a look at the locks. Afterward, I'll meet you at the hotel where she was staying and we can look through her belongings together. Who knows, maybe the notebook is there." He didn't wait for my answer, but lifted the phone receiver. "Hey, Dusty here. I need a green and white with a deputy for an hour? Great, send her up."

I stubbed my cigarette against the side of his metal trashcan. I let the butt fall inside. My emotional holiday was over. Haylee was truly gone. The adventures of the Scary Marys—Haylee's name for us, referencing the Holy Mother—had come to an end. It felt surreal, impossible at best. Haylee was the strong one, the survivor. Everyone knew that. I was only along for the ride.

I pulled a fresh cigarette from the pack. "I need coffee. Isn't this the land of Starbucks?" I said.

"This is the land of Peet's, Starbucks' predecessor. And you better hold off on that cigarette until you get outside."

A female deputy wearing a uniform the color of a grass stain entered the office and introduced herself as Wilson. Her eyes went straight to the bronze Buddha and her eyebrows arched as if she were looking at the devil. My kind of people.

"Deputy Wilson, can you get Ms. Kaleigh some coffee, and afterwards drive her down to the Belvedere Club. I want her to look at the outside locks. Don't go inside." The sternness with which he delivered the last phrase was clear. He was afraid I would freak again.

The Ladies

Deputy Wilson turned the patrol car into the drive of the Belvedere Club. The incline, now empty of the emergency vehicles that had blocked it just hours ago, held only one other car, a black limousine. Its suit-clad driver leaned against the hood reading a paperback.

Deputy Wilson parked ridiculously close to the limousine's rear bumper, her posture stiff with aggression. The driver looked up from his book, but didn't budge. I grabbed my camera case and hopped out. I wanted to get a look around without the deputy in my way and with any luck, her irritation with the driver would distract her awhile. As I climbed the flagstone path, her short, staccato questions fired at the man faster than he could reply.

"Look, I'm just doing my job," the driver said, sounding annoyed.

In the terraced garden near the Belvedere Club's entrance, mingled among tulips and calla lilies, another flower show of spring dresses was in bloom—organza on parade. I counted five, no six, women clustered together clucking. Setting down my camera case, I raised my Nikon and started shooting.

The double shots in my Caffè Americano had kicked my brain back into gear and my earlier blackout was a distant memory. Whoever invented espresso shots deserved a Nobel Prize.

As I neared, the group of women—all wearing hats that would draw envy from British royalty—enfolded me, devouring me like fresh grain.

"Oh look, the press," said the woman wearing the

sunflower-yellow chiffon dress. A full plumage of yellow and orange rested on her head.

I snapped a shot.

"And the cops!" exclaimed another woman in a rose lace tube dress. Her hat was a pillbox with a set of spikes fanning out of the rear.

I snapped a shot.

"This is so exciting," yellow woman said, crowding me. "And what paper are you with?"

"The *Chronicle*, I hope," said another voice.

"Want our picture?" asked someone behind me.

Without waiting for my reply they drew together and posted broad smiles. What else could I do? I snapped the shot.

"Now who are you?" I asked. I grabbed my camera bag from the ground and searched for my old notebook. I still carried it, but used it mostly for photography notes like where, when, and what exposure.

Yellow lady stepped up first. Her perfume reminded me of my grandmother. She was shorter than I and probably somewhere in her late seventies. Despite a frail appearance, she spoke in an excitable tone. "Odilia Keith. That's O-D-I-L-I-A Keith. Want me to spell Keith?"

"I got it." I sketched a quick facsimile of the feathered hat so I'd remember which one she was once I downloaded the images.

The tall thin woman wearing rose limped in slightly behind Odilia Keith. She swung her left hip forward, propelling her as she walked. Hip degeneration.

"I'm Penny Tabor," she said. "T-A-B-O-R." Her accent was English, but not London, more coastal.

"Penelope," Odilia Keith said.

"Oh, of course, Penelope; Penny for short. That's P-E-N-E-L-O-P-E."

The others joined us, all saying their names at once. I coughed on a sugary cloud of perfume and longed for breathable air or at the very least, a cigarette to cut the sweetness.

"Ladies, please, one at a time," Odilia Keith said. "Gloria, you go next."

As I sketched the green floral crest of Gloria's wide-brimmed raffia hat, Deputy Wilson burst into the circle.

"What's going on here?"

Odilia Keith squealed. "The fuzz!"

Everyone started talking at once. Deputy Wilson pulled a whistle from her pocket and blew. The ladies' gloved hands flew up and over their ears.

Deputy Wilson pointed to the red crime scene tape across the entrance door. "As you can see, this is a designated crime scene. The Belvedere Club is closed until further notice."

I wanted to set myself apart from Deputy Wilson. I might need to interview these women again. "I'm afraid your Thursday get-together is cancelled," I said in a friendlier tone.

"Of course the luncheon is cancelled," Penny said. She leaned towards her good hip. "We received emails this morning. We've just come 'round to catch a glance. Perhaps you could tell us what happened?"

They drew closer still.

"A woman was killed," Deputy Wilson said. "If you have any information regarding this crime you need to contact the Marin County Sheriff's Department. Anyone have anything they want to tell me?"

Like a confession.

The hats bobbed as the ladies looked from one to the other. The silence was broken when a flock of sparrows took flight from trees overhead.

"Okay folks, let's clear out," Deputy Wilson said, "and

whoever's with the limo, get it out of the drive. This is a crime scene." And to me, "Have you done what you came here to do?"

I pointed to the door. "I'll get right to it."

Like a breath strip, the group's enthusiasm dissolved. A huff. A complaint. Another complaint. Yellow clad Odilia Keith, the smallest of the group and obviously the pack leader, raised a gloved hand in the air and said, "On to the city, girls."

The gaggle started down the hill, holding their hats in place as they shuffled. I wondered how Penny Tabor's hip could handle the steep incline, but she kept up. I took a few steps toward the entrance, and turned and shot one last photo of the ladies on their descent.

The door had a disk tumbler lock. I was pretty sure Haylee couldn't have opened it; for one thing she didn't have the right tools. I wondered if one of the reasons she'd sent for me was to get her inside. Perhaps something beyond this door held a clue to her death. One way to find out.

Kneeling, I reached inside my camera case, pulled out my pick kit, and went to work.

"What are you doing?" Deputy Wilson asked, leaning over me, blocking my light.

"Checking the lock like Dus… ah, like Lieutenant Arkansas said." Calling him Dusty didn't feel right, especially not to his subordinate.

"You don't go inside."

"I won't, but would you mind looking around the building and checking if there are any other doors I should see?"

"Don't go inside!"

"I won't. Geez."

I inserted the tension wrench and applied a little torque to the plug, but had trouble getting the tumblers to bind. I inserted a rake pick, wiggling it in and out. Once all the tumblers were trapped, I turned the plug and the lock clicked. I stood and pulled the door open.

The compass windows allowed enough daylight to illuminate the room beyond, but the entrance—where I stood with crime scene tape blocking my path—was dark and ominous. Death has an odor. I'd only smelt it a few times, but I recognized it now. I wanted to enter, to step across the threshold, but my feet held their ground. I needed to look around, to search for clues as to why Haylee would enter without waiting for me to arrive.

"Don't you go in," Deputy Wilson said, pulling up behind me.

"Any other doors?"

"There's another one around the side and toward the back."

"Probably the kitchen." I closed the door and jiggled the tumblers back into locked position. "Let's go."

The door at the rear was indeed the kitchen door and had a pin tumbler lock. Haylee couldn't have opened this one either. I could barely open that type except with a pick gun, but mine had been stolen by my soon-to-be ex-husband. "I've seen everything I need to." I didn't need to try the lock because if I came back alone, I'd enter by the entrance door.

As we headed back to the car, the Easter Parade was still in session at the bottom of the hill. The higher voices drifted upward. A margarita-colored silk skirt ruffled on a light breeze. Sun played through the sheerer cloth.

"I have another question for the ladies," I said, and rushed down the drive before Deputy Wilson could stop me.

"Oh, hello again," Odilia Keith called as I approached. The yellow and orange feathers in her hat fluttered on a puff of air. "Would you like more pictures?" The women shuffled together ready to pose.

"I'm good with the visuals, but I have a few questions if

you wouldn't mind?"

"Shoot," Odilia said and laughed. "Isn't that what you say in the business, *shoot*?"

Barely a hundred pounds and chock full of spunk. I directed my first question to her. "Where can I find a list of your members?"

"We're all on the website," she said.

"The Belvedere Club has a website?" I said, wondering why I didn't already know that.

"Of course. We might look old, but we aren't dinosaurs."

"Why?" Penny Tabor asked, her rose pillbox hat askew on her flat mud-colored hair. "You think one of us killed that poor woman? Are we suspects?"

Like earlier, they spread around me as if to attack. "No, not at all. I hope to speak with everyone who might have come in contact with Hay—I mean, Ms. Macklin, the journalist. Did anyone have a problem with her interviewing style or with the story she was writing?" It was a long shot, but it would keep me from having to interview them individually later.

"Francine," Odilia Keith said, her lips pursed.

"Oh yes." Penny nodded, her hands propped on her hips.

"Francine," the others repeated, hats bobbing in agreement. All speaking at once, they offered up bits of information.

I raised my hand as if they were school children. "Whoa. Quiet."

The voices died down and I continued, "Thanks. Now, who is Francine?"

"Francine Starling. She's a trouble maker," Penny said.

"Always wants to change this and that. Never happy," said the woman in the orange floral print whose name escaped me.

"And she had an argument with that reporter," Odilia

added.

"Haylee? She argued with Haylee? When was this?"

"At the luncheon," said Gloria.

"What luncheon?"

"A week ago. We meet every Thursday," Odilia said.

"What was the argument about?"

"Oh, who knows," Odilia said, tipping a lace-gloved hand in my direction. "Francine's always arguing with someone."

"We don't pay her much mind anymore," Penny added.

I jotted "Francine Starling" in my notebook, while the ladies yammered on. "Anyone else have a problem with Haylee, or the article?"

"What about Tony?" Penny said, shifting to her bad hip and massaging it at the same time.

"Oh yes, he's Sicilian," Gloria said, her gray eyes twinkling beneath the broad green brim of her hat.

Odilia Keith nodded. "That's right, our little Tony is Sicilian. You know the Mafia began in Sicily."

Mafia? "Who's Tony?"

"He's our chef," Penny said, a hint of pride laced with the words.

I remembered Dusty had said the chef had found Haylee. "Tony what?"

"Amato. A-M-A-T-O," Odilia said.

I wrote Tony Amato's name beneath Francine Starling's. "Great. Anyone else?"

They looked from one to another to see who had more gossip. Penny's hand shot from her bad hip into the air. "There's Stevie. He's been to prison. Maybe he killed her."

Prison. I tightened the grip on my pen. "Who's Stevie?"

Penny limped closer, her tone turning conspiratorial. "He lives across the street from me, lives with his mother. She's an invalid. He was in jail."

"How did he know Haylee?"

"Not sure he did, but he's a criminal," she said.

With the back of her hand, Odilia slapped Penny's arm. "Just because he's a criminal doesn't mean he killed anyone. He didn't even know the vic." Odilia winked at me for confirmation. "Vic is short for victim, right?" And back at Penny. "The guy wouldn't kill someone he didn't know."

I crossed Stevie off my list. Two names: Francine Starling and Tony Amato. A good start. I jammed my notebook into my camera case and headed back up the drive toward the idling patrol car. Behind me Odilia and Penny were still arguing about Stevie.

"Plenty of people kill people they don't know," Penny said. "Haven't you heard the term psychopath?"

Deputy Wilson was tapping the steering wheel when I slid into the passenger seat. As she pulled away, I noticed that the limo was gone.

The Dog

Marin Suites in Corte Madera sat smack dab between the sheriff's office to the north in San Rafael and the Belvedere Club, to the south. Deputy Wilson dropped me off and I claimed the reservation that Haylee had made, although technically, I didn't need one any more because my job was done.

Lieutenant Arkansas, Dusty, had left a message with the desk. (The only cop I'd ever called by his first name was my dad's partner, Bucky. Come to think of it, that probably wasn't his first name.)

The message said the autopsy was still in progress and he'd meet me at one p.m. rather than eleven, as we'd planned. I asked the desk clerk which room was Haylee's, but the little New Delhian wouldn't tell me. Probably the Sheriff's Office had already alerted management and asked that the room not be disturbed. I knew the rules. I wouldn't disturb anything, but I had to get a look at Haylee's room before the deputies hauled off her belongings.

My suite contained a cozy sitting room with a sofa and two matching chairs. To the left of the sitting room, a kitchen stretched lengthwise complete with the essentials: fridge, stove, microwave, and coffeemaker. A dining area separated the two rooms with a round table and four chairs. Straight back from the doorway and through the sitting room was the bathroom. To the left, behind the kitchen wall, the bedroom wrapped around a king size bed. The curtains, upholstery, and paintings were all bright greens, yellows, and oranges with a tropical isle motif. Any second I expected to smell pineapples ripening.

After tossing my knapsack on the bed next to my camera case, I grabbed the phone to call Terrance.

"Where are you?" he asked without a hello.

"You should know, you sent me."

"California? What are you doing there? Get on a plane and get back here. There's no more story out there."

"Uh, Haylee's dead. Murdered." The words scraped across my tongue like a lie in the confessional. "You don't think that's a story?"

"Not for us. Who on Capitol Hill cares about a dead reporter in California?"

"For one, I do!" I threw the handset across the bed.

Luckily for him, he was three thousand miles away because I was having fantasies about choking him until his slimy tongue turned purple and jumping up and down on his antique writing desk until it was reduced to kindling.

Terrance's voice carried across the room. "Briana…Briana."

I wanted to scream, I wanted to punch something, preferably Terrance, but instead I flopped over the mattress and picked up the handset.

"Get back here or I'll fire your ass," he said.

It occurred to me that I could start an email rumor that he had crabs. "Speaking of asses, your sympathy's choking me up here."

"Yeah, sympathy. Sorry. I know you two were close," he said. "It's those lamo cops out there keep calling, asking for this and that. Can't get a dang thing done around here with the phone ringing off the hook. Now, they want me to send Haylee's computer out there. Sent Rod out looking for a box and haven't seen him since. He's probably lost on the beltway again."

He drew in one of those nasal breaths which sounded like someone sucking the chrome off a bumper. "Listen, you're a good reporter. Come on back, I'll give you your old job back. That should cheer you up."

"Buckets. And, I'm a great reporter. Problem is, without Haylee, there's nothing for me to come back to. I'm staying until they find out who killed her and why. If you're nice to me and I mean really, really nice, Terrance, I might give you the story before I sell it to the *San Francisco Chronicle*." I disconnected.

Let him gnaw on that. He'd already lost one good reporter; how would the execs take to his losing a second? With both of us gone, there was no one left to handle the formidable crime scene in D.C.. How long could the *Dispatch* survive on political reporting alone?

Thing was, I had no idea what I was thinking. All I wanted to do was keep my brain engaged so it wouldn't stop on the one fact I did know: Haylee was gone.

Three years ago when my daughter Siobhan died of SIDS, it was as if my insides had been smashed to pulp from a three-hundred-foot freefall. I broke down. The doctors called my mental holiday a psychotic break. I called it hell on earth. But Haylee was there for me. Every day. She carried me back to the land of the living, but my emotional health took much longer to heal. By the time my soon-to-be ex-husband Conor walked out, I was so deep into the bottle I barely noticed his absence. Everyone had given up on me, everyone but Haylee.

I kicked off my sling backs and dumped the contents of my knapsack on the bed. I was wearing one of the two pairs of pants I'd brought. Otherwise, there was a U2 tee shirt for sleeping and a Donna Karan skirt and jacket set, which I carried to the closet and hung up. I hadn't planned to be here more than a day; I'd packed for two. Maybe it wouldn't be much longer than that. I'd forgotten to ask if Dusty had a suspect. I assumed he would have told me, but I had to stop assuming. From what I'd already seen, things were done differently out here.

Digging through lenses and filters, I found my notebook at the bottom of my camera bag. I flipped through the pages until I found the one where I'd scribbled Haylee's room number. I'd called her once and had a vague recollection that it was two-ten, but before I broke into some stranger's room I wanted to be sure. Two-ten.

The suites, which opened onto a rectangular courtyard, still sported old-fashioned Schlage Single Cylinder Deadbolts. Any decent hotel on the East Coast would never offer such a burglar friendly system. My apartment door back home had three different lock types. But out here, locks were like curtains, mostly decorative, because as I walked along the balcony, jasmine scenting the air, I noticed that most suites had the kitchen and sitting room windows wide open. Anyone with half a mind could pop a screen and enter with little noise and even less trouble. *Good-bye laptop.*

When I reached two-ten, I checked the doorknob. Someone from D.C. wouldn't leave a door unlocked. Sure enough, it was locked, and the windows closed tightly.

For the work I was about to do, I had a special handbag of black cotton that could be rolled into a small pouch and stored inside a normal leather handbag. In use, like now, it hung over one shoulder and across my chest where the bag part rested on my stomach. When I leaned forward to slip the picks into the lock, I appeared to passersby to be digging through my handbag for the key. My youngest brother Mel had taught me this trick using a backpack. He'd become a low-grade burglar during his rebellious teen years. Now, he was an accountant.

I slipped the feeler pick into the opening and checked the tumblers. Five. Not even a challenge. I slipped in the shim and felt tumbler after tumbler align. With a little added pressure I sensed rather than heard the succinct click of success. Trying the handle again, I was rewarded. But as soon as I stepped inside, I knew the room wasn't Haylee's. For one thing it was neat. Haylee could make mincemeat out of a hotel room faster than she could boot a computer. For another thing, the suitcase on the sofa before me was a masculine brown. Not Haylee's color.

I closed the door and crossed to the balcony rail. Below, two boys splashed around in the courtyard pool, their voices reverberating upward. A woman wearing a sea-foam green bikini stretched out on a chaise lounge. She had the figure of someone who shouldn't wear bikinis. At the other end of the patio, a colorful beach towel lay draped over a plastic chair and a couple of paperbacks were stacked on a side table. I wanted to scream, "It's March!" What was wrong with these people? Okay, it wasn't snowing, but seventy-four was hardly a heat wave.

Defeat weighted my shoulders, splaying me down against the rail. I propped my chin on my stacked hands. Bad weather, dirty air, and security were what I knew best. What was I doing in this land of perpetual sunshine where everyone was friendly and accommodating? Accommodating, but slow. In the time it took the desk clerk to check me in, an East Coast equivalent would have checked in four people and taken a coffee break. Must be the heat. Heat slowed people down. But it wasn't hot! I bet if I looked really hard, I'd see goose bumps on Miss Bikini mom. But I was obsessing, something I tended to do when I didn't want to focus on the problem at hand.

Had the police already confiscated Haylee's belongings and the hotel re-rented the room? No, Dusty said he was coming over after the autopsy. Next option. She'd changed rooms. She sometimes did that if she didn't want someone to find her. Did that mean she had known that she was in danger? Haylee? I turned back and scanned the row of rooms. Much to my dismay, there was something else Haylee never traveled without.

I licked my lips twice to get ample air flow. Clapping my hands to the beat, I began to whistle *Mary Had a Little Lamb*. Feeling (and surely looking) like the village idiot, I approached the rooms, moseying and whistling past the row of doors. At the end of the balcony, I turned right and continued along another row, whistling and clapping, my bag bouncing against my stomach. Reaching the end of that balcony, I again turned right until I was directly across from two-ten. Here, I hit pay dirt. To be sure, I stopped clapping, but kept whistling. A high-pitched bark followed by a faint scraping noise reached my ears.

The barking came from one of two doors side by side. By flattening my left palm against the door at the left, I tried to feel the vibration of eager paws. I rested my right palm on the other door and whistled one more chorus. A slight movement in the door to the left. I tried the knob. Locked.

"Fifi?"

The door vibrated. How many dogs went haywire to the tune of *Mary Had a Little Lamb*? It must be Fifi, Haylee's toy poodle. Haylee had feared that someone might dognap her prized mutt so she'd taught the dog the trick to help her find Fifi should some crazed soul ever succeed in snatching her. A starving refugee wouldn't steal this dog. Skinny and high-strung, Fifi was like a coke whore in a bad mood. Anyone would rather step on her than steal her.

I've had nightmares about the anguish Haylee would suffer at the creature's demise. And to my regret, I had long ago promised Haylee, with a crossed heart and a Girl Scout salute, to take care of her treasure should anything happen. Would putting Fifi in a trash compacter fulfill my obligation?

I reached into the handbag and dug for the pick and shim. The second lock went much faster since I knew what I was dealing with. I opened the door. The white fur ball lunged, raising up on her tiny hind legs and placing her front paws on my slacks. Our normal relationship was one of mutual distain—Fifi avoided me and I spit on her. This physical contact was new, leaving me a little unsettled. I lifted her into my arms like I'd seen Haylee do many times before. The lump returned to my throat.

"Stupid dog, look what you've done."

Fifi ran her tongue across my chin. *Yuk.*

There was only one reason for such behavior. I carried her through the dark and stuffy sitting room to the kitchen. A bowl of water sat below the refrigerator next to an empty food bowl. "Need a bite, do you?"

I put her down and she promptly tried to jump back into my arms. "Wait a minute." I picked up the food bowl and opened the refrigerator. A single can of dog food sat on the second shelf of the otherwise empty interior. I filled the bowl, adding a little extra for comfort, and set it on the floor. Fifi sniffed at the food and looked up at me longingly.

"What?" Did she sense something was wrong? Did she miss Haylee? The chocolate eyes bore into me.

"Eat!"

I shoved open the curtains.

A kaleidoscope of light caught in her rhinestone collar and shot around the room. Fifi whined. A dark, crusty path ran from each tiny eye down the pristine white fur along both sides of her muzzle making her look as if she'd been crying all morning.

"Okay. Here's the deal. Haylee's gone. It's you and me, kid. Get used to it. And no more of that licky-licky crap, got it?"

I fled, returning to the sitting area. Fifi didn't follow.

I inched toward the bedroom where it looked as if Haylee's suitcase had exploded. Clothes lay on the dresser, the floor, the bedside lamp. I peeked into the empty dresser drawers and rummaged through the pockets of her suitcase. No notebook. In the bathroom, towels draped the toilet seat. I checked her makeup case, which was now empty, its contents strewn across the counter. Knowing it was fruitless but needing to be thorough, I examined the shelves beneath the sink.

I saved the sitting room for last, clued in by the three rows of yellow Post-It®s stuck to the island painting hanging behind the sofa. This was where she had worked. I checked under and around the sofa and chair cushions, but I'd been right from the beginning—she'd taken the notebook with her. Next, I went to the Post-It®s. Starting in the bottom right-hand corner and moving left, I tore them off and stacked one on top of the other until I had the lot in the order of Haylee's working mind. Dusty would have a fit, but it was the only advantage I had and maybe a bargaining chip for the future.

Right about that time, there was shuffling on the concrete outside the door. I stuffed the Post-It®s into my back pocket. The word "unlocked" registered just as the suite door flew open. Framed in the doorway were the New Delhian desk clerk and Lieutenant Arkansas.

The Mess

Dusty stepped into the room. "What are you—"

Dog nails clicked-clacked across the Linoleum as Fifi rushed around the refrigerator and scampered towards the open doorway. Barking wildly and with teeth bared, she lunged for Dusty's leg. He jumped back, reached into his hip holster, and pulled the Glock free with his right hand.

"Don't shoot!" I leaped and scooped Fifi into my arms.

"What the hell is it!"

Fifi kept barking, high-pitched and incessant, while wrestling against my grip. "Haylee was a beautiful woman and a first rate reporter, but like everyone, she had her faults. Meet Fifi."

"No dogs allowed," the desk clerk said, wagging a finger.

"Named after Fifi Brindacier. It's French."

Dusty holstered his gun. He gestured to the desk clerk. "You can leave us, thanks."

"No dogs allowed," the desk clerk said, more forcefully.

"Better known in English as Pippi Longstocking," I said. "It means string of steel."

"Yeah, more like string of yarn, soon to be a yo-yo if it comes after me again." Dusty waved the New Delhian away. "I'll take care of this. Thank. You."

The clerk stopped outside, his gaze locked on Fifi. Dusty turned back to me. "No dogs allowed."

"Dog? What dog? Close the door so I can let this sewer slug out of my arms."

"If it tries to bite me again, I'll shoot it." He closed the door. "How did you get in?"

"It was unlocked."

"Of course, why did I bother asking? The clerk told me someone, who looked a lot like you, asked which room Haylee was in. You didn't know which room to break into?"

Fifi stood between us, her little head bobbing to one and the other.

"I heard Fifi barking. I knew she'd be hungry. I checked the handle; it was open. Management must have come in because Haylee would never leave the door open."

"Management? Then why didn't *management* know about that thing?" He nodded to Fifi. "Open your handbag." He slipped his hand under the strap of the bag slung across my chest.

"I didn't take anything. All I did was feed the dog, and you showed up, pistol blazing."

"Got it. That's your story and you're sticking with it. Now, open your bag."

I pulled the black bag over my head and let him take it. As he fished through it, I used the diversion to make sure the Post-It®s were tucked down flat in my back pocket.

He pulled out my leather pick case and held it in the air. "Unlocked, huh." He dropped it back in and rummaged around until he found the pick and shim.

He held up one. "What's this?"

"A homemade shim."

Satisfied, he tossed me the bag.

Fifi leaped to the sofa and curled in a ball ready to ignore us. Dusty surveyed the suite. He walked past me and peered into the bedroom. "You do this?"

"What?"

"Someone searched the place."

Really? What had he seen that I'd missed? I joined him. "How can you tell?"

He gestured with an open palm. "Just look," he said.

The misunderstanding registered. "No. This mess is

standard Haylee."

He cut his eyes my way.

I plucked a sweater from the carpet and draped it across a chair. "She's a believer in the chaos theory."

"Not sure I've heard that one."

"From chaos comes order. Plus, she pays housekeeping to stay out and overlook Fifi."

He glanced at the poodle as if weighing what I'd said. He had a natural scowl that made it hard to read his thoughts.

He entered the bedroom and began slamming drawers. "We need to look for the notebook. I spoke with Evidence. It definitely wasn't with her at the Belvedere Club."

Not being a patient person, a second fruitless search was too painful to endure. I returned to the main room and sat with Fifi on the sofa. I thought of caressing her white fur, but chose to pick at my nail polish instead.

After the bedroom, Dusty moved on, naturally, to the bathroom.

"It's not in there either," I said and bit my lower lip.

Arkansas looked my way. A flash of anger disappeared behind another expression that didn't look good.

"I spoke to your editor. He said you used to be a pretty decent investigative reporter."

"A great reporter," I said. "Terrance confuses his adjectives."

"What have you found?"

"You first."

He opened the counter below the sink and looked in. "Still waiting."

"Come on, I'll tell you everything, I promise. Work with me. Tell me about the autopsy."

Ignoring me, Dusty lifted the towels one at a time using the tip of his pen.

I sprung off the sofa. "It's not here! I've checked

everywhere, the bedroom, the bathroom, and under the cushions in here. Haylee was waiting for me at the Belvedere Club. She was about to break a story. The notebook was with her. Look, I knew her better than anyone. I knew how she worked, how she thought. You and me—we want the same thing here. Let me help."

He straightened and stepped over to meet me. He stood so close that the rose-scented soap on his skin made me want to gag. More than half a foot taller, he was intimidating. I hunched my shoulders while waiting for him to either punch me or yell at me. Instead, he took a step away and clasped his hands together over his chest. I looked up to see if he was praying. He wasn't.

"Perhaps you've heard of 'Tampering with Evidence' or better yet, 'Hampering a Police Investigation?' This *is* a police investigation. I don't give a damn about your story—"

"My story?"

He held up a hand and continued in a monotone voice that was just a little scary. "You will tell me what I want to know, or I'll lock you up for any number of infractions. I am investigating a homicide." He sidestepped me and walked into the kitchen area.

Okay, my "helpful" strategy hadn't worked. But, I had others. I scurried after him. "This isn't about a story. I want justice. For Haylee. She was my best friend. Look, I'm a cop's kid. I won't get in your way. I know the rules. With any luck I can recreate her investigation of the Belvedere Club and stumble onto whatever it was that got her killed."

He faced the sitting room, his gaze locked on the island painting. "What can you do that I can't?" He walked towards the painting, stopping before the sofa.

"I told you. I knew Haylee. She was very good at goading people. A pro. She could push a lie until she got the truth."

He leaned across the sofa and ran his index finger over the

painting. "Something was stuck here. Stand by the table."

I shuffled over to where he'd been standing and sure enough, the sun's reflection outlined the position of each Post-It® I'd removed. All three rows and six columns. I swallowed hard.

Fifi jumped off the sofa and ran to the door, scratching it with her paw. "She needs a pee-pee break. That's the signal." I looked around for her leash. It was balled up on the dining table. "I guess I'll keep her with me, or do you plan to interrogate her?"

"Take her and all of her stuff. I don't want you in this room again. Do you understand? I'll arrest you in a heartbeat." He turned back to the painting.

The Mother

I caught up with Haylee's parents at the Civic Center. Down the hall from the Sheriff's office, I clung to her mom while her tears soaked my shoulder. Nadine Macklin was the kind of mother we all want but very few are blessed with. At five-foot-four and a head of graying blond curls she could wrap her sturdy arms around you and make you feel safe, even from yourself. This time it was my arms around her, trying to give back some of the comfort she'd given me over the years.

"My baby," she sobbed. "My poor baby. Did you see what they did to my girl?"

When Nadine had learned that I'd grown up motherless, she took me on a shopping spree, teaching me how to measure my breasts and turn the number into a bra size, teaching me what bras to wear with which clothes, teaching me when to add cleavage and when not. It sounds silly, but at the time my little more than boy-size breast had gone braless because I hadn't a clue of such things. When I was sixteen, my father had dumped a box on my bed and told me I might need some of the things inside. My mother's affinity was for white lace, most of which had yellowed by the time I had a glimpse. And let's say her breast size, after so many children, was a bit more generous than the Lord had seen fit to bestow on the Kaleigh's only daughter.

I'd stapled one of her lacy brassieres tightly around my chest, but the empty cups, angling out from my armpits, crumpled under the weight of my sweatshirt making a lumpy, distorted mess. That was my first and final attempt at wearing a bra until I met Nadine Macklin.

"My Haylee," she cried. "My little princess." Her voice bounced, the corridor distorting her words into gibberish.

Her Irish brogue thickened when she was upset. Haylee had loved to imitate her mother's accent almost as much as she liked a good joke. *Jasus, handhum over ere.* When she was on a roll, we'd laugh for hours.

"Did you see what they did to my girl?" Nadine's hands trembled. She wasn't focusing anywhere in particular, but kept her eyes in constant motion as if she didn't trust her surroundings.

I swallowed the lump constricting my throat. "Can I get you some coffee? Something to eat?"

Nadine was allowed to fall apart, but I had to hang on because Haylee expected me to. There comes a point in every child's life when she learns that her parents are only human. My parents died before I experienced that lesson, but on every level I was experiencing it now and my heart was ripping apart. I was the adult, leading Nadine to a row of plastic chairs and lowering her down.

Mr. Macklin trailed behind on a cell phone, arranging with United Airlines for the return of Haylee's body once the Sheriff's Department released it. His eyes were red rimmed, but his voice, strong. Irish men weren't afraid of tears; their pain was their devotion to life.

"We tried to stop the autopsy, but they wouldn't listen. I can't bear them slicing my baby up, her soul seeping out."

I didn't state the obvious: Haylee had already been cut up by someone other than the coroner.

"Who would have done something like this?" Nadine shook her fist. "Ooooo, the world's a wicked place. She was such a pretty girl. Everyone liked her. Didn't everyone like her? That nice boy Micky wanted to marry her. Why didn't she marry Micky and give me lots of grandbabies? I want my grandbabies." She dropped her head into her hands, her body rocking with her sobs.

Micky was Haylee's high school sweetheart and so opposite that their marriage wouldn't have lasted forty minutes, although technically, long enough to make a grandbaby. That wasn't the life Haylee had wanted. A good looking guy, Micky was popular, which afforded Haylee a certain prestige. Don't get me wrong, she'd liked him well enough to struggle with her emotions, but he had no ambition, no goals, while Haylee dreamed of traveling the world, of doing something important with her life. Early on, her ambitions mystified her working class parents. Haylee had always planned to give her mama grandbabies, but later, after she was established in journalistic circles.

"That's settled," Mr. Macklin said as he stuffed the phone into his shirt pocket. He sat beside his wife and patted her hand.

I didn't know what to say to comfort him, so I remained silent hoping to convey my sentiments telepathically.

He gestured with two fingers as if to say he understood, and then spoke to his wife. "Sheriff says they'll need our girl another couple of days, maybe a week." Stretching his arm around Nadine, he gave her a gentle squeeze, comforting himself at the same time. "Briana, if you're still around I'd appreciate it if you would keep an eye out. Make sure Haylee gets to the airline."

What did he think she'd do—oversleep?

"Of course she'll be around," Nadine said, turning her tear streaked red nose from her husband to me. "You will, won't you?"

"Terrance wants me back in D.C.," I said, softly.

"Nooooo." The pitch of her distress was so high, I took a step back. Nadine hopped up, grabbing both my hands in hers and squeezing.

"You must stay!" She leaped in the air, taking my hands

with her. "You're the only one I trust." She crouched down and peered over my shoulder back towards the Sheriff's Department. She lowered her voice and leaned closer. "He has idols on his desk."

She crossed herself with the sign of the Trinity. "You must find out who did this. Make it your quest." She squeezed my hands and leaped again. "Promise. Promise me. Haylee's depending on you. This is a quest for Haylee."

Closing my eyes, I nodded. "Sure, I'll do what I can."

"I knew we could count on you, but you promise me one thing—you'll work with the police, you won't do this on your own. Haylee'll be looking out for you, but I couldn't bear losing you, too. There's evil here. You stay safe, promise." She patted me on the shoulder before whipping me into an embrace that jarred my teeth. "We're heading back to the airport now. I want to get back to Boston, feel the need to see Jeffrey and the boys. Take care of my girl. I'll see you back in Boston."

Jeffrey was their son and his wife had given birth to twins a few months ago. Haylee was their godmother. Her last remark must have referred to the funeral, because I had no other plans to return to Boston. Like me, they weren't quite ready to use terms with such finality, terms like funeral.

"I'll wait to hear from you," Nadine said as they turned and walked hand-in-hand down the corridor. Midway, she turned back and mouthed the words, *your quest.*

Quest of Celtic legend denoted a spiritual need, or goal. Whether real or imaginary, romantic or adventurous, a quest was always thought of as heroic. Haylee's mom was asking me for a heroic ending, commanding me really, to give value to Haylee's death. As a journalist, I knew most death was senseless. I'd seen a man die over something as stupid as a soccer bet. Nadine hadn't meant to imply that the lieutenant wouldn't find Haylee's killer, but that he couldn't reward

Haylee for her sacrifice. A bunch of falderal, but it meant something to me.

But what was I thinking? I was in the land of liberals and Deadheads, same sex marriages and tree sitters. How was I going to solve a homicide without knowing anyone, without connections, and without particularly warming to the lead investigator?

A great sadness enveloped me. Haylee's death would affect me in ways I had yet to imagine. To stop the threatening waterworks, I thought about my promise—my quest. It was a relief really, because I couldn't go back without looking Haylee's killer in the eye. My soul couldn't rest until hers did.

The Trail

After a fretful night of little sleep and much tossing, I was waiting in Dusty's office when he arrived the following morning. I'd stopped at Peet's Coffee and bought him a Caffè Latte. Nothing a hard working lieutenant liked more than good coffee. I was finishing my third.

"To what do I owe the pleasure?" Dusty asked, wearing an expression of displeasure as he walked around his desk.

"To whom. Madge Talis, your press officer. You know her, she writes your press releases, interfaces with the public, P.R., stuff like that. She said it would be all right for me to ride along with you while I write my article on the high conviction rate of the Marin County Sheriff's Department."

"High?" He dropped the fax he'd been reading on his desk and picked up the coffee, smelled it, and put it down. "Thanks, but I don't do caffeine."

Was he kidding? Or insulting me? The group of fat seated Buddhas at the end of the desk eyed me with contempt. On the brighter side, it was more for me. I tossed my empty cup in the trash and reached for his latte.

"What do you wash your donuts down with? Prayer?" I tore my gaze from the tormenting statues. "This is the first homicide in three years and the two before that were successfully solved. You don't think that's high? Your press officer does," I said without waiting for an answer. The fact that I was talking extremely fast hadn't eluded me. Two morning lattes were my norm, but I'd ordered the third in an attempt to fight off the symptoms of jet-lag. Four might just kill me. I pried the cup from my lips. "Where are we on the autopsy? Have you confirmed the ETA?"

Dusty closed his eyes and ran the tips of his fingers from his crown down to his heart. With eyes still closed he spoke. "There's no 'we,' you are not investigating this homicide." His eyes flickered open. "I don't know how things work in D.C., but out here, the police investigate crimes, not reporters." He'd lost the Jesus sandals and jeans and was wearing a pair of dark slacks and a yellow short-sleeved golf shirt. He appeared taller, more imposing. In the right light, some women might call him handsome.

I'd had a rough night, trying not to think about Haylee. Whenever I settled down and tried to sleep, favored images and haunting promises awakened my not too stable emotions. In the end, I'd thrown on my tennis shoes and a pair of slacks, tied back my hair, and set out on a run, figuring if I kept moving, my sadness wouldn't have time to catch up.

Around two a.m., a patrol car pulled up beside me and the deputy asked me who I was running from. When I informed him I was out for a jog he told me that although Corte Madera was fairly safe, it was never safe for a woman out running alone in the middle of the night. I agreed that no one was safe now that Paris Hilton was out of prison and mumbled something about insomnia. He suggested Hops and Valerian. I had no idea if this was a comedy team or a local rock band, but concurred that it sounded like a plan.

I set my coffee cup on the desk and tapped my newly painted fingernails. "On my side, I've reconstructed the first part of Haylee's research on the Belvedere Club. It's mostly about Mrs. Weathersby, the founder of the lineage."

Actually, I'd stuck Haylee's Post-It®s on my bedroom mirror and read through them about a hundred and fifty times, hoping something might pop out. Tony Amato's name was there and so was Francine Starling as were half a dozen other names. "I've printed a list of the Belvedere Club's active members from the website and I've started a list of the club's employees. Who have you already interviewed?"

Dusty slid deeper into his chair, and then leaned back, creaking the springs. Wheels turned in his strange brain, I could almost hear the clicking of the spokes. He crossed his arms over his broad chest and glared at me. He had to know I was a good source. Reporters, in general, were good sources because we understood the investigative process, and I knew almost everything there was to know about the victim. If I could ever get Fifi to talk, I'd know everything.

"You really want to do this to yourself? What kind of masochist are you? She was your best friend."

"To start with, I'm the kind that wants justice for those I love. And if I can help in any way, shape, or form, it's my duty to do so." I was propelled forward probably from too much synthetic energy, boiling below the surface. "Besides my father, my brother, Garret, is a cop too, with the Boston PD. Call him, he'll tell you I'm not a nut." Actually, I had no idea what Garret would say about me because we'd fallen out of touch after I had married Conor.

Time seemed to freeze between us. I had more arguments, but was having trouble organizing my thoughts as they raced through my skull at the speed of light. Tapping his fingertips together, Dusty let out a sigh that seemed to go on forever. Finally, he opened his top drawer and pulled out a file folder, dropping it on the desk between us.

"My only two deputies are busy interviewing the Belvedere Club's members—yes, I have my own list. I'll let you help and we'll call it a ride along, but the moment you get in the way, or I feel you're more trouble than you're worth, you're out. Questions?"

Haylee's file. It had been in the desk the whole time I'd been waiting for him to arrive. I'd like to say I hadn't thought about searching his office, but in truth, the only thing that had stopped me was the sergeant in the opposite office. I reached for the file.

Dusty's hand came down hard on top of it. "You sure?"

I nodded.

"First, you never told me about the locks," he said.

I wasn't sure if he was referring to my picks or Haylee's room. He must have seen my confusion because he clarified himself.

"The locks on the Belvedere Club's doors, could Haylee have opened them?"

"Oh. No. The front one isn't too complicated, but both the front and rear locks were above Haylee's expertise. Someone let her in or the door was open."

He lifted his hand for an instant and then dropped it back on the folder. "As a rule the Belvedere Club is kept locked. They had some break-ins during the late eighties and since have kept it locked up."

"Then they should invest in better locks."

"What should I read into to that?"

"One woman's opinion." It was time that I shut up if I hoped to get back inside the Belvedere Club, but my vocal cords seemed to be running on automatic. "So we can assume that the killer had access to a key—a member or an employee," I said.

"Or a husband, child, or employee of a member. Only one Belvedere Club employee had a key—the chef—and he isn't married. All active members have keys." He opened the folder and added the fax from his desk. "The analysis on the painting behind the sofa in her room reveals glue. Do you know what she might have glued up there?"

Now was my moment to come clean, but we were getting along so nicely. "Who says it was Haylee? Maybe it was a previous occupant."

Dusty removed a photo from the folder. "These are as graphic as it gets."

My hand stopped midair as I realized what I was about to see. "Do you have a loop or magnifying glass?" I asked. He was right, I couldn't look at those photos and hope to maintain objectivity, but I'd long ago learned that if I looked at photos with a photographer's eye—I could look at anything. I'd shot lots of crime scenes, and one extremely gruesome bloodbath in a downtown bar, and I'd never had a problem as long as I was looking through the viewfinder.

Dusty reopened the drawer and pulled out a fifteen-x loop and slid it toward me. When he passed the photo, I laid it flat on the desktop and without looking, maneuvered my hand over the face. I placed the loop on the incisions and scanned the photograph for information. It wasn't Haylee, because I wasn't looking for the things that made her Haylee. I was looking at a victim what defined the crime: the wounds, their angles, and any visual details such as her clothing.

"Cause of death?"

He handed me another photo. "Asphyxiation."

"Official terms, please."

He lifted a yellow form and read from it. "Respiratory failure due to aspiration of blood."

I flinched. She'd drowned in her own blood. "Okay, she was stabbed. Stabbing requires getting close to the victim. We can deduce that it was someone she knew, maybe even planned to meet. The jab-slash pattern hints at personal anger—again, someone she knew. Yesterday you mentioned defensive wounds, anything under the nails?"

"You sure you aren't a cop?"

"My father and his partner used to do this as a parlor game. They weren't detectives, but they helped solve a number of cases for the Boston P.D. just by brainstorming."

"There was a green—forest green—fuzzy cloth under one nail. It didn't match any of the clothes we collected from her room. Of course, someone may have lifted something before we got there."

I glanced up and wasn't surprised to find him smirking. "Forest, no, I can't think of anything. The only green I remember her wearing was more an olive and it wasn't fuzzy, it was silk. Her nails? Haylee was manic about her nails. Were they broken?"

He flipped through the coroner's report. "Most were."

That was oddly reassuring. "She put up a good fight."

"Your turn," he said. "What else have you come across in your reconstruction of the victim's research?"

"Haylee, her name is Haylee."

He jammed the coroner's report back in the file. "I don't use names. For me, it's not personal, it's a job. You better understand that if you plan to hang around."

He was right, of course. It couldn't be personal for me either if I hoped to get through the investigation. I'd been denying my grief for the last twenty-four hours. The sensation was something akin to being chased by the four horsemen of the apocalypse.

I unfolded the list I'd printed of the Belvedere Club members' names. "This I found interesting. The acting president, Charlotte Warren and another woman, Annette Vaughan, are the only unmarried members. All the others are listed as their husbands' wives: Mrs. Percy Keith, Mrs. Lawrence Tabor, Mrs. Olivier Starling."

"Women's lib hasn't hit the society set—big deal. Why's there a check by Mrs. Gary Larkin?" he asked.

"Oh right. Haylee once dated a Gary Larkin, but I looked up Mrs. Larkin's photo and she's in her fifties."

"This is Marin County—everyone's had work. Add another five to seven years. Maybe the parents?"

"This guy didn't come from money." What I couldn't say was that his name wasn't among Haylee's Post-It®s. "He was a chauffeur for the White House. Haylee dated him during her stint as a political reporter. He would supply her with the dirt on who was doing what to whom and for how much."

"I'll look into it."

"I guess you've already interviewed the chef, the man who found her," I said.

"Tony Amato, he didn't have much to say at the crime scene." Dusty gathered the photos and shoved them in the file. "Of the Belvedere Club members that we've interviewed, none spoke with the victim outside the luncheon she was invited to attend. Also Amato inventoried the kitchen, no missing knives."

"Premeditation?"

"Looks that way. The weapon, a smooth edged knife with a four-inch blade, was carried to the scene. We've been unable to locate any of the kitchen staff. I was headed over to talk to Amato again this morning."

I almost lurched out of the chair. "Can I go?"

"You should lay off the caffeine." He rose. "I was going to invite you, on one condition."

"Anything."

He laid his hands flat on the desk and leaned towards me. "You're there as an observer. Ob-ser-ver, don't speak."

I made a zipping motion across my lips and grabbed my camera bag.

The Chef

Dusty's car was an unmarked black Sentra, parked between two green and white patrol cars.

"Where's your car?" he asked.

I pointed to the rented white Saturn parked at the end of the lot.

"No camera. Put your camera in your car."

"But—"

"No camera."

I huffed. And he pointed.

I did as commanded, but then felt naked sliding into the passenger seat of Dusty's car. Even as a print journalist, I'd always carried my camera. I believed in *a picture is worth a thousand words* theory not to mention photos made great evidence. How did he expect me to function without my engine?

While we drove through San Rafael, down two-laned, tree-lined streets, Dusty was silent. In my mind, I rifled through different conversational subjects, but found I wasn't much in the mood to talk either.

"I think I need another latte," I said.

"Are you kidding, you're so wired I could recharge my cell phone on you." He glanced across me and out the passenger window. "Besides, we're almost there."

We crossed a busy four-lane road into a more industrial section of town lined with warehouses, a Molly Maid, several transmission repair shops, a Patio World, a few car rental companies, and lots of body shops. Quite a different Marin County from the lush rolling hills and opulent homes I'd become accustomed too.

Dusty parallel-parked in front of a three-story, clapboard building with two Mexican children playing cards on the front steps. They took one look at the Nissan and disappeared into the building.

"Do we look like truant officers?" I asked. Curtains wavered on the third floor as I stepped from the car. Dusty caught the movement and looked over at me.

"Remember—"

"—I know, you chief, me, observer."

The patter of little feet echoed on the floors above us as we entered the building. The interior was dark and dank, the double glass doors offering the only light source. There was an acidic odor I couldn't identify and wasn't sure I wanted to. Paint peeled from the walls in strips and I thought about lead poisoning, one of my last stories before my demotion. Several of the mailbox doors were broken and hanging loose, a few listed names in black scrawl, most were blank. Linoleum tiles, marked with age, buckled and peeled away from a concrete foundation. At the rear of the hallway, directly in front of us, was a set of wooden stairs. Tony Amato's apartment was to the left of the staircase.

When Dusty knocked, Tony opened the door quickly as if he'd been expecting us. Maybe Dusty had called ahead. I preferred surprise visits myself. A person's composure or lack thereof goes a long way to defining character, but obviously Lieutenant Arkansas didn't see Tony as a suspect. I did. I saw everyone as a suspect especially the person who finds the body.

"Prego, prego," Tony said, gesturing wildly with a chubby hand. He was a short man with a taste-tester's belly, which wasn't camouflaged under a dirty white tee shirt. A doughnut of black hair circled his head and his eyebrows were thick enough to scrub his pots and pans.

His apartment looked like it had been decorated by his

grandmother. The style was reminiscent of the early sixties when mass production outweighed aesthetics or comfort. The few pieces of decent furniture were scratched and worn past their prime. A couple of family portraits adorned the walls, but without adding any symmetry to the room. Porcelain figurines of the Virgin Mary dotted the bookshelves which held everything from a broken toaster to a stack of National Geographic magazines, everything except books. A leather-bound Bible lay on a side table, its surface heavily ringed with moisture stains.

"Sit, sit," he said, motioning us to an orange plaid sofa covered with a protective plastic sheet. "What can I help you with? I've already told you all I know."

His Sicilian accent was slight, but he wore the same charming smile characteristic of every Sicilian man I'd ever met. I didn't trust him for a minute.

"I've tried to locate several of the kitchen staff to verify what you told us about the knives, but every address you've given me is either a business or non existent," Dusty said.

Tony didn't seem surprised. "Mexicans," he said, puffing. "Illegals. You know how it goes."

"I don't know how it goes," I said, forgetting my vow of silence, but Dusty didn't seem to notice as Tony informed me that unbeknownst to him, he must have hired illegal immigrants. He repeatedly assured Dusty that he'd called their contact information, his head bobbing with emphasis.

"But not their addresses?" I asked.

"I don't go to their houses. Why would I go to their houses? How would I know they lied?" He emphasized each word with hand gestures and the digits were flying as he again assured Dusty that he thought they were legal. There was no mention of work permits.

"You told the officers that you'd seen Ms. Macklin before," Dusty said.

"That is correct, yes, at the club."

"How often?"

"Once she came to see Mrs. Warren. Another time she spoke with the kitchen staff." Tony chuckled. "She talked to the men, you know, try to make them angry. She asked them if they felt…um." His hands flew into the air as if to pull his words from space. "You know…that they weren't allowed in the dining room."

"Discriminated against?" Dusty asked.

Tony nodded. "Yes, discriminated, that's the word."

"Did anybody talk to her?"

"No, nobody. That was the last time I saw her. Well, before the morning, you know."

"About that," I cut in. "Haylee's body was in the front room and I thought the room was off limits to men."

"Off limits, no. No." He shook his head. "Only when the ladies are there."

Dusty understood where I was going and continued. "How did you come across the body? Where do you keep your fish cooler?"

"The cooler? In the storage behind the kitchen. I parked in the front and went around back to get the cooler. When I go back to my car, I see the front door open. I go in and that's when I find…well…you know."

The smell of spicy beef wafted through the apartment from an open window. My stomach growled as Dusty continued with the questions.

"And you didn't see anyone else?"

Amato shook his head. "No one."

"What about the owner, Charlotte Warren, how often does she come to the Belvedere Club?" Dusty asked.

"Mrs. Warren, she come on Thursday. Always Thursday."

"So when did Ms. Macklin speak with Ms. Warren?"

"Thursday. Last Thursday. We have sea bass. I remember

because the young one came to the kitchen and told me how good it was." He rubbed his fingers and thumb together like he was grounding herbs.

"Was that the same day she spoke with the kitchen staff?"

"No, no. That was…Tuesday. Grocery day."

Dusty closed his notepad and stuck it in his breast pocket. We stood to leave, but I remembered one of the Post-It®s with Tony Amato's address. "Did Haylee ever come here?"

Tony shook his head. "Here? No. Never." He reached for the door handle and shrugged. "Why? No. Never." He flashed his Sicilian smile.

As we walked to the car, I thought about what Tony had said about the immigrants. "Does this mean you'll never find anyone else who worked in the kitchen?"

"Probably not," Dusty replied.

"Convenient for Tony, isn't it? No one to verify his information. I would think that makes him a top suspect."

Dusty slid behind the wheel. "Why's that?"

"No one to verify that he found Haylee. Maybe he killed her, cleaned the knife, and called the police. Maybe the murder weapon is still sitting in the Belvedere Club's kitchen."

My suspicion of Tony came from one of Haylee's notes. Written under Tony's name was the word "Dirty." That might mean anything from Health Code violations to making obscene overtures and now, to hiring illegals. Underneath "Dirty" though was Tony's address, which I verified on the outside of the building. If Haylee hadn't been here, why did she have his address? Of course, I couldn't share this information with Dusty unless I was ready to share everything. And I wasn't.

Dusty started the car. "Forensics went over the kitchen knives. I don't read Tony as the type who'd want a lot of police attention. He's already guilty of hiring illegals. If he was a murderer, he'd be hiding out up north with the rest of his staff, not helping the police."

"Aren't there laws against hiring illegal immigrants? Aren't you going to charge him with something?"

"California has about three million illegals. If we didn't hire them we wouldn't have any restaurants, malls, or repair shops. Marin County is so filthy rich, it's hard to find anyone willing to do manual labor. For our own sake, we turn a blind eye."

"That's ridiculous."

"Welcome to the Bay Area. I know teachers who can't afford to live near where they teach so they're forced into a two hour commute each way."

"What about you? You're a government employee," I said. "Do you commute?"

"That I am and I live on a boat, no rent, low utilities, it's the only way I can afford to live around here. Most of my colleagues live up north."

" 'Up north. Up north?' Does this place have a name?" Irritability strained my voice. The four lattes had worn off, leaving me in a slump worse than any jetlag.

"Well, there's 'up north' and '*up north.*' The first refers to the northern part of Marin County like Novato, or a little further like Petaluma in lower Sonoma County. The second refers to the wine country, Napa, Sonoma or even a little east like Sacramento. That's where we'll find Mr. Amato's staff. Traditionally, when the local Mexicans want to disappear, they go up to the wineries and work for a while. In return, when they want to disappear from up there, they head this way. It's an evolved network, very efficient. It keeps the INS ignorant, law enforcement in a tizzy, and the economy rolling along like a steamboat."

And allowed Tony Amato anonymity. I ran through the Post-It®s in my mind and wondered who I would interview next if given a choice. "Have you spoken with the Belvedere Club's president—Charlotte Warren?"

Dusty shot me a glance of pure annoyance. "Acting president. I have an appointment after lunch and no, to your next question."

"Come on. Observer. Promise." I held up three fingers of the Girl Scout pledge.

He didn't answer right away. My previous attempts at begging hadn't borne fruit so I leaned my head back on the headrest and fell asleep.

The Mansion

Charlotte Warren lived in Belvedere on Beach Road up the hill and around a bend from the Belvedere Club. Painted orange sherbet with whipped cream white trim, the house resembled a giant birthday cake. The fixtures were shiny gold and three chimneys topped with white chimney pots poked out of the terra cotta roof like candles. The good news was that the other houses on the block, at least those not hidden behind walls of shrubbery or monogrammed gates, were nowhere near as garish.

Like most of the houses on the island it offered heart-pounding views of San Francisco Bay. Dusty informed me it was one of the original homes built at the turn of the century when San Franciscans used the bayside town as a weekend retreat. He also said that he didn't remember it being orange.

Charlotte greeted us at the door and led us into a sitting room lined with fluffy, bulbous curtains. The room was an antique dealer's paradise with an eclectic mix of European styles—the light feminine flourishes of France and the heavy bold carvings of Spain. And, as antique shops often do, the interior smelled of death and of those who have gone before us.

As Charlotte offered us a seat, I wondered about servants. A house this size couldn't function without servants. No sooner had the thought popped in my mind when a short Spanish woman appeared in a maid's black dress complete with starched white apron, attire I thought existed only in porn movies. She set a tray of tea cups on a gilded Louis XIV coffee table.

Charlotte dismissed the woman and took charge of the

teapot. "May I offer you some tea? White tea, the Chinese tea for royalty."

Charlotte was taller than I, but nowhere near Dusty's height. She wore heavy pancake makeup like actors use to create their iconoclastic looks. In her case, I wondered if she was covering some type of scarring, childhood acne perhaps. Her hands were covered in beige cotton gloves. Over the gloves she wore several rings, a sapphire the size of an ice skating rink on her left ring finger. Between the makeup and gloves it was impossible to guess her age. I assumed Haylee had had the same problem because several Post-It®s listed the lineage from Belvedere Club's founder, Mrs. Weathersby, down through Charlotte's brother's birth, but not one for Charlotte. Charlotte's name had been jotted as if an afterthought at the bottom of her brother's Post-It®.

Dusty introduced me as Haylee's friend and Charlotte's face clouded with genuine concern.

"My dear, I am sorry about Ms. Macklin. This whole affair has upset me so much I haven't slept a wink since. I feel responsible. I even called my no-good brother to see if we should compensate the family in some way." Her dark eyes clouded with tears. "I only met her once, but she was such a lovely woman…beautiful skin. Such a shame." She dabbed the corner of her eye with a cloth napkin from the tray. "I'm sorry Lieutenant. I know you have your questions." She paused again and dabbed her other eye. "I'm sorry." She took a deep breath, the sapphire finger draping her chest. "I didn't think it would be this hard."

She turned back to me. "I would like to call her family. I understand she wasn't married, perhaps her mother. Do you think it would be all right?"

Her sincerity threatened to take me to an emotional place I wasn't ready to go to. She had a soft maternal look that reminded me of Haylee's mom. I wanted to curl into her arms so we might comfort each other. Instead, without meeting her gaze, I answered, "I think Mrs. Macklin would appreciate that."

She handed us teacups, using the moment to gain control of herself.

I said a prayer to Saint Francis de Sales, the patron saint of journalists, for his continued guard over my own emotions until my quest was done.

The White Tea wasn't white, but a foggy khaki color with a light, slightly sweet taste. Not herbal. Fresh. Dusty probably loved it, but I preferred more of a punch. A cigarette would probably improve the flavor, but Dusty's lecture at lunch about lung cancer and the risk of secondhand smoke warned me off from even asking. Taking another sip, I leaned back on the Queen Anne sofa and let Dusty do his thing. Charlotte smiled graciously while answering his questions, most were about her interview with Haylee. He came to the subject of her brother, which interested me for another reason.

"You mentioned a brother?" Dusty said.

"Charles. My twin."

"Twins?" The word popped out of my mouth.

"He's the older. Six minutes. Never lets me forget it."

That answered the question of the Post-It®—the same birth date. Because he was older, Haylee had listed his name at the top of a shared square.

Dusty put down his tea and retrieved his notepad. "Where does he live?"

"Over in Ross. Mother left me the Belvedere Club, had too. According to the trust, it can only pass to a daughter, granddaughter, or other blood female relative. This house was left to him, but since I don't get along with that tart he married, he moved to Ross. We don't see each other often."

"Do you have children?"

"Oh, I never married. I'll have to leave the Belvedere Club to his daughter, eventually. Hopefully, she'll have more class than that mother of hers."

"Does Charles's wife belong to the Belvedere Club?" he asked.

"Oh, no." Her hand flew up. "She has the manners of a fish monger."

Things were getting a little more interesting and even though I wasn't allowed to join the conversation, I scooted forward while Dusty continued his questioning.

"Do you know if Ms. Macklin interviewed Charles or his wife?"

"I have no idea. Can't see why she would—boring people really. I hate to say it." She twisted a curl around her index finger.

"Could you give us Charles's address? We may need to speak with him in the future."

"He's always at that company of his. You can find him there. Securitec."

"Securitec," Dusty repeated, almost to himself. As Charlotte nodded, an odd expression curved Dusty's lips. "Do you have anything to do with Securitec? Do you work?"

Good question. How did she maintain her lifestyle? Although, looking around, I realized nothing in sight had been purchased in the last fifty years. Nothing except that silly maid's uniform. Who'd paid for that? I'd interviewed plenty of people with servants and that was the first uniform I'd ever seen. Maybe I was obsessing. Servants weren't slaves, they were paid employees. I was offline, headed into dangerous territory. Her response popped me back to the present.

"Securitec is Charles's baby. I work with the charities that the Belvedere Club sponsors, mostly with St. Mary's."

"Does this tea have caffeine?" I asked as I let her pour me

a second cup. I'd had two espressos with lunch. Dusty shook his head.

"A little, but not enough to hurt you." She poured Dusty a half a cup more and told us about the charity work she was involved with, all of which matched Post-It®s on my mirror.

My eyes fell on her gloved hand gently wrapping her teacup. I remembered Odilia Keith's fine Italian lace gloves. "Why do all the club members wear gloves?"

Dusty's head turned so fast I swore I heard a snap. I realized my observer position was in danger because I had questions that he wasn't asking.

Charlotte put down her cup and glanced down at her hands. "Silly, isn't it. They don't all wear them, but you are right, many of the older women do. My mother started the trend when she hit fifty. Thought her hands looked seventy so she started wearing gloves." She tugged at the top of each glove in the unconscious way people touch the part of the body that they are talking about.

She continued. "If anyone asked her about it she'd launch into a monologue on how gloves are a society staple in Europe. How Jackie Kennedy brought the fashion to America, but we weren't chic enough to catch on. If gloves were good enough for Jackie, she'd say, they were good enough for her. Of course she made me wear them too. She didn't want anyone to guess it was an age issue. Now…it's habit."

"How long has your mother been dead?" I asked. There was no date listed after her birth date on the website, yet Charlotte was designated as the acting president.

"Mother's not dead, although…" she trailed off. "She's reached an age where she needs looking after. She can no longer care for herself."

Dusty twitched uncomfortably and before he said something useless, I changed the subject.

"I understand Francine Starling had a disagreement with Haylee at last week's luncheon. Do you happen to know what it was about?"

There was a visible slump in her posture. "Ah, Francine. What can I tell you? Francine Starling grew up spoiled rich and she likes things her way. No compromises. She not a bad person, mind you, she just expects attention."

Dusty scribbled on his notepad as Charlotte continued.

"From what I remember, the argument wasn't with Ms. Macklin per se, it was one of the other women who mentioned Francine's daughter, a subject chosen to set her off. And it did. Francine's daughter is an embarrassment to her family."

Charlotte picked up her teacup, took a sip, and continued more animated. "The girl lives in the wilds of Montana or somewhere, hunts her own food, sleeps in a tepee. I believe at some point Francine ordered Ms. Macklin not to mention her daughter in the article. Whether Ms. Macklin was joking or egging Francine on, she mentioned she would like to interview the girl. Well, Francine lit into her as only Francine Starling can. It appeared that Ms. Macklin found it all rather amusing. It ended with Francine stomping out which she does quite often, to be sure."

Dusty asked another few questions while I tried to picture Haylee and Francine's argument. If Haylee thought mentioning Francine's daughter might reveal another side of Francine Starling or her status in the Belvedere Club, Haylee'd have no qualms about goading the woman. The question was how far could spoiled Francine Starling be pushed?

Charlotte walked us to the door. While she and Dusty discussed a few other trivialities, I glanced at a recess cut into the wall. A red porcelain bowl sat inside with a brass spigot hanging over it. What I found odd was the gray square painted around the recess. It was so out of character with the rest of the decorations. A moment later, I registered the anomaly—it was a painting. The recess wasn't a recess at all, but a faux perspective. The gray rectangle, a frame.

"Interesting," I said, pointing at the painting as Charlotte opened the door for us.

She squeezed my hand with an unspoken sign of emotion. "It was nice to meet you. Lieutenant Arkansas said he'd give me Mrs. Macklin's number. I'll give her a call straight away."

As soon as the door closed behind us, Dusty's energy ramped up. "Any other information you forgot to tell me like who told you about this argument?"

"It's probably not important. When I went back to check the locks at the club some of the members were mulling about."

As we walked back to the car I told him about the ladies and all their suspicions, including Tony Amato and Stevie.

"I think we can rule out Stevie, but in the future, you let me decide what is important or not," he said.

"Tony's a stronger suspect than Francine Starling."

"If Tony Amato murdered Haylee, he wouldn't have called in the discovery. I know the type. He would have been long gone," Dusty said.

We stopped by the car and took in the clear San Francisco skyline.

"Charlotte's no good brother, as she calls him, is one of the biggest business tycoons in the county," he said. "Big business and crime are synonymous. If Haylee interviewed the brother, maybe she found something there."

"Is Securitec our next stop?"

"No way. I have to speak with the Sheriff before I mess with someone at that level. I'm not taking on that responsibility alone. Anyway, check the time. It's Friday afternoon. Mr. Warren's probably already headed for his weekend hideaway."

The Break-in

Dusty dropped me at my car and suggested I visit the wine country over the weekend. For the next two days, he was unofficially working Haylee's case, but didn't foresee any interviews or need for my assistance. He politely gave me his home number in case I thought of anything important, and then told me not to call.

Back in Corte Madera I ran into the maid leaving my room. "No dogs allowed," she said, snapping the door shut. "I'm not cleaning there."

I'd forgotten to put the *Do Not Disturb* sign. I slipped her thirty dollars. "What dog?"

She looked the bills over and grinned. "What dog?"

Fifi and I strolled through a family neighborhood of one-story bungalows on the other side of Tamal Vista Boulevard. It was near enough to the hotel that we wouldn't get lost, yet far enough that we wouldn't be seen by any hotel employees. While Fifi tugged me along by the leash, I scanned a map of Northern California, thinking a trip to the wine country might be a good idea. "Up north" I might run into at least one of Tony's ex-employees. This was faulty logic on my part, I realized. I wouldn't recognize any of the kitchen staff and only had the names from Haylee's Post-It®s so unless these fleeing illegals came up and introduced themselves, there was no way I would find even one. Sometimes the brain skips along and hums, sometimes it trips and stumbles.

"What a cute dog."

I lowered the map to find a woman in cut off jeans and flip-flops squatting to caress Fifi. In my mind's eye, I saw Fifi biting off her hand and me being hauled away by animal control.

"You…ah." Oh, too late. She'd made contact and Fifi appeared to enjoy it, rubbing herself against the woman's bare legs.

When the woman tilted her head up in my direction, long strands of faded blond hair fell away, revealing a face deeply tanned and richly freckled. "How long have you had her?"

I checked my watch. "Not long."

"She's so affectionate."

Fifi tilted one eye in my direction.

"She is?"

The woman stood and continued down the sidewalk in the opposite direction. Fifi and I watched her go.

When we returned to the room, I filled Fifi's food bowl with nuggets. I'd been overfeeding her in an effort to compensate for my own loss. But it now seemed like a good time to curl up with a bottle of Irish whisky. Then, I remembered the photos.

I had deliberately put off downloading the crime scene photos, but I was eager to download those I had taken of the ladies. Putting faces to names helped me stay organized.

I slipped my memory card into the laptop. There were only four new images. Was it possible? I overshot as a rule. In the first image I tried to name each woman. Odilia Keith, in flaming yellow and orange, was forever marked in my mind as the leader of the pack. There was Penny Tabor and her pillbox hat and bad hip.

Odd. Standing behind the group with her back to me was a woman I didn't remember meeting. I counted heads, or I should say hats, and sure enough, there were six. My notebook showed only five names.

I looked over all four photos, but the mysterious woman only appeared in the first. I had a vague memory of someone walking out of frame, but Odilia Keith's enthusiasm had held my attention by that time. And the limo…

I ran to the Post-It®s. They were still stuck to the bedroom mirror in the order of Haylee's research.

Amanda Weathersby (1880-1829) SF Philanthropist Club Founder 1st President	Patricia Weathersby (1879-1859) Amanda's only Daughter Married Robert Perreault 3 children 2B 1G	Patricia Perreault President Until 1935 Passed to only daughter Charlotte Lehman	Charlotte Lehman (1904-2064) Had 2Boys - 2 Gals Ran club 1935-1960	Amanda Warren (1925-) Charlotte Lehman's eldest daughter	Amanda Warren Current president (1960-) 1991 daughter charlotte became acting president
Compass Founded 1914	St Mary's Catholic Charities	Rummington Alzheimer's Clinic mother	Tony Amato Duty 10 Woodford Rd	Lunch Thursday 12 noon	Francoise Starling Club
Annette Vaughan Club	Ines Espinoza Waitress	Juan Sandova Kitchen	THURSDAYS	Woman Only	Charles Warren (1955-) Charlotte

The top row was background on the Belvedere Club, the Weathersby lineage, births, deaths, family. The single, new piece of information was about the twins.

The middle row began with the three charities funded by the Belvedere Club and its members: Compass, founded in 1914 to aid homeless families and young girls and women drawn to the Bay Area by the Panama-Pacific International Exposition; St. Mary's Catholic Charities which provide money for AIDS patients and Food Banks; The Rummington Alzheimer's Clinic in Santa Rosa. Scribbled under the last charity was the word "mother." I'd assumed Charlotte's mother had begun that particular endowment, but now I realized that must be the Alzheimer's clinic where the mother lived.

Enough guessing. I needed to find out for sure. Could the sixth woman, the one hiding from the camera, have been Charlotte's mother? How sick was she? Or perhaps it was the sister-in-law, Charles Warren's wife. Being a non-member would explain why she didn't want to be photographed.

The second and third squares in the bottom row listed two Belvedere employees. One waitress was highlighted in pink, Ines Espinoza, who, according to Dusty, was one of the

MIAs. What had Haylee interviewed her about? According to Haylee's work ethic, the Post-It® following the employees indicated either new information or a new subject. The following yellow square had Thursday written on it. I already knew Charlotte Warren visited the Belvedere Club on Thursdays and had lunched with Haylee. There was nothing interesting there. I went back to Tony Amato's square. It listed his full name, full address, and the word "Dirty" with a capital "D." Still a mystery.

Dirty, Dirty, Dirty. I had a hard time believing it was a health code violation. When it came to his cooking, Tony came across as serious, remembering each day by what meal he prepared. His home was a pigsty, but he'd said Haylee hadn't been to his place. Yet, capital "Y," she had written his address on the Post-It®.

I dug through my knapsack lying on the bed. The Sheriff's Department had asked Haylee's mom to bring some photographs of Haylee for the investigation. The ones they hadn't taken she'd given to me. I chose a headshot taken at an awards banquet where Haylee's story on the Washington homeless had won her an award for investigative reporting. The headshot didn't show the pale pink Valentino gown she'd worn, and her gracious expression masked her determination.

Reliving the evening, I fell easily into the buzz generated from the other tables like locusts in my ears. The hall had smelled of overcooked chicken as waiters served prepared plates. Terrance had a date, a whiney piece of work with pinched features. Haylee had brought me as her escort, another of her ploys to drag me out of my funk, whether I'd wanted help or not.

Knees first, I sank onto the bed. The emotions I was holding at bay were swelling. It wouldn't be long before they overtook me. I had to find Haylee's killer before that happened because without Haylee, I might not make it through my grief, this time.

Do, don't think. I grabbed my keys and headed for the parking lot. Those were the words Haylee had burned into my brain after I had lost my baby, Siobhan. *Do, don't think.* I could have sworn I heard Haylee's voice, whispering the phrase into my ear.

* * *

The Belvedere Club's drive was empty, but I parked farther down the street and walked back. In full sunlight a patrol car could easily spot my Saturn in front and decide to check it out. The lower parking lot was public parking and there were two other cars already parked there, but I preferred to stay as hidden as possible.

I unlocked the entrance door, ducked under the police tape, and pulled the door shut behind me. My momentary panic was overruled by my practicality—I didn't have much time. In the entrance I scanned the names beneath the photos of past presidents. All were listed on the website. From there I pushed through the swivel door to the right that led into the kitchen, figuring I'd save the main dining room for last, while not entirely sure that I could face the room again.

Indirect sunlight filtered through foliage. I had to switch on a light to have a good view. Tony kept his kitchen clean. Except for traces of dark fingerprinting powder, the room was spotless and smelled of chlorine bleach.

The rear door had been printed as had the handle on a door to the left of the industrial refrigerator, which was probably the storage room where Tony retrieved the fish cooler. Using a paper towel—the prints had been taken but I didn't want to leave mine—I opened the door and peered inside. Shelves of oversized canned goods lined one wall, while shelves stacked with pots and pans lined the other. A four-foot wide freezer was straight ahead and on top, the famous fish cooler that had brought Amato to the Belvedere Club that morning.

Back in the kitchen, I walked around not really sure what I was looking for. Maybe something out of the ordinary or something that caught my eye. The knives were stuck to a horizontal running magnet behind a wide cutting-board counter. I counted over thirty. Did Tony really know how many he had?

I pushed through the door back into the club. A corridor ran off to the right. It led past the restrooms to an outdoor patio. Sliding glass doors opened in a way that joined the patio to the building. Today, they were locked with two steel plugs. Fingerprinting power covered the plugs.

The two identically decorated restrooms displayed floral wallpaper in tones of pink and lilac. Both were spacious and elegant: gold fixtures, marble flooring, cloth hand towels, and fresh flower bouquets with flowers pouring over the sides.

I paused before entering the main room and took a breath. Here was where the struggle had occurred. According to Dusty, the body hadn't been moved.

Why had Haylee gone inside? Had someone let her in? Or left the door open for her? And why?

The room looked pretty much the way I remembered: the rosewood floorboards, linen-clad tables circling the room, and a larger rectangular table as the centerpiece. The chalk markers were as I remembered too, but I tried to ignore them by walking the perimeter of the room. Behind the large table I squatted to look under the tables.

I hoped that Haylee, in the middle of fighting off an attacker, might have left me a clue. That was what I would have tried to do. She'd been expecting me. I should have been here.

It occurred to me that even if she had left a clue, the

sheriff's department might already have laid claim to it. I needed to ask Dusty.

The sun was setting and the room had grown darker. The chalk markers appeared to glow neon. I needed to leave. Sooner or later a patrol car would roll by. Or would they? Dusty had to assume that whoever killed Haylee had access to the Belvedere Club. Certainly, he was keeping an eye on the place.

The Apartment

The muted light of dusk softened the wreckage in Tony's neighborhood. Unlike before, the street in front of his apartment house was packed with cars, bumper to bumper. I drove around the block twice before finding a parking space on a service road behind the building.

As I turned the corner while walking back, a group of Mexican men, smoking foreign smelling cigarettes, blocked the sidewalk. One said something to me. Another said something to him, none of which I understood, and they all shuffled aside, allowing me to pass. Times like these, I wished I'd paid attention in high school Spanish.

Across the front of Tony's building every window but one was lit and many were open, allowing a jumble of salsa and bachata music to seep into the street. Even louder were the television announcers, sly and convincing, and the familiar jingles, creating instant recognition. The one light I didn't see was at the side left corner, which, if my calculation was correct, was Tony's apartment.

I slipped into the building and rang his bell despite the lack of light beneath the door. I rang a second time in case he was cooking something that made a lot of noise like…fried chicken. I walked up the hall and rang the first bell I came to. Blocked by an interior chain, the door opened two inches. A woman with spikes of gray hair leaned into the crack, cocking her head so that she peered out with one eye. As soon as I spoke, she slammed the door in my face.

"Hello. Hola." I banged, but she obviously had no qualms about ignoring me.

Okay, I needed to work on my interrogation techniques.

There were no other apartments on this floor, so I climbed the stairs to the third floor, figuring I'd work my way down. This was what Haylee would have done. She was organized and meticulous to the point that her information gathering techniques were almost maniacal. All that aside, I still hadn't a clue what type of information she might have been looking for.

When I reached the top floor landing, I saw a young girl sitting in the hallway, her back to me. Long dark strands cascaded over her shoulders as she dropped a small red ball and scooped something up in her hand. Jacks. I didn't think kids still played jacks. I didn't think there were still toys on the market that didn't operate without a computer chip. The ball rolled away and as she reached for it, I saw that she was the girl I'd seen outside earlier when I'd come by with Dusty. When she spotted me, she crawled to her knees, and started to stand.

"Hi, is your mom around?"

"Mom!"

A curly headed woman stuck her head out a doorway halfway down the hall. She took one look at me and spewed off something in Spanish to her daughter which, from the slump of the child's shoulders, must have been a reprimand. The girl stood and disappeared into the doorway. The woman, drying her hands on a dishtowel, took a few steps in my direction.

I held out the photo of Haylee. "Sorry to disturb you, but I'm looking for my friend and wondered if you'd seen her around here." She glanced at the photo, but didn't take it from my hands.

"The blond." She nodded and then shook her head.

Well, which was it? "Have you seen her?" I asked again.

"No." She looked up. "Sorry." She spun around and went into her apartment, closing the door behind her.

She'd said "the blond" not "a blond" which might simply be a fault of English grammar, but the one thing I did remember from high school was all the romance languages were very specific with their articles. It seemed like a strange error to make, but before I could dwell on it further, footsteps thundered up the stairs behind me. I turned to see a smaller Mexican woman juggling two large paper bags and hustling two big-eyed kids, the taller one a girl and the shorter, a boy. They crossed the hall and the woman tried to adjust the grocery bags while reaching into her handbag. Everything, including her tiny frame, looked ready to topple. I rushed forward and removed one of the brown bags from her hands.

I smiled with what I hoped was a non-threatening smile. "Let me help."

My intrusion startled all three. The children fell silent and the woman gave me a suspicious nod.

"Thanks," she said and reached back into her handbag for her keys. I offered to take the other bag, but she assured me she could manage.

The children scampered inside. I followed as the lights came on. Hanging on the wall across from the door was a huge wooden cross with the likes of Jesus nailed to the center. It was the only wall decoration in the living room. Near the kitchen was a circular table laden with cereal boxes and used bowls. She motioned for me to set the bag there.

"Thank you," she said.

I handed her Haylee's photo. "I'm looking for my friend. Have you seen her around here?"

She took the photo and barely looked at it before she said, "Yes, she was here."

"Do you remember when?"

"The day? No."

Her English was very good and as she removed her sweater, I noticed she was wearing hospital scrubs with a medical insignia on the front pocket.

"Do you know why she was here? Did you speak with her?"

"I spoke with her, yes. Why do you want to know?" she said.

Suspicion clouded her face and she began inching me back towards the door. I reclaimed the photo and introduced myself. I figured the local paper had probably run a story about the murder, but with any luck they hadn't used Haylee's photo.

The woman didn't offer her name, but gestured towards the photo in my hand. "She is a newspaper lady, too."

A roar of clatter burst through the room and the little girl ran across the apartment toward the kitchen followed by her brother. The woman called out in Spanish, and then turned back to me. "She said she was writing about Tony, what a good chef he is."

"Yes, that's right. Did she ask you about Tony?"

She nodded, her eyes tired.

"Can you remember what you told her? It might help me find her."

"Just that Tony is a wonderful man. We all…." She gestured towards the outer apartments. "We all have children to raise and no man to help us. Tony helps us. If we have a problem with the apartment, he fixes it. I have friends who wait months and months to get things fixed where they live. Not Tony. He's a good man. A good Catholic."

Yeah and so is the pope. That's what we said in the neighborhood when someone mentioned a good Catholic. I was Irish. I knew lots of good Catholics and some not so good. From her description, Tony Amato didn't sound like a killer, but maybe an opportunist. Before I spoke, I checked in with the Jesus across the room. "Does Tony expect anything extra for his trouble?"

Her expression went from confused to angry faster than I could blink. "Tony's a good man. Not like that."

Good hadn't led Haylee here. Maybe she'd interviewed Tony at his apartment. But why had he denied that she'd been here? Was it something to do with illegals? He hired them, maybe he rented to them.

The woman rested her hand on the door above the handle and pulled it open a little wider.

I had to work fast. "How long have you lived here?"

"Three years."

The kids rushed into the room, running in the opposite direction, feet pounding despite the carpeting. They wore uniforms, the kind required at private schools. I couldn't see her answering a question about her immigrant status and I didn't want to alienate her further.

"What school do your kids go to?"

But she didn't like that question either. Her scowl said that she found it too personal. Again she spoke in Spanish and the kids returned and jumped onto a worn leather sofa. "I must make dinner, we're running late tonight. If your friend comes back, I'll tell her you were looking for her."

I thanked her as the door snapped shut in my face. I continued down the hall, knocking on doors. No one else admitted to having seen Haylee until I reached the end of the second floor. An Asian woman of slight build stepped into the hallway, pulling her door closed behind her. She recognized Haylee and handed back the photo, smiling. "She ass about Tony."

"What did she ask?"

She giggled in a way that made me wonder about her age. Her black hair shone with health and vitality and there wasn't a wrinkle on her flawless skin. She looked too young to be living on her own.

"She ass about Tony's girls."

Tony's girls? "Do you remember which day that was?"

"Monday."

The beginning of the week. "Do you have kids?" The woman upstairs had mentioned they were all single mothers.

"No. No kids. You?"

I shook my head. "You like Mr. Amato? Tony, is he good to you?"

"Tony, berry nice man." She giggled again, but didn't elaborate.

"Did my friend ask you anything else? Anything about the Belvedere Club where Tony works?"

She shook her head. I thanked her because I couldn't think of anything else to ask. I started down the stairs, wondering what Haylee had been onto, but feeling certain she hadn't come to hear these women rave about Tony Amato's kindness. She wasn't that kind of reporter. Where was the story in a good landlord? As I hit the bottom step, the shadow parted and Tony stepped out.

"Hello again," he said.

Surprised, I grabbed the banister and felt it wobbled beneath my grip. "Mr. Amato. I knocked earlier, there wasn't an answer."

"So you thought you'd bother my tenants." His chubby jaw was set. "I just got back. Mercedes called. Said you were upstairs, asking questions."

I assumed Mercedes was the young woman I'd helped with the grocery bags. "Seems Haylee was here too, asking questions."

"My nana came to this country with almost nothing. She told me story after story of her hardships." His hands started moving with his words. "Like Juanita told you—" he poked me in the chest. "I help these ladies out, help them get on their feet, make a family for their kids. Nothing wrong with that, is there?"

Juanita? If she was the one with the grocery bags, who was Mercedes? "Sounds pretty noble. Why'd you lie about Haylee being here?"

"Tell you the truth. She wanted to do a story on me. I told her no, absolutely not. No need for the cops to know about that, is there?"

"Why not?" I asked.

"Come on." Again with the hands. "Okay, look, maybe some of these ladies are still waiting on their green cards. The police get involved, employers get questioned, next thing you know someone's out of work. It's hard enough finding jobs these days. Look at me, I'm not working again until the police reopen the Belvedere Club."

I thought about the loss of a great journalist and couldn't drum up an ounce of sympathy. "My heart goes out to you. Why didn't you want a story? Most people would love to see their name in print."

"Same reason. Draw attention to me, you draw attention to these ladies, their struggles. Can't do it. Listen, I'm sorry about that journalist, but I promise you, the only thing I know about her death was what I saw yesterday morning."

The Sicilian smile.

The Internet

While the laptop booted, Fifi sat on her haunches, looking up at me with pleading dog eyes. Boy, did I hate that.

"What? I already fed you." I threw my hands in the air as if to enunciate. "You've made your pee-pee. What more could you possibly want? A cigar? A glass of Port?" I shifted my position and tried to move the laptop to the sofa, but the cable was too short. Fifi didn't budge. She batted her lashes and whined.

"Stop! I'm doing everything I can. I don't know who killed Haylee. If I did, you'd be the first to know." I was losing it. I was talking to a dog. I grabbed my camera bag and pulled out a cigarette. I lit it and drew in a soothing breath. "Ah, go out and play."

I checked my email first and found a menacing message about expenses from my editor's assistant. Next, I went to the Internet browser and did a search for "Tony's Girls." The giggling Asian woman stuck in my mind like an annoying TV jingle. The way she'd said "Tony's Girls" several times.

Ash dropped in my lap as the first page of the search came up. It was anything but wholesome. *How to get Laid* was the first subject. Beneath that, was the second listing *Tony's Boys and Girls.* My stomach turned as I clicked this site open. It was a series of children's drawings with the artist name and age printed below. *Shew.*

The next site was a page from an author's website, but on the fourth try I found what Haylee had found. On a black background, a line drawing of an apartment building filled the screen, not just any building, but one that looked suspiciously like Tony Amato's. Inside each drawn apartment was the photo of a young woman. I clicked on one face that looked vaguely familiar. The image opened into a screen of streaming video. A woman sat on a bed, watching television. She wasn't dressed in a particularly sexy way, a long tee shirt that revealed a triangle of orange underpants. Her pose wasn't at all provocative, but I found myself holding my breath.

As I watched, the woman barely moved.

I backed out and clicked on another face and a window popped up asking for payment. The wheels of commerce. Viewing time was billed at a dollar a minute. Since I still didn't know what I was looking at, I grabbed my wallet and typed in my MasterCard number. This time, a different bedroom opened with a different woman, drying her hair with a towel. She was wearing a light blue robe. Juanita. The woman I had helped with the groceries and who had raved about Tony's kindness. An Internet porn shop. Was this how the women were earning their green cards? *Tony's a good man.*

Would this have gotten Haylee killed? How important was it and to whom? At best, it was a "sensation" piece guaranteed to draw voyeurs: *Porno Apartment*. Not Haylee's style of story. A journalist's job was reporting, not judging. Of course nowadays, with corporate returns more important than news in the newsroom, today's journalists weren't as impartial as they should be. But Haylee was. She wouldn't write a piece that wasn't newsworthy, no matter how sensational it was or how many readers it would grab. So where was the story? Where was the danger? Had she confronted Tony about running a story? She knew better. He still may have found out.

At that moment, Juanita's two children ran into the room wrapped in worn striped towels. She dropped her wet towel on the bed and went to work, patting down the children who laughed and squealed with delight before running out of the room stark naked. A shiver ran up my spine.

Stubbing my cigarette out in the saucer I used as an ashtray, I reached for the telephone. Either these women didn't know they were on camera or they did. Internet porn was one thing. Child prostitution, a whole different game. I dialed the number Dusty had left me.

A loud barrage of music burst through the connection. I had to say Dusty's name a couple of times before getting a response. The music muffled as if he had stepped into a closet and his voice came through clearer.

"I told you not to call me," he said.

"I wanted to let you know I went back over to Tony's apartment house."

"Ah, hell. Hold on, let me go to my car."

"Where are you?" I asked.

"I'm at a bar, trying to forget I've got a half-rate reporter covering my ass."

"Hey buddy, cover your own ass! I thought you might like to know that Tony Amato's running an Internet porno ring, pedophilia included." I disconnected. Let Mr. Sourpuss chew on that.

Almost immediately, the phone rang.

His disposition was unimproved. "It cost me sixty cents to use that call back function. Don't hang up again. Now, start from the beginning."

I related my conversations with Juanita and the Asian woman, realizing if he had a camera in her apartment, Tony probably watched while I had spoken with Juanita. His remark about harassing his tenants carried new meaning as I told Dusty about Juanita's kids and estimated their ages. He didn't say a word.

"You still there?" I asked.

"This website, what was it again? There's no doubt that

it's Amato's building?"

"Www dot world wide beauties—all one word—dot com." I knew he was writing it down because he mumbled the words back to me. "As we speak, a woman on the second floor is brushing her teeth, and not very neatly, I might add."

"All right. I'll send a car over to check it out. I'll let you know what we find."

Now, this Buddhist sheriff probably thought I was going to sit tight and have another cigarette. Whoa be the innocent. I switched off the laptop, grabbed my camera bag and met Fifi at the door.

"You have to stay."

She barked, and barked again.

"Shhhh. Oh, all right, but you're staying in the back seat."

By the time I'd parked and walked back to the apartment building, Dusty had arrived. I had to give him credit; he didn't appear all that surprised to see me. A San Rafael black-and-white pulled up, double parking on the street, its flashing blue lights illuminating the night.

Dusty said something to the driver and the lights went dark. He motioned me to the patrol car.

"Give me your flashlight," he told the driver. The officer handed him a black handled light and he turned to me. "We'll go check out the apartment where you saw the kids. If we find anything, we'll radio these guys up."

"You're going to need more than two cops if there's a camera in each apartment," I said.

Dusty looked at the driver. "Told you she was smart."

The driver laughed and I wondered what Dusty had really said about me. I resolved to let him do his job. I had uncovered Tony's secret; now, all I wanted was to prove he killed Haylee.

"Lead the way and don't turn on any lights," he said, gesturing forward.

We climbed the staircase using the flashlight to guide us through the musky darkness. When we reached the third floor landing, Dusty knocked at Juanita's door. He held up his badge when she cracked the door open. She saw me and her face froze, something close to terror filled her eyes.

Dusty introduced himself and Juanita did likewise. "Would you step into the hall, please."

Juanita glanced down at the worn house robe she was holding closed at the neck. Not the image of an exhibitionist. Dusty was assuming there weren't cameras in the hall. I glanced upward, wondering if he was right. Technology had created lenses the size of a pencil eraser. They could be planted anywhere, in the ceiling, a darkened corner, beside a door frame. When Juanita stepped out, Dusty pulled her door closed.

"Are you aware of an Internet camera in your bedroom?" His question was so formal that Juanita asked him to repeat it, but as the words sank in, Juanita covered herself with her arms. Her rapid eye movement betrayed her thought process and I wondered if she was fabricating an excuse or working out some other detail.

Finally, she grabbed the door handle and threw it open. "Show me!" Like a marine, she marched us through the apartment, her tiny shoulders puffed up as if expanded by air. Once in the bedroom, Dusty turned to me. "Where was she standing when you saw her?"

"Oh please, I know about angles." I mentally reconstructed what I'd seen while sliding into the spot where Juanita would have been facing the camera. In front of me was a beat up dresser with a three-by-three mirror attached.

Juanita must have read the surprise on my face. Her hands flew to her hips and she said, "See, nothing. No camera."

"Wait," Dusty said. "Stand aside."

He switched off the overhead lamp and switched on the

flashlight. He directed the light at the overhead lamp and then at a fire alarm. Next, he lit the mirror and like magic the camera became visible as if the glass were transparent.

"There it is," he said.

Juanita's tense face went slack. She sank onto the bed, hanging her head, and sobbed. My stomach tightened. She wasn't faking, she hadn't known, and now, most likely, she was terrified that she was going to be arrested. What little she said, she said in Spanish and more to herself than us. This probably meant that every woman in the building had no idea she was being filmed.

Within seconds of finding the camera, Dusty had radioed the cops below. A whirlwind of footsteps, voices, and movement carried up the staircase. I rushed after Dusty into the hallway and down the stairs.

"He was halfway out the bathroom window," one of the officers said over his shoulder. Both officers were leading Tony out the front door with his hands cuffed behind his back.

Above us heads popped over the railing and we heard a mix of languages being spoken. I heard Juanita's voice and several exclamations followed. *Dios mio*, my God, I recognized.

The old woman from the apartment next to Tony's cracked open her door and Tony's head turned. A mix of Sicilian passed between them and the door slammed shut. A bolt jammed into place.

The entrance quickly clogged with police and tenants and children. Everyone seemed to be yelling, but no one was audible. I had my camera out and had snapped off a picture of Tony being led out and another shot of the barrage of officers arriving, but now it was time to tie Tony to Haylee. I turned behind two officers and followed them back toward Tony's apartment. Dusty met me in the doorway and grabbed my shoulder and spun me around. "This is a crime scene. You can't go in there."

"Hey, you owe me."

"Oh, right. Thank you very much for being a good citizen. Now, beat it. You aren't going in."

"This gives him a motive for killing Haylee?"

"You think?" His blond eyebrows rose in mock disbelief.

I jammed my camera into the camera bag. "Let me look around. No photos."

"Can't do it. Policy. We have to wait for a search warrant. I'll call you if we find anything."

"Like a knife," I said.

"Oh? Is that another tip? Let me write that down." With his hand so tight around my arm that I felt the bruising, he pulled me to the front entrance. "Go. He's guilty. We'll find the evidence. I know you think we won't be able to without your fine instincts and keen observations, but trust me, we will. Don't worry. I'll call you and you can get on a plane and fly home. Believe me, I want that knife as much as you do."

The Miscalculation

Something cold and wet crawled across my face jarring me awake. Two brown marbles hung inches from my nose. Oddly enough, I took this as a sign that I was still asleep, dreaming. Nothing this bizarre belonged to the realm of reality. Fifi's, pink tongue slid across my cheek and eyelid. I shoved her across the mattress and sat up, wiping my arm across my wet face. Six-thirty.

"Have you lost your mind?"

After pure exhaustion, I'd finally fallen asleep and now this. Six-thirty. "What do you want?" I plucked the sleep from the corners of my eyes.

Fifi barked.

"What?"

She leaped off the bed and ran from the room. I stumbled after her and found her waiting by the front door.

"Now? It's illegal to walk dogs before nine. This is California, they have rules." I slumped back to bed. Fifi followed, running and barking as if I'd stolen her food bowl.

"Shut up."

She kept barking, the high pitch jarring.

The blanket tangled around my feet so launching a kick was futile. "You're going to get us thrown out." But she already knew this, didn't she?

"I should have let Dusty shoot you." I slid from the covers and pulled on a pair of straight-legged slacks and covered my nightshirt with my blazer. I grabbed a handful of sandwich bags from Fifi's suitcase (yes, she had her own) and headed for the door.

By the time we returned, the cool morning air had revived

me and there was no returning to the warm haven of dreamland. Besides, Fifi wanted breakfast.

With nothing left to do at this ungodly hour, I carried my coffee back to the bedroom and read over Haylee's Post-It®s for the five-hundredth and thirty-third time. I tried to work Tony Amato in as the killer. Usually when Haylee was on to something the Post-It®s got rearranged to follow the story, but all I had that related to Tony was the word "Dirty." Nothing else fit, not the charities, not the employees. If she'd stumbled onto "Tony's Girls" while visiting the apartment building she might not have had time to add it to the Post-It® organization. That was a big possibility and happened more often than not, but the other thing that bothered me was why did she die at the Belvedere Club? If Tony was trying to shut her up, it seemed more likely he would have killed her somewhere that wouldn't link back to him.

Last night, I was sure I'd found Haylee's killer, but by the light of day confusion had set in. It was ten-thirty on the East Coast and a decent hour to call Terrance, although I generally preferred calling him at indecent hours.

"Hey chief, the police arrested someone last night; he's looking good for Haylee's murder."

"Tell me what you got," Terrance said.

"Guy's name is Tony Amato."

"The cook?"

There was a clicking sound coming through the line and I wondered what Terrance was doing. "Chef, yeah. He owned an apartment house where he rented cheap apartments to immigrant single mothers while he secretly recorded them for an online porn site."

"Killed Haylee to shut her up?"

"That's what the police think," I said, not adding my doubts.

The clicking stopped. "Hardly a big story. Happens all the

time. Remember that guy in Baltimore?"

"Haylee had busted him, too." It was a similar story. A Saudi had his apartment house wired for video and Haylee had discovered it while using her interviewee's bathroom. The only difference, it had been an upscale building with apartments going for five and six thousand a month. This new information made sense in the scheme of Haylee's find, but something Terrance had said bothered me, although, I couldn't quite draw out what.

"Listen, write up the story, email it, and catch the next plane back here. I have a couple of stories breaking. Some exciting stuff. Call me when you arrive."

Terrance's attitude was almost human which didn't sit well with my already doubting self. I went back to the dresser and stared at the yellow Post-It®s, rerunning our conversation in my head. What had he said…? And it hit me. *It happens all the time.*

It does happen all the time. The electronic age had spawned all kinds of perverts. There was even a website dedicated to video shots up women's skirts. The reason Haylee had noticed the camera in the bathroom in Baltimore was because she'd just read a story about the same situation down in Florida. This story wasn't Pulitzer and Haylee knew it. She'd already written a similar one with a much more interesting money angle. This one lacked two of the three ingredients, drugs, sex, money. A regular story contained one ingredient; a Pulitzer had to include two, hopefully all three.

My gut had it right. Tony didn't kill her.

The Schooner

With Fifi snarling in the backseat, I drove north to San Rafael and the Sheriff's Department. I was afraid to leave Fifi yapping at the hotel, afraid I'd come back to find my things spread across the sidewalk.

Parking in a back lot, I raised all the windows tight and locked the door behind me, wondering if it was warm enough yet to roast a dog. Maybe, if I stayed for lunch. When I reached the sidewalk, I turned back and looked at the Saturn. Fifi was no longer barking. She tilted her head to the right, watching me.

"Oh, all right."

I returned to the car, cracking the four windows enough for Fifi's snout to inch through. "I'm not doing this for you; I'm doing it for Haylee."

I tilted my head back and looked heavenward. "If you want Fifi with you, give me a sign." We Irish believe in Heaven and some of us believe dogs are allowed.

The office was sparsely populated, which allowed me to really grasp the beauty of the design. Deputy Wilson was manning the front desk and acknowledged me with a nod.

Thursday, when she'd driven me back to the Belvedere Club and after I'd bought her a latte, I'd learned that she was a rookie and that she was stuck on the desk until someone in the field needed to partner-up. "Still no partner, I take it."

She smirked. "No one wants to play with the new kid." And then more jovial, "Your name's been bandied about lately."

"What can I say…" I made a grandiose gesture. "When you've got it…"

"Here's a heads-up. Most cops don't like non-cops solving their cases."

"Dusty doesn't mind, he thanked me."

"Dusty's a little, well, let's just say not every lieutenant asks you to call him by his first name."

"I get what you're saying. Thanks," I said. "Listen, I was wondering if I could speak with him? I know he's not officially working—"

"He's not here right now. He was in till two a.m. booking a prisoner."

"Amato, I know. Do you think I can reach him on his private number?"

She looked incredulous. "You have his private number?"

I checked the time on the wall clock. "He gave it to me."

"His private number?"

I reeled off the number including the four-one-five area code.

She leaned over the counter, propping both elbows. She brought a hand to her chin and puckered her lips, staring at me a minute longer than was comfortable. "Know where he lives?"

"Oh, good idea. I should drive over. Yeah, he lives on a boat, somewhere here in San Rafael."

She raised an eyebrow, surprised I knew that much. A sly grin curled her mouth. "Go south on 101 to the next exit. At Second Street turn left. Past the strip mall, on the right, you'll see Lowrie Yacht Harbor. That's where his boat's docked. It's blue."

"Dark blue, light blue?"

"Robin's egg," she said, looking cheeky.

Anyone who had spent any time with cops knew they had a strange sense of humor. I didn't know if the "robin's egg" was her joke or Dusty's, but I was sure that sending me unannounced to the harbor was hers. I'd sensed a certain incongruity among Dusty Arkansas and his coworkers. I didn't need Deputy Wilson to spell it out for me. I needed to speak with Dusty so I wasn't about to waste time questioning her motives.

I passed a lumber yard, a tackle shop, a yacht rental, some skuzzy apartment houses, and a long line of marinas. Lowrie Yacht Harbor was the last marina on the right before the area turned residential. I parallel parked behind a beat up camper with its bumper hanging off and a recycled bread truck that had been painted several shades of yellow. A wooden rowboat was tied on top.

I hooked the leash onto Fifi's collar and walked her over to the clapboard office. Peering inside, squinting between the leaves of numerous plants lining the inside window, I saw two men, sitting on opposite sides of a battered desk, feet up, watching television; neither was Dusty and neither looked like he wanted company. Below, concrete steps led down to a wooden pier, which wove left and right around the harbor. Other piers split off from this main axis. So many boats. Many in shades of blue or with blue sail covers. Hands down, blue was the color of the sea, not a purple or a red or a green in sight.

Fifi and I went right, choosing a pier dotted with new redwood planks set in among older, blacker, rotting ones. Below, stagnant water smelled like dead fish although I didn't spot any floaters. Even Fifi held her nose in the air, hoping to catch a fresh breeze.

Soon, we came to a white boat with a large blue-green awning. Something about the boat made me think it was Dusty's. Probably the *No Smoking* sign glued to the cabin door. I looked for some other indication that this was his, like a Salvation Army clothing rack. The sign, though, made me want to light up, just on principle. I pulled out a cigarette and stuck it between my lips.

But if you get right down to it, blue-green fell more into a turquoise category. Robin's egg was more blue. I dropped the unlit cigarette back into my bag and we continued.

Up on a rise behind us, a row of two and three-story apartment buildings built side-by-side sat on a point of land jutting into the bay. Weekend life—gleeful children, Spanish pop, mariachi music, and repetitive hammering—burst forth from the buildings, all of it echoing off the still water like a sounding board. Between the stench and the noise, I couldn't imagine a hell any worse.

On a schooner deck near the end of the pier, Dusty sat, beneath potted lemon trees, cross-legged on a red tapestry, palms pressed together, and chanting with his eyes closed. He was wearing charcoal sweatpants and a tee-shirt which read, *If you fall from the roof, leave your anger on the eave.*

The schooner looked like an old pirate's boat with carved wooden rails, a wooden bowsprit, a wooden deck, and oxidized copper portholes that cut into the cabin. Robin's egg blue was the cabin's color, the hull, a weathered white. Everything needed paint and the deck needed resurfacing. Miniature orange trees sat in clay pots midway back on each side of the cabin, blocking passage to the bow. And as if noise from the apartments wasn't enough, two leather straps hung, one on each side of the cabin dangling three brass bells. When the wind blew, I bet they really sang.

When we halted in front of the cockpit, Fifi barked. Dusty's chanting faltered, but didn't stop. Fifi must not have liked the pitch. She barked again.

Dusty opened one eye.

"What's with the Kumbaya?" I asked. A strange smell drifted by. Incense.

He exhaled and his body appeared to deflate thirty pounds. "I'm trying to get grounded. This case has been unusually nerve-racking. At first, I thought it was just you—

high-strung, uptight, edgy—you know what they say about redheads, but that boss of yours..."

"Terrance?"

"Right, Terre-rant. Has anyone ever punched him out?" he asked.

"Anyone besides me, you mean."

"To your credit, I'm sure. Boy, am I glad this case is almost over. Have you come to say good-bye? Good-bye. Enjoy your flight." He closed his eyes and inhaled a deep breath, expanding his chest.

"Tony didn't kill Haylee."

"Of course he did." His voice was higher, almost comical, because of the inhalation.

"The story—it's not a Pulitzer. It's missing one of the big three."

"Not listening." But his eyes opened and he exhaled.

"There's sex. But no money," I said.

"You didn't see that equipment. Computers, routers, DVD recorders. Lots of money there. Personally, I'm thinking of changing professions."

"Did you see his apartment, his clothes, his furniture. And no drugs. A Pulitzer needs more than one."

Following the smell of sandalwood, Fifi and I mounted the plank that led to his deck. It wobbled slightly and I wondered if Fifi floated.

"You're insane and your little dog too."

"Haylee was specific," I said. "She said the story was a Pulitzer and that code means drugs, sex, money, or at least two of the three. Get it?"

"Am I supposed to?" The praying palms fell apart and he rested his hands on his knees. "We have Tony. We have the video. We have statements from tenants that they didn't know about the cameras. And something you don't know is that we have several yellow Post-It®s from the trash in

Haylee's room with "Tony's Girls" and several tenants' names written in Haylee's handwriting. She knew what was going on and Tony knew she knew because he was watching the monitors. Now—"

"Did you find the knife?" I asked. "Haylee's notebook? Anything that suggest a meeting that night? And Haylee was at that apartment building a full four, count them, four days before the murder. Why did he wait so long? She might have broken the story at any time."

I had Dusty's attention now.

He uncrossed his legs and stood up slowly with a pained expression. Something cracked and his hand flew to his back. "Look, there's an FBI guy in San Francisco checking out Tony's computers and I have two of my people and half the San Rafael Police department going through Tony's recordings. I'm sure in a day or so we'll have the evidence we need to charge him with the murder. He tossed the knife, probably in the bay across from the Belvedere Club. Chief says, eventually we'll send down divers, but first we need to place him at the scene." He massaged his lower back. "Go on home. You did a good job. Your friend would be proud."

"Proud, proud of what? I've botched a murder investigation by giving you just what you wanted, a scapegoat. You've got the wrong guy, and you can care less. Case closed, is that it? Well, I care and I'm going to find the murderer with or without your help."

I stomped my exclamation, and Fifi and I turned on our heels, all six of them, and left.

The Research

Back at work, I mulled over the new information that Dusty had mentioned, Post-It®s left in Haylee's trash. They confirmed what I believed: she'd uncovered Tony's story, but decided not to run with it because she had something bigger on the horizon. That was why they'd ended up in the trash rather than stuck to the painting with the others. Looking over the three rows, I mentally worked each square back into its place in the lineup. What else had been removed? Or added?

The Post-It®s preceding Tony Amato's name listed three charities: Auxiliary Aid, St. Mary's Catholic Charities, and The Rummington Alzheimer's Clinic. These three, according to the Belvedere Club's tasteful Website, were the only charities the club sponsored. Two main fundraising events, a Christmas Auction and a Spring Ball, supported the charities while annual dues supported the club. Last year the Belvedere Club had raised one-point-two million dollars. As my pop would say, *Not bad for the petticoat brigade.*

Fifi scratched at the door and whined in that wheezy way she had of making me want to dropkick her to Germany. The ball of fluff wanted another bathroom break. I ignored her for the first twenty minutes and looked up each charity on the Internet. Finally, fearing she might dig a hole right through the door, I complied. It wasn't just maddening that she had a bladder the size of a raindrop, but every person we passed had to stop and chat about how cute she looked, or tell us about their aunt's, sister's, niece's, wife's dog. And whenever we passed someone else with a dog it was like the invasion of Iraq all over again. Yes, Fifi was friendly, but only to dogless strangers.

After our stroll around the rear parking lot, I emptied Fifi's water bowl, and went back to the Post-It®s. The square after Tony's referenced the Belvedere Club's lunch. The last in row two and the first in row three, were women's names: Francine Starling and Annette Vaughan. With Tony Amato out of the way, my focus switched to Francine Starling, my second suspect.

The Internet coughed up gobs on Oliver and Francine Starling, society page after society page. There was a spread in *Architectural Digest*, Mrs. Starling draped across the edge of a country French lounge sofa. She looked comfortable in front of the camera, no...it was more than that. Francine Starling was commanding; she owned the space—literally and figuratively. I had rarely come across someone who could use the lens the way she had, but fashion shots weren't my specialty.

Annette Vaughan was another story altogether. I couldn't find anything on the Internet except her name listed as one of the Belvedere Club's members. The ladies that I'd met at the club hadn't mentioned an Annette Vaughan so I had no idea why Haylee had written her name on a Post-It®.

From the side table, I pulled out the hotel phonebook and looked up Starling. Marin County was broken into each city alphabetically, and I found an Oliver Starling in Belvedere. There was nothing for A. Vaughan or Annette Vaughan although there were plenty of other Vaughans in every city in the county.

The call to the Starling's residence was answered on the third ring and I was passed off to Mrs. Starling who must have been standing nearby. I introduced myself as Haylee's colleague and mentioned that I was out here finishing up the story she had begun.

Francine Starling was professional in her condolences, a

little like she was reading from cue cards. Her enthusiasm rose a decibel when she spoke of the story. She was glad it would still run. If the Internet was a good measure, she liked her publicity.

"Many of Ms. Macklin's notes were lost. I'm afraid I only have your name and another name, Annette Vaughan."

"Oh, Annie, of course," she said.

"Would it be possible for me to come by and ask you a few questions?" I crossed my fingers.

"This morning!"

"Too early. How about this afternoon? I only have a few questions and I wanted to perhaps get a photo if you don't mind." The photo op should cement the deal.

"Oh, dear..." She paused long enough for me to worry, and then continued. "I suppose this afternoon would be possible, let us say around two. Do you have the address?"

I read the address from the phone book and she confirmed it. I had four hours to fill. I could call every Vaughan in the book to see if anyone knew an Annette or I could smoke a cigarette.

I grabbed Fifi's leash and shook it. "Want to go for a walk?"

She remained curled on the sofa.

The Photo Op

After a quick meatball sub and a stop at Peet's Coffee, I was back in sunny Belvedere looking for Francine Starling's address. I pulled up to a steel gate mounted with a coat of arms and initials that didn't fit Oliver or Francine Starling's in any language. Pressing the speaker phone mounted at the entrance, I announced myself to someone with a Russian accent, and the gate begun a slow roll out of my path. Before it was fully open, I drove in and down the sloped drive, curving around in front of a house built into the hill. The redwood paneled exterior was landscaped with large boulders and juniper bushes.

A plainly dressed woman in her mid-fifties opened the door and led me past an oppressive portrait of Mr. Starling and into a living room.

"Mrs. Starling will be with you momentarily."

Large framed windows faced San Francisco. The Transamerica Pyramid defined a skyline dotted with clouds while the image became part of the room. The effect was like living outdoors. Off to the side, I spotted the country French lounge sofa from the magazine layout. I chose a more centrally located sofa covered in a wine-colored velvet. There I waited until Francine Starling made her entrance.

Francine didn't make me wait anywhere near as long as I had expected. She must have been eager to get the article to press. A tall woman, she moved like she had a steel rod implanted in her spinal column. Her chin was perfectly parallel to the floor. Her hair and makeup were professionally done. No doubt she'd called a stylist immediately after our phone conversation. The smell of fresh hairspray preceded her into the room. She wore a floral Valentino skirt that I'd recently seen in Vogue magazine and a knitted top, belted at the waist.

What Francine Starling wasn't wearing was gloves. Age—I guessed somewhere in the sixties, but she'd had work done. Her face looked as white and lifeless as a peeled potato.

I stood and held out my hand, introducing myself. For all her tense appearance, her handshake had the strength of a limp tulip. She slid a crystal vase filled with zinnias across the glass table before lowering herself on the other end of the sofa. Her back remained erect. "Do you want to start with the photographs?" she asked.

While every hair is still in place. "We can." My camera was sitting in my lap. "I saw the photos from the *Architectural Digest* spread and I'd like to try for another angle."

"Certainly. How about the Secretary?" She glanced over her shoulder to a carved secretary against the rear wall. "It's been in my husband's family for generations."

The secretary was a faux Louis XIV in oak, quite popular in the 1950's. How many generations was she talking about? "Perfect."

Francine leaned across the top of the secretary and tilted her head provocatively. Next she straightened, laying only her arm—elbow to hand—along the top. She tried two more positions until she found the one that suited her. It was easy to see that she was an old hat at photo ops. She knew about lighting, she knew angles. She picked up a Mont Blanc and pretended to pen a letter. "If you stand there," she pointed. "You can catch the light coming in from the windows and won't need a flash."

I bit my tongue and snapped the shot, not that I intended to use it.

"You'll want another one, to be sure," she said.

"I have a preview, it was good. Why don't I get another one with you standing and resting your hand on the back of that chair?"

Hand on chair—how difficult could it be? But she tried several other poses until I saw her face warm up the lens. She wanted control of the shot, but I didn't relinquish my lens easily. Instead of letting her repose, I repositioned myself and shot a third time, before she could object. "That should be good," I said. "Now, do you remember your conversation with Ms. Macklin?"

"Certainly. We were seated beside each other at the luncheon." Francine gestured me back to the sofa. She sat at the other end.

"That would be the Thursday luncheon?" I turned off my camera and put it back in the bag. "A week before she died?"

"That's right. She had a wonderful sense of humor."

Yes she did. A shadow fell over me and I knew I needed to refocus the conversation. "What sort of things did you talk about? What type of questions did she ask?"

"About the club, naturally. How I became a member and how long have I been a member. Questions along those lines. Like a lot of the members, I inherited my membership from my mother." She stood. "May I get you something? Some coffee or perhaps, tea?"

"Thank you, I'm fine." I pulled out the photo of the Belvedere Club ladies that I'd printed earlier at a local camera shop. There was still the question of the unidentified fifth woman who had shown up Thursday morning. "Do you recognize the women in that photo?"

Francine had barely glanced over it when she answered. "Of course. They are all members. There's Gloria, Penny, Odilia—"

"Who's the woman with her back to the camera?"

Francine glanced at the photo again. "That's Lenora Larkin. Her husband is Supervisor Larkin. He used to work at the White House, you know."

"Really? In what capacity?" It couldn't be a coincidence. Haylee's ex-boyfriend—Gary Larkin. I looked at the image and tried to match it to the one of Mrs. Gary Larkin that I'd seen on the Belvedere Club's website. So Gary had a preference for older women.

Francine handed the photo back to me. "Oh, I don't know. I understand it was a while ago. He probably worked in the Clinton Administration." She walked to the picture window and looked lovingly at the view.

One mystery solved. Gary's new wife hadn't wanted me to see her. I made a mental note to ask Dusty what he'd learned about Gary Larkin, but I had to concentrate on the problem at hand. Haylee was an investigative reporter. Since I didn't know what she was onto, I had no idea what direction to take. I decided to start with the lineage. "Do you know Charlotte's mother, Amanda Warren?"

She turned back to me. "Well, of course. She was the Grande Dame when I joined." She crossed the room and sat on the chaise.

"Grande Dame?" I asked.

"That's what we call the head of the club."

"Oh, the President?" By her reaction, I saw she didn't like the word. "Who is always a descendant of the original founder?"

"That's correct."

Her inflection said this was a contentious point so I removed my notebook from my camera case. "Does it bother you that the only way to be a Grande Dame is through birth?"

"Now, you sound like that other reporter. Grande Dame is a figurehead. The title holds no real power. It's a women's club, for goodness sake, not a sports team."

I bet. Francine Starling was a woman who needed to be queen bee. It must feel like a wedgie riding up her ass that she never could be. I tried to remember Haylee's exposé on men's clubs. "What about the exclusivity issue? Women only? Are you anti-men?"

Francine returned to her end of the sofa and reached for the crystal vase moving it back to its original position. "My goodness, no, I'm not anti-men. Some of my favorite people are men." She laughed at her own joke. "Everything has to be so Politically Correct these days. Can't like-minded people come together without it being a crime?"

Oh, snippy. With a curl of my lips, I let her know I got it. "What are the like interests of the Belvedere Club?"

She slid a small ceramic bowl next to the vase of flowers and looked at the arrangement with a cocked head and earnest expression. "That's better, don't you think?" She relaxed by laying her hands in her lap. "We're a group of a certain social status. That status has its obvious rewards and also its not so obvious drawbacks. At the Belvedere Club, we…network."

I imagined the networking—where to buy the freshest flowers, who did the best nails, the best tummy tucks. Life was hard. I couldn't wait to hear about the drawbacks.

"Most of our husbands are important men—some, very important men. As their wives and because of our social standing we are expected to raise money for museums, orchestras, this illness and that. At the Belvedere Club, we decide how *we* want to contribute to the community. We don't do it because we are expected to, but because we choose to. Does that make sense?"

It actually did in some diamond-crusted feminist way. "One-point-two mil. I'd say you've done quite well."

She beamed.

"Do you feel Charlotte Warren has done a good job as

acting president?"

She shot to her feet and marched back over to the San Francisco view, leaving her back to me. "You aren't going to let this go, are you? I know you've talked to the others, how else would you have their pictures?"

Since I couldn't see her face I had no idea what she might be feeling. I stood and walked around the coffee table. "I heard a rumor that you argued with Haylee about your daughter."

"My daughter?" Francine turned. "You were misinformed. I did have a disagreement with that reporter, but my daughter has nothing to do with it—she's not even a member of the club, yet." She huffed before continuing. "I don't believe Charlotte should be president. There, that's what started the disagreement."

"Oh."

"Don't look so shocked, Charlotte is fully aware of my sentiments as are the others, which I'm sure they've regaled in telling you."

"What's your problem with Charlotte? Or is the problem the whole lineage thing?"

She stared at me for a minute and then grimaced. "I'm afraid that's all I have time for today. I have a dinner party for twelve this evening."

I'd lost her. Always thinking of the article. She wanted to secure her place in the story and speaking out against the president would damage her image.

"Would you like another picture or two?" she asked me. "No, well then, I'll walk you out."

I picked up my camera bag. "One more question if you don't mind."

Her expression said she did and her stiff shoulders said she did, but I asked anyway.

"I'd like to speak with Annette Vaughan, but I haven't

found any contact information on her. Would you happen to have her number?"

She smiled. "It's in the club register. I'll get it for you."

I walked myself to the door and Francine met me with Annette Vaughan's number scribbled on a message pad. She tore off the number and handed it to me, saying she'd like to see a copy of the article when it was finished.

The Gardener

Outside the Starling home, I removed my cell phone and punched in Annette Vaughan's number. I figured it was too late for an interview today, especially if she needed to get her hair and makeup done, too. I didn't really know what else to ask either, but I wanted to speak with everyone that Haylee had spoken with. I never knew when a jewel would catch the sun.

Annette Vaughan sounded cheerier than Francine, her voice lower, but more expressive. Without hesitation, she told me to come right over. She spieled off directions to Mill Valley and instructed me to come through the back gate as she probably wouldn't hear the bell.

Traffic in Mill Valley was awful due to the two lane road in and out. I passed, bumper-to-bumper, through the shopping district and out the other side into tree-filled hills. Annette Vaughan's house was on a narrow street lined with parked cars, leaving a single lane passable. I found a space at a cross street and had to walk back. The house was pale yellow clapboard with white trim. White rose bushes lined the front, with yellow tree roses lining the front walk like a promenade. All very storybook charming. I found the gate at the side of the house and let myself into the yard.

A woman, wearing a blue smock and floppy hat, knelt in the grass and was digging in a raised vegetable garden.

"Ms. Vaughan?"

Brushing off her gloved hands, she stood, dry dirt falling from her blue jeans. "Are you the reporter?"

I introduced myself and thanked her for seeing me.

"Should I stop or do you mind if I continue while we talk?

I really want to get these tomatoes planted today. Looks like we're going to have a dry spring," she said, glancing up at the sky.

"Please." I motioned to the tomatoes and lowered myself to a patch of grass next to her.

A braided ponytail hung down her back. Annette looked younger than Francine Starling and Charlotte Warren by about ten or fifteen years and she lacked the stuffiness the other women exuded like cheap perfume.

"I just love gardening. Keeps me grounded," she said, smiling as she dug.

"'Grounded.' What exactly does that mean?"

Annette chuckled. "One of those New Ageisms, I suppose. 'Grounded,' 'centered,' 'balanced.' Where are you from?"

"Boston area mostly. I'm currently living in D.C.." Even as I said it, I wondered if it were still true.

"For me, 'grounded' means getting my feet back under me. Lots of things out there to trip you up. Know what I mean? Things like what happened to your colleague." Annette popped the plastic off a tomato plant and shoved the plant into the hole she'd dug. "Such a nice person. I only met her that once at the Belvedere Club, but I liked her instantly. Did you know her well?"

"Haylee was my best friend." I don't know why I said that, but it probably had something to do with her easy going manner.

She drew in a breath and the newly soiled gloves came to her mouth as if she wanted to hold back her words. She wasn't bothered by the dirt marking her cheeks. "I am so sorry, I—"

I sucked in my own breath and held up a hand to end this conversation. "How long have you been a member of the Belvedere Club?"

She bent back over the dirt and picked up the hand shovel. "Almost fifteen years, now. My mother passed away from breast cancer and I inherited her membership," she said, plunging the shovel into the earth.

Now it was my turn to be sorry and I said so. "Does that mean that Francine Starling's daughter will inherit her membership?"

"I suppose so, but I doubt she'd want it. Francine's daughter is a free spirit. Most likely, Francine will offer the membership to someone else in the family."

"That's allowed."

"That's the only way to get a membership. Mothers usually pass them to their daughters, but it can pass to another family member like a sister or a cousin."

I made a note, but something didn't make sense. "If you must inherit your membership, how did Charlotte Warren get hers? Her mother is still alive."

Annette brushed her forehead with the back of her glove depositing some fresh dirt on her skin. "You can pass your membership to another family member at anytime. Dying isn't prerequisite."

I pointed to her forehead. "You've got some dirt," I gestured.

She wiped at where I pointed, but only manage to further sully the spot.

"Here," I said. "Let me." I wipe away the soil and she thanked me, but I'd completely lost the thought I was vaguely pursuing. "Do you enjoy being a member?" I thought this question might lead somewhere. Annette was obviously of different ilk than Francine Starling and Charlotte Warren.

"I love it. They're a wild bunch. Don't be fooled by their impeccable manners. They can get as trashy as a twenty dollar whore—in their own way, mind you. Could you pass me that plant, there?"

I popped the tomato plant from its plastic container and handed it to her. "I have a hard time picturing Francine Starling trashy."

"Huh, Francine is an intelligent woman reigned in by a lifestyle that dictates to her husband."

"She has a choice," I said.

"Not Francine, or any of the other women raised in that society. Believe me, I know. I was well on my way to being exactly the same until my mother died. Their fathers were the emperors, all powerful. That position is now held by their husbands. It's all they know. It's a different generation." She filled dirt in around the tomato.

"Look at Charlotte Warren. She never married. She made a choice."

Annette Vaughan rolled back on her knees and looked me square in the face. "Have you met Charlotte?"

"Yesterday."

She looked me over as if wondering what to say. "You didn't notice...." She shook her head. "Charlotte's, well...Charlotte's special." Annette went back to her digging.

"I found her sincere, intelligent, helpful." I though back to the meeting, to the maid in the ridiculous uniform, to the antique furniture, to Charlotte's friendly demeanor, and wondered if I'd missed something.

"Oh, Charlotte's all those things." Annette pointed at another tomato plant. "and...she's special. She's had choices."

I passed her another plant and watched her put it in the ground and cover up the roots with dark earth. "Because of the lineage? Or because of her mother?"

"Amanda Warren, Charlotte's mom, what a character. In a different way, mind you. Amanda's what we call an eccentric."

In my book they were all eccentrics, but I'd yet to meet Amanda Warren so my ruler for comparison was limited. "I understand Francine Starling and Haylee had an argument during the luncheon. Do you know what it was about?"

"I don't remember." Annette didn't look at me when she spoke.

"Someone said it was about Francine Starling's daughter. Francine said it was because she doesn't want Charlotte Warren as the Belvedere Club's president."

"That's true." Annette lowered the shovel and rolled back on her feet. "If Francine Starling had her way, she would vote Charlotte out of the club altogether, but we all adore Charlotte. It'll never happen."

"Why did Francine stomp out at the luncheon? It's been my experience that when someone stomps off, he or she's hiding something."

"Well then, Francine Starling has quite a lot to hide."

The Argument

Sunday morning, I was awakened by a call from Haylee's mom. She sounded better than she had the last time we'd spoken; I sounded worse, she pointed out.

"The Sheriff is ready to send Haylee home. I've booked O'Brien's for the wake on Friday. The funeral's at our church, of course. You'll be back?"

"I don't—"

"You have to be here. You have to speak. Haylee would want you to speak," she said.

"I thought you wanted me to find Haylee's killer."

There was a long silence at the other end before Nadine spoke. "Hon, the police have the guy. Why don't you know that?"

"The police have *a* guy. He's not the killer."

"Lieutenant Arkansas seems to think he is."

I sat up and picked at my nail polish. "The guy was running an Internet porno ring. Haylee had already published a similar story. She never would have—"

"Hon, you need to let the police do their job. Trust them. You've been upset by losing Haylee. You're biased."

"Nadine, I—"

"Get yourself back here. We've a room for you here at the house. Friday's Haylee's day."

Arguing seemed pointless, but I'd never known her to be this closed-minded. I supposed she needed to believe Tony was the killer. She needed the certainty. And she needed Haylee back home. I bit off my thumbnail while promising Nadine that I'd fly back to Boston before Friday.

She was wrong about another thing though—I still hadn't

faced losing Haylee. A light airy feeling had settled over me in the last day or so and although it was agreeable, it wasn't natural. Not for me. So I had reason to worry. I am a professional, I reminded myself, same as I did whenever anxiety swept in. My biggest fear was that my denied emotions would rise up and slap me down when I least expected, leaving me defenseless. The sensible thing was to keep moving forward, and when that failed, I ran.

Desperate for a diversion, I returned to the Internet. For most nonprofits, financial information was available to the public. I tried to locate the financials for the three charities. The Auxiliary Aid billed itself as a Traveler's Aid Charity originally founded to help young girls and women drawn to San Francisco by the Panama-Pacific International Exposition. More recently, they helped house and feed homeless families until they got back on their feet.

St. Mary's Catholic Charities ran food banks around San Francisco, catering to the city's large homeless population. They also assisted AIDS patients with home care, hospital visits, and financial options.

The Rummington Alzheimer's Clinic was based in Santa Rosa, which I found odd since the other two were nearby in San Francisco. Santa Rosa was about fifty miles north of Belvedere. Fairly new compared to the other charities, the clinic was built in 1975, and the Belvedere Club had been a financial supporter since 1982. The Rummington Alzheimer's Clinic didn't have a webpage, but I found an address and phone number in an online medical directory.

While I was pouring my second cup of coffee, Fifi went into a barking spasm that was sure to be heard downstairs and across the courtyard in the manager's office. Online, I had found collars that sent an electrical shock through the dog when it started to bark. I was warming to the idea.

After slamming the coffee mug down, I reached for her

snout just as someone slammed a fist into my door, banging fiercely.

"Look what you've done," I said.

She kept barking, and my visitor kept banging.

"Stop!"

The room fell silent. Fifi eyed me suspiciously like she was expecting a kick. I threw out my index finger and set my eyes in a stern grimace. She didn't move, so I crossed the room and threw open the door ready to deal with the next problem. Without a greeting, Dusty charged in.

"How did you know?" He lumbered across the room, sending Fifi scampering under a chair. "What have you found? Do you have the notebook?"

"Whoa. Rewind. What are we talking about?" I asked, returning to the dining table. I clicked out of the Internet. This deliberation on my part filled Fifi with courage. She crept halfway out from under the chair and barked once at Dusty.

"Look. I've been fair with you, took you on interviews, shared autopsy info."

Fifi barked again, causing him to raise his voice, which caused Fifi to continue barking. I covered my ears with my hands.

He pointed at Fifi with his hand in the form of a gun, his thumb cocked. "Either shut the thing up or I'm going to put it out of its misery."

Hmm, decisions, decisions.

I reached down to gather up the ball of fur, but she dashed back under the chair where I couldn't reach her. "Stay there," I said, as if it was my idea and turned back to Dusty. "You were…yelling something. What?"

"I don't yell!" And a strange calm settled over him. He sat on the arm of the wing chair opposite the television and rested his hands in his lap. He reminded me of a psychotic killer I'd once interviewed. The killer also changed emotions at the blink of an eye. How dangerous was Lieutenant Arkansas?

His voice was without emotion. "Amato. How'd you know he wasn't the killer? The notebook. You have it, don't you?"

I dropped down on the sofa a safe distance from Dusty. "I told you, I knew Haylee, knew how she worked. All I had was a guess, but from your theatrics, it looks like I was right."

"If you have that notebook—"

I raised my right hand. "On the Bible, I don't. But I'm not the least bit surprised about Amato. What cleared him?"

"His recordings. The Internet business dialed directly into his recording equipment which was an automatic setup. Looks like he did his sleeping during the busiest period, and did his editing in the early morning hours when the phone lines were less active and he could free up the equipment. A time stamp on a few recordings puts him on the equipment at the time of Ms. Macklin's death. Also a witness. A resident coming home from work on a night shift saw his car parked out front of the building and a light under his apartment door. Circumstantial, but the time stamp is exact. It's invisible on the recording. Amato didn't know it was there. Now, you're telling me you guessed that?"

"The story didn't fit the Pulitzer angle."

"Oh, yeah. The big three, sex, money, and rock and roll."

"Sex, money, or drugs. Laugh if you want, but there are specific criteria to our code. It's what makes it a code."

"Why did you need a code?" he asked.

"Terrance. He's an ass. So where do we go from here? What's next?"

He looked down. "Maybe you can tell me? If you don't have the notebook, what sent you back to Amato's?" His face tensed although his hands were gently crossed in his lap. He scared me more than a little.

I called for protection. "Fifi. Come Fifi." Maybe if I threw her at him, I'd have time to get away.

"Out with it or you'll have more than just your editor to worry about."

Once, I'd been charged with hampering an investigation. Jail wasn't a lot of fun. You had your sobering addicts, your insisting innocents, and those who just didn't give a hoot. Luckily, I knew card tricks.

"Promise you won't get mad," I said.

"I never get mad. It's not my way."

"Good to know." I stood and motioned him into the bedroom. The charities would involve considerable investigation, not something I could effectively do alone and certainly not by Friday.

I spoke fast, hoping to keep him thinking rather than reacting. "I found those in Haylee's room. Each one has a subject that she researched. One led her to the story that got her killed. Under Tony's name… you see it? That's as far as I've gotten."

The yellow squares, strung across the mirror, drew his attention.

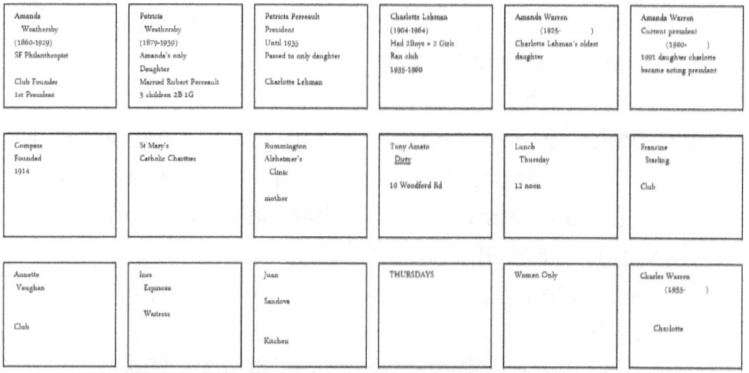

He clutched his palms together and brought the double fist to his lips. His jaws tensed and released, tensed and released.

For the longest time he remained silent.

"The order's important?" he asked when he finally spoke.

I clucked my tongue.

"The last one is—"

"Charles and Charlotte Warren's birth date. Mrs. Warren is technically still the Belvedere Club's owner, but her will bequests it to Charlotte, who as we know, is already running it."

He dropped his hands by his side. "But Charles's name is at the top. If that's the last one doesn't it point us in their direction?"

"Possibly, but not necessarily. This order is a working order. At any point, something else might have emerged, like Tony did. She picked up on what he was doing the first time she went to the building. Don't ask me how. But she never moved his Post-It® to the end and she threw out the others referencing the porno scam. Why? My guess is that she was already working on a bigger story."

Dusty read over the squares. He pointed to the first row, and then to the last square with Charles' name on it. "This should be in the first row. Why isn't it?"

"I think we have to follow her research to answer that. After Tony's square we have these two names, both Belvedere Club members. I spoke with each woman yesterday afternoon. Francine Starling is the one who had the argument with Haylee during the Thursday luncheon. No one can agree on what caused it. Annette confirmed that Francine Starling doesn't want Charlotte Warren running the Belvedere Club. And Gary Larkin of Mr. and Mrs. Gary Larkin once worked at the White House although no one can tell me what he did there. I called Odilia Keith to confirm that Supervisor Larkin is fifteen years his wife's junior. But note there isn't a Post-It® with his name on it. You didn't find any other Post-It®s in that trash did you?"

Dusty still didn't look at me when he spoke. "An argument with a member, and Haylee's ex-boyfriend—these are your suspects? None of this seems like a motive for murder."

"Check before Tony's square, we have the three charities sponsored by the Belvedere Club. If we think of the club or its members as the money then we're looking for sex or drugs or both to fit the code."

He chuckled, but more with tolerance than humor. He didn't take his eyes off the Post-It®s.

"Auxiliary Aid, ever heard of it?" I asked.

He scratched his nubby head. Another long pause before he spoke. "Their big drive is during the holidays. Make people feel guilty for having a job, a home, give to those less fortunate, that kind of thing."

"Ever hear any negative publicity?"

"Nope. Far as I know, they're on the up and up, have to be with that kind of publicity each year."

"What about their financials? Can you have someone look into them?" I asked.

"Not without good reason." He read off the second charity. "St. Mary's Catholic Charities. They have a magazine, saw it in a waiting room once."

"That's it?"

"It's all I know."

"Maybe we can hire a private investigator."

"Funny," he said. "You're a million laughs." He read the third one. "The Rummington Alzheimer's Clinic."

My favorite. "Odd, don't you think?"

He let out a sigh, long and slow and turned towards me crossing his arms over his chest. "How so?"

"Well, the other two are bona fide charity organizations with their own charters while this is a private clinic."

"The detective in me thinks you want to start there."

"Clinic equals pharmaceuticals equals drugs. Add donations and you have money."

"And money plus drugs makes your theory—the what is it—Pulitzer?"

I snapped my fingers and winked. For such a big guy, he was pretty quick. I only explained it three times.

He massaged his head, pretending to think, but I knew he wasn't. "Sex," he said, his eyes cloaking me like a big brown blanket.

"Pardon me?"

His voice was lower and he drew out his words. "I like the sex angle better. A big clinic like that, there might be a sex angle, and there's Gary, the ex-boyfriend. Funny that he should make an undocumented appearance."

I wasn't sure if he was teasing or not.

He continued, his voice going back to its normal range. "Know what I think, and mind you, I'm only a stupid lieutenant without code words, but I think you're trying too hard. Your Pulitzer theory, your Post-It®s theory. Now, who's looking for a scapegoat?"

An emotion I couldn't identify tightened my chest. I ran from the room, Haylee filling my mind. I so wanted to speak to her, but I knew better. Fifi must have sensed my turmoil because she crawled out from under the chair and followed me to the computer. Reaching, I scooped her up and hugged her close. "How are we going to live without her?"

"Did you say something?" Dusty drew up beside me. "Or are you talking to the dog?"

The sarcasm said it all. I put Fifi down.

"I'll look into the charities, but I'm more interested in knowing why Charles Warren's name is the last in the list. I'll call if I have any more questions," he said.

"What? No, no, no. If you're interviewing Warren, I want to go with you."

"You lost your privileges when you withheld information. Take comfort that I'm not arresting you."

"I haven't withheld anything. You saw the Post-It®s. There's nothing there. Without Haylee, they mean zip."

He walked to the door. "I've spent two days digging up evidence on the wrong man, time I might have spent better, thank you."

"You would have found out about Tony, eventually. I probably saved you time!"

He shifted his weight. I saw I'd made a direct hit, but he refused to give.

"I'll call," he said, closing the door behind him.

I returned to the bedroom, Fifi at my heels. The mirror was empty, the Post-It®s gone.

The Boyfriend

I'd deal with Dusty's snit later. I had something more pressing on my agenda. The Marin County phonebook didn't contain a listing for a Gary or Lenora Larkin so I pulled up my electronic phonebook on the laptop, hoping to find the name of someone who'd kept in contact with Gary over the years.

Unfortunately the Haylee-Gary period was lodged back in our party-hardy days, most of which I don't remember. The two numbers I had—one for a cousin of Haylee's and another for an ex-coworker—had been disconnected. I deleted the entries from my phonebook and punched in Odilia Keith's number, one of the chattier Belvedere Club ladies.

I apologized for bothering her again, even though I knew she loved being part of the investigation. This was the type of gossip you couldn't pay for and, no doubt, the moment we disconnected she'd be calling the others to let them know I'd phoned for the Larkin's number.

A soft-spoken woman answered the Larkin's phone. Probably the help. Since Mrs. Larkin employed a limo driver I doubted she answered her own phone. I asked the woman to speak with Gary.

"Briana, I can't believe it! Where are you?" His voice carried the same excitement I remembered, although I didn't detect a hint of his southern twang.

"I'm here. How are you?"

"Here! In California?"

"Marin," I said.

"Oh right. I read about Haylee. I'd just seen her too, it was so weird. I can't believe she's gone. How are you holding up?"

The mention of her name hit me like a punch to the throat. Hearing Gary's voice, the past had embraced me like a long lost lover. I'd completely forgotten why I'd called. "Could we meet for a coffee or something?"

"That'd be great! Let me TIVO the game."

We exchanged locations and decided to meet at a coffee shop in the Town Center, a small shopping complex near my hotel. I hooked Fifi's leash on and snuck her out the back.

* * *

The only thing I recognized about Gary was his smile and even that had been whitened. His wavy ponytail had been replaced with a short, cropped style. His slightly heavy build was trim and dare I say, muscular. He wore a pale gray linen suit with a white tee shirt underneath.

"You look great," I said as we hugged.

He mirrored the sentiment, but he was lying. The emotional toll of Haylee's death was wearing me down. The black circles beneath my eyes were widening with each day. And I'd paint my nails, then chip half the paint away. I hadn't even combed my hair for this meeting and couldn't remember brushing my teeth all day. If I were a man, I'd have a mean five o'clock shadow.

Gary ordered us two espressos while I tied Fifi to a table in the courtyard.

"Do they have any suspects in Haylee's murder?" He asked, dropping into a chair next to me.

I took the coffee he offered, but before I answered him, he continued.

"A deputy came by the house and questioned my wife. She belongs to the club where it happened."

Another thing Dusty forgot to share. "You mentioned that you saw Haylee, when was that?"

He looked down at Fifi curled by his feet. "We hooked up

for a coffee, right here actually." He picked up his espresso and drank.

He'd looked away when he answered me. He was lying. This was the first time since he'd arrived that he'd looked away. I tried to digest what that might mean. I wasn't some great friend of his, only someone from his long ago life. I pulled my cigarette pack from my handbag. "So you're married? And Supervisor? How did that happen?"

"My wife. I met her when I came out here to start my limo business."

I took out a cigarette. "How's the business going?"

He pointed to a *No Smoking* sign and forced a regretful smile.

"As Supervisor can't you do something about that?" I asked.

"Hey, it's California. I don't smoke anymore either. Business, pretty good, can't complain. Had some rough patches in the beginning, but Lenora is wonderful. She's helped me a lot. The political thing was her idea."

I bet. She was trying to legitimize her boy-toy.

"And it's not just Supervisor," he continued. "I'm on all these boards—all voluntary—they don't pay shit, I mean, you know what I mean."

"Sure. What other boards?" I shoved the cigarettes back in my bag.

"Oh, there's the Child Care Commission, the Design and Review Board, the Alcohol and Drug Advisory Board—don't drink anything stronger than coffee these days." He picked up his cup.

"Me either."

He laughed. "Funny what the years have done to us."

"Did you find Haylee changed?"

He looked away. "Not much. Well, yeah." He turned back. "She said you're a photojournalist. You like it?"

"Journalist pays more, but I still get to write captions. With all these boards it sounds like you're working towards a political future. Are you planning to head back to the White House?"

"Have to get elected first. Lenora says volunteering for all those boards helps me get voters. And we're active in a lot of charities too—always networking." He opened his jacket and pointed out his Special Olympics tee shirt. "Also there's the Wildlife Fund, and Lenora's on the board of the Auxiliary Aid. We meet a lot of influential people through that one."

On the board of a Belvedere Club charity. Another coincidence? "Sounds like you and your wife are really happy…and busy. I just can't get over the fact that Haylee didn't tell me she'd run into you. That wasn't like her unless—"

He glanced around the courtyard and everything became clear to me.

"—unless she had something to be ashamed of."

Our eyes met. He swallowed hard and looked away.

"Gary, did something happen between you two?"

"I told her not to worry about it." He picked at his paper cup trying to unfurl the lip. "My wife, well, my wife's older, more sophisticated." His southern accent made an appearance. "She's not that interested in sex anymore—it wasn't always like that—she's basically told me to do what I want, just don't let anyone know. Lenora's wonderful, but—"

"I get the picture." I still couldn't believe Haylee didn't tell me. "Do you think Lenora knew about you and Haylee."

"I didn't tell her."

Would Haylee? "Have you spoken to the police?"

"Why should I? he asked. "I don't know what happened. I was at a fundraiser that night."

"Was your wife with you?"

He lowered his head and leaned over to caress Fifi. "Of course."

The Squeeze

I didn't know Lieutenant Arkansas well, but from the finality in his voice and the puff of his chest, I felt certain he'd meant what he'd said. I was cut from the loop. There would be no more ride-alongs, no more brainstorming information, nope, nada. He'd tolerated me because of my relationship to Haylee, or maybe, as he'd said, he needed an extra hand. Either way, he no longer trusted me and maybe I was a tinny-winy bit to blame. Unfortunately for him, he underestimated me, which made me feel a little sorry for the big guy. I started my calls at six a.m.—nine a.m. on Capitol Hill.

At nine-twenty Marin Sheriff's time, Madge Talis, the press officer, escorted me into Dusty's office. He was on the phone, but as his glance passed from Talis to me, I knew things were going to get ugly.

He disconnected and stood, rather than motioning us to sit. He was hoping to make it quick. "Madge," he said with a nod. "I'm a little busy today. I need to get to San Francisco."

"I don't want to hold you up. I believe you know Ms. Kaleigh."

Dusty tilted his head in my direction, but didn't greet me.

"She has official permission to accompany you on any and all interviews regarding the Macklin case. In return she promises that nothing will be printed until okayed by me. She—"

Dusty stepped forward, closing in on Madge and using his height as psychological manipulation. "She's hampered my investigation—"

Madge, not easily intimidated, held up a hand. "Official

clearance, I said. You can argue all you want, but this comes from farther up."

"Fine. Let's talk to the Sheriff."

Madge paused and looked my way. "Higher than the Sheriff."

"There is no higher," Dusty said. He eyed me in a way that made me want to duck and take cover.

Madge forced a chuckle, pretending everything was okay. "We're clear then?"

Dusty pointed to the telephone. "That was Belvedere's sergeant. He's back from vacation and wants the case. Maybe I should pass her and the case over to him."

"That's not how it works and you know it," Madge said. "You started the case, you finish it. If he wants to help, it looks like we can use all the manpower we can get. Another reason to make use of Ms. Kaleigh here." She leaned her head towards me without really looking at me either. "And her connections."

With that, Madge left, leaving Dusty and me facing each other, and me without a Kevlar vest.

"How high?" he asked.

"Ever heard of a Senator named Barbara Boxer? She really loves this state."

"Bull. I don't believe you. You don't know Boxer, you pulled a hustle and when I find out how, you're doing time." He grabbed his jacket off a coat hook and head out. I scurried behind him, hoping he wasn't headed to the men's room.

* * *

Without a word, we drove twenty minutes south to San Francisco. Dusty hadn't allowed me a cigarette before leaving so again I was picking at my nail polish as the Sentra climbed 101. At the top, I admired the view of Mount Tamalpais, the hiking trails streaming down the side. After a tunnel and a downward slope, the Golden Gate Bridge came into view. It wasn't golden, not even yellow, or orange, but a dull, muddy, rust color like the primer coating my Honda back in D.C..

"Why do they call it the Golden Gate Bridge when it's red?"

Silence.

A flock of seagulls swooped down under the bridge and out of sight. Out on the Pacific, a barge, led by a tug, was heading beneath us towards the bay. The sun was high, the clouds sparse, and the morning was one of those we Easterners don't really believe exist outside of the movies.

Dusty's icy calm bothered me and not just because a gun was hooked to his right hip. Okay, hanging him up with his superiors probably didn't sit well with the big guy. It wouldn't have sat well with me either. But he'd left me little choice. I couldn't look into the charities on my own; a serious inquiry required authority. And I knew better than to make enemies with the police because they ultimately had the upper hand. If Dusty's little tiff lasted too long, I could see myself squeezed out of the investigation altogether. I'd called in my only ace—a friend of a friend of a friend—I couldn't use her again. I'd need another angle.

"Ever heard of a quest?" I asked.

Silence.

"Like the quest of Gawain? The Holy Grail? Of course, there are lots of quests, like spiritual—spirit quest, for planets—planet quest, for data—data quest."

Not so much as a grin.

"A quest for the Irish is like a goal, but stronger, much, much, stronger. Sort of like our reason for being, a preordained mission."

Dusty's knuckles on the steering wheel appeared to relax. Perhaps it was my imagination. I rambled on.

"My quest, if you think about it, is to make sure Haylee's

killer is punished. That's my quest for Haylee and for myself. Were that enough, I could sit by and wait for you to catch the killer, hands down."

Dusty relaxed into his seat. I waited for him to switch on the radio to drown me out.

"But you see, I have another quest and that's for Haylee's mother. She needs to understand why Haylee was killed by this person. She needs validation for her daughter's life."

He winced before speaking as if to do so was causing him great pain. "Celtic grief counseling?"

"You've got it! We Irish aren't big on therapy."

The interior fell silent again, the engine humming as we slowed for the toll plaza. I waited it out, hoping he would say more. I didn't have to wait long.

"That gives you the right to make others look bad?"

"That wasn't my intent, never my intent, and if I did, I apologize. I'll compliment your investigative skills, praise your interrogation technique, and flatter you like an oil baron if it will help bridge this riff. Come on, let me hang around while you investigate. Don't shut me out like this. Who knows, I might be of help."

After a long pause, Dusty glanced across the seat. "Buddhism teaches that each individual is responsible for *her* or his own liberation from anguish."

What was he talking about? "I can appreciate that, but Haylee's mom isn't Buddhist and I owe her, more than you can ever know."

He sighed like he was wasting his words, which—let's face it—he was. "The camera stays in the car. This is an investigation, not a story."

"Fine. And I have some information for you. I saw Gary Larkin yesterday. He says that he and Haylee hooked up."

"You mean—"

"Sex, yeah. I was really putout about it because I believed

him. Can you believe that, I believed him over my best friend?"

Dusty honked at a red Miata when it cut in front of him. "But your friend didn't tell you, did she?"

"Exactly. And why? Because it never happened. But Gary says it did?"

"Because it did."

"No way. He's married. Haylee wouldn't sleep with a married man even if he had a signed invitation from the wife, which, according to Gary, was the way it happened."

"Is this another code thing?"

"She had morals and I don't see her ignoring them for some guy she hadn't thought about in years."

"She was far from home. Maybe in the heat of the moment—"

"No way. He's lying," I said.

Dusty watched the road rather than continue his fruitless argument. I knew Haylee.

"So where are we going?" I asked. "I think we should start with the Auxiliary Aid. It's bound to be smaller than the Catholic Charities and we can move ahead faster." Truthfully, I didn't care where we started or what Dusty thought of my suggestion. I'd made it because I wanted to show him I was ready to be helpful. Instead, I got a rise.

"We'll start where and when I say. As far as I know, I'm still heading this investigation. Madge has nothing to say about that."

The Charities

We drove through the Presidio, the oldest, continuously operated military base in the country from 1848 when Mexico signed California over to the United States until 1994 when it closed. Dusty explained that it was now a National Park, but that George Lucas, of *Star Wars* fame, had won a bid back in 2001 to build a nine-hundred square foot film studio inside the park. He pointed out the newly constructed studio as we drove past. We took Arguello Boulevard to California Street and turned left. Dusty pulled out his notepad and checked something, probably an address. I didn't ask and he didn't share. Farther up California, we parked in front of a weathered two-story building of gray stucco. The worn wooden sign out front had once read "Auxiliary Aid." The current version was "xil ar id" with a hint of where the capital "A"s once lay.

I started to tell Dusty about Lenora Larkin's involvement, but he cut me off with a raised index finger.

"Not a word."

I suspected he didn't mean right now, but if I opened my mouth during the interview, he'd find sufficient cause to lock me in a cell somewhere and lose the key. It was nice being friends again.

The director was a cheerful woman of about fifty. She wore no makeup yet her cheeks were rosy red due to a web of broken capillaries. Her hair, mostly gray, was pulled back away from her face by an elastic band. Her blue jeans were fitted and a knotted navy blouse revealed a thick huggable waist.

Her personal office was the size of a laundry room,

overstuffed with manuals and dustier than the Sahara. Its only redeeming feature was that it overlooked the street allowing plenty of light to illuminate the filth. When asked, she found the financials, lightning quick, all without breaking her conversation with Dusty.

"Since Sacramento cut our funds, we're always trying to drum up donations from one source or another, Lieutenant Arkansas. I'm used to people asking to see our financial report." On a photocopier that looked older than me, she photocopied the spreadsheet and offered it to Dusty.

Even to my skeptical sensibilities, she came off like a woman with nothing to hide. Although, a corpse might be lying beneath the stacked manuals and we'd never notice with all the other crap scattered around. She answered Dusty's questions about the charity's charter directly and without pause. An icon of honesty.

Dusty waved the rolled spreadsheet in the air. "I thank you for your time." He handed her a business card.

"I understand Lenora Larkin is on your board," I said.

Dusty took a step back.

"Why, yes. She's an amazing fundraiser. We raised sixty-two hundred at our last soiree." Pride resonated in her voice.

"Last Wednesday night?" I said.

"At the Harbor Museum."

I looked at Dusty before I spoke again. He was looking at the director. "Was Mrs. Larkin there?" I asked.

"No. She was ill, but her husband joined us."

The room fell silent while I filed away Gary's second lie.

Dusty cocked his head at me, his expression neutral, but his eyes angry. "Anything else?" he said.

I made the zipper motion across my lips.

He pointed to his card still held in the director's hand. "If you think of anything else...."

"You know, Lieutenant, the San Francisco police force

does a drive for us every spring."

"You're kidding. How do they find the time?"

Her expression showed that she hadn't caught Dusty's sarcasm, or else she was too embarrassed by her own brazenness to acknowledge his. Either way, it was time to move on.

"Maybe you should have left a donation," I said once we were in the car.

If he could growl, I'm sure he would have. Instead, he tossed the spreadsheet at me and started the engine. "And maybe you should have told me about Mrs. Larkin."

"Did you tell me that she'd been interviewed?" I asked.

"Why should I?"

"Because I told you about Haylee and her husband."

He pointed at the spreadsheet. "Sex and money. It fits."

"There was no sex." I peeled open the financials and started comparing deductions and deposits. How did they spend their dollars?

Dusty turned left a little too fast and I fell over into the door just as my cell phone rang. "Ratboy" Terrance's moniker lit the screen.

"Briana, that you? Where are you?" Terrance asked.

"California. Ever thought about getting treatment for that A.D.D.?

Dusty shot me a menacing look. Did he not want me to take the call?

I shrugged. "Amato wasn't the guy who did Haylee. Lieutenant Arkansas and I are interviewing more people."

"I don't care. It's been five days, I want you back here. Now."

Dusty took another hard left and I fell over again. The spreadsheet drifted to the floorboard between my legs. "Would you stop that?" I said to Dusty.

"Briana?"

"What Terrance? Can you hear me? Terrance? You're breaking up."

"Don't play that stupid—"

"Oops. I think I cut him off." I switched off the phone so his call back would go to my answering service and he could never prove I'd snaked him.

"A little too easy, don't you think?" Dusty said.

"But it works. Every time. The beauty of technology."

"Back to Larkin—what if they did sleep together and the older woman saw the younger woman as a threat? Maybe Ms. Macklin's murder has nothing to do with the story she was working on."

"The wife had the opportunity, she wasn't at the fundraiser, but the motive falls flat," I said.

Dusty was silent, probably working this new information into the other interview of Mrs. Larkin. I had to get a look at the interview notes myself.

We pulled up and parked before a huge stone church with steeples cloaked in barbed wire.

"Still following the money?" I asked.

Dusty passed me on the sidewalk, but didn't reply.

I hurried after him through an iron gate and up a grand set of marble steps, where a statue of St. Patrick stood on one side and St. Kevin on the other. More saints, some I recognized and others I didn't, popped from the church's façade. My hand found its way to the stonework that looked old and Italian. I felt the years—the wind, the fog, the rain— carved in its surface.

Dusty stopped before the doublewide entry doors and he pulled out his notepad. He flipped through the pages until he found what he'd been looking for. He turned and headed around to the left and away from the massive doors.

Through another gate we found a smaller, normal size door with a brass plaque that read, "Office." A bell was to the side with another sign underneath that read, "Please ring."

"Anything you need to tell me ahead of time?" he asked.

"I'm good."

"Speaking of money...," Dusty said, reaching for the buzzer. "This place must cost a mint to maintain."

"The Catholic Church is one of the richest institutions on earth, I doubt very seriously if their charities maintain this building."

"Don't tell me—you're Catholic."

"And you're a heathen."

"Buddhist."

"Same difference."

His next rebuff was stifled when the door swung open and a priest, wearing a simple black smock, greeted us. He led us down a dark corridor into a brightly lit office where several other priests in similar costume sat behind desks, looking busy and pretending to ignore us.

"We can talk in here," the priest said, motioning to a conference room with an ebony table and matching chairs. There was solemnity in the way he closed the door behind us. Like the confessional. Should I drop to my knees?

A yellow legal pad and pen lay on the table delineating the priest's station. When we sat, the priest tore off the top sheet of paper and handed it to Dusty.

"Here is Ms. Jeffers' number. Unfortunately, she isn't in this week. She's having some minor surgery. As I mentioned, we don't actually run the charities here. They are handled by the Women's Auxiliary."

I shifted in my chair so Dusty would see my self-satisfied grin, but he didn't look my way and the grin soon grew too heavy to hold.

"This church is pretty impressive. Must require a lot of maintenance," Dusty said.

The priest whistled. "That she does."

Now, Dusty looked at me. He didn't want to ask the next question, but felt he had something to prove.

"Go ahead," I said, urging him along.

He wasn't going to give me the satisfaction of being right again so he reworded the question. "Can you tell us what exactly the Catholic Charities support?"

"Certainly. The Charities are part of an association created to help the community in the broadest sense of the word. The National Charities, one of the largest social services networks in the US, sponsor relief on a major scale like victims of nine-eleven, or hurricane relief when Katrina devastated New Orleans and the Gulf Coast. As for the local chapters, they work on a smaller scale within communities."

The priest put down the pen. "For example, here in San Francisco, we have one of the first and one of the largest HIV AIDS outreach programs. We encourage our parishioners to work with those afflicted and we work to educate the community about the disease. Most of the documentation used by other chapters originated with our program."

"Isn't the church anti-gay?" Dusty asked.

"That is a theoretical question, Lieutenant, and my stance is no, it isn't anti-gay. But I can see by your expression you don't agree with me. No matter, the charities are about helping those in need, whatever their situation, whatever their religion."

"Even Buddhist?" I bit my tongue.

Dusty's eyebrows shot up.

The priest nodded. "All religions. Another one of our programs is funded by the US Department of Housing and Urban Development. Counselors provide homebuyer information, mortgage delinquency solutions and other housing options for those in need."

"Sounds like a multilevel organization," Dusty said.

"Oh, it is. Local chapters, state chapters and of course, the national chapter. On the other hand, you must realize that the association has been around for a long, long time. Whereas the needs of the community continue to change, the method of running the association hasn't changed much. Ms. Jeffers can help you with that, the details, I mean."

"Thank you for your time, Father. I'll give Ms. Jeffers a call."

The priest showed us out and as we left, Dusty hung back to look over the church's façade, probably caught up in its evergreen appeal. I had experienced the same feeling the first time I saw the National Cathedral in DC. You didn't have to be religious for its classical beauty to draw out your spirituality.

The Clinic

Before heading to Santa Rosa, Dusty allowed me a cigarette. He said it was a long drive and he didn't want me complaining the whole way, but I knew better; it was the big bear's way of saying I'd been forgiven.

We left San Rafael and drove north on 101, conversation sparse at first, finally Dusty asked about Haylee. "Tell me about her," he said. "What kind of person was she?"

Maybe it was because my coffee fix was wearing thin that I thought about our morning routine. On even days, I brought the lattes, on odd days Haylee fetched. She hated odd days. It wasn't uncommon for her to call at the last minute and beg me to stop at the coffee shop on my corner. Her excuses ranged from having to buy her mother a birthday, Earth Day, or first day of autumn card—because she knew I was a sucker for her mom—to mini-emergencies like Fifi having diarrhea.

"She was a good person." As I heard my trite words, it felt as if a giant boulder were crashing down on my chest, cutting off my breath and circulation. My fingertips went numb.

I looked out the window for something, anything, to change my thoughts and was immediately rewarded. "Oh, look, a duck."

Dusty glanced where I was pointing. "What?"

"That duck, there on the side of the highway. Someone might hit it. Shouldn't you stop?" I turned my head as we passed it.

Dusty snickered. "First off, and I know you're a city girl so I won't hold this against you, but it's a heron not a duck, and secondly, it can fly, as can ducks."

"What's it doing next to the highway? It's going to get hit."

"Must be some swampy water below. It won't get hurt."

Dusty's cell phone made a noise that sounded like a burp. He pulled it from his jacket and fiddled with the keypad while keeping one eye on the road. "Good news." He shoved the phone back in his pocket. "Amato was arraigned this morning. One thing out of the way. Now, you were going to tell me about Haylee."

A dark green pickup truck sped around us and Dusty followed it with his eyes.

"I'd rather not."

"Come on, tell me something she liked to do, a hobby or sport."

"No!" My voice came out in a screech, but rather than apologize I stared out the passenger side window.

This drive was becoming the longest in history. The countryside didn't offer up another duck and my imagination was running low. High in a sky so clear that it looked painted, the sun tracked our course, heating the interior to where the air vent, directed on my face, was of little use. "How much farther?"

"The quiet too much for your uptight sensibilities? What is it with those shoes anyway? Aren't they're cutting off your circulation?"

Shoes? I glanced at my two-toned Ferragamo pumps, and across at his leather loafers. I held back the remark which came to mind, realizing that without meaning to I'd cancelled out that warm and fuzzy thing we had going. All I knew was I couldn't think about Haylee, let alone talk about her. Not now, maybe not ever. I turned back to the passenger window and pressed my face into the cool surface of the glass.

"How come you don't have a partner?" I asked.

"Because I don't."

Must be his congeniality. The highway narrowed to two lanes and lush green hills replaced shopping malls and car dealerships. When I was a child, my aunt had told me stories of the fairy hills back in Ireland, and from her description I imagined them to look much like the gleaming emerald hills around me. I scanned the mounds for caves where fairies might live. I checked the air for a reflection of a fairy wing and found comfort in the childish exercise.

"Doesn't all this sunshine give you a headache?" I asked.

"A headache? Just remember to wear sunscreen?"

Shoot. I knew I'd forgotten something.

A bold green sign listed Santa Rosa as the next three exits. I watched as we passed each of the three. "Do you know where you're going?"

"Do you?"

We left the highway at the next exit and made a series of turns through a clean but densely populated residential zone fitted with speed bumps. Dusty slowed to a crawl over each bump. The last left turn put us on a two-lane road which led away from civilization, between two cow pastures, and well into a treeless countryside. The colors were crisp and vibrant, the bright sky like nothing I'd ever seen before. I had noticed this phenomenon the morning I arrived, but had attributed it to the blooming flowers and trees, and the magnificent bay views. Now, with only wildflowers and grassy fields to catch the sun, I realized there was more to the lighting effect. A lack of pollution? Different latitudes? How can the same sun, giving the same light, offer such varying illumination on two different coasts?

I started to ask Dusty, but he pointed across the seat and turned right into a long drive. At the entrance, two red brick columns bordered the freshly laid asphalt. A quarter of a mile up, we came to a brick building trimmed tastefully in white stone and the name in gold letters by the door—The

Rummington Alzheimer's Clinic.

The clinic was the only building for as far as I could see. Grapevines stretched across the piece of land to the left and along a terraced piece of land behind the clinic. To the right, a paved parking lot and an area with walking paths and cement benches. Landscaping was sparse. The only trees were two birches near the road. The patch of grass near the walking paths was neatly trimmed.

A domed ceiling gave the reception area a light, airy feeling. Sectional stuffed chairs linked together creating small sofas. We didn't have to wait. The receptionist walked us down the office wing at the left to the director's office. When we entered, Dr. Rummington stood. He was slightly taller than Dusty and noticeably thinner in his expensive three-piece suit. He spoke with a British accent and his mannerisms were somewhat affected as he motioned us to chairs.

He took his seat behind a cherry wood desk, wide enough to safely separate him from our germs. "How may I be of service, Lieutenant?"

Why did The Rummington Alzheimer's Clinic bear his name if he was only the director? But remembering my vow of silence, I kept the question to myself and waited to see what direction Dusty would take.

"From my reading, I understand that you're a pretty famous guy," Dusty said.

The doctor smiled. "Not hardly sir, I've had a few theories that have panned out, that's about it, I'm afraid. I'm surprised you even recognized my name. Few people outside the research field do."

"Famous enough to have your own clinic."

"It's not exactly mine. It was renamed after my research in nineteen eighty-five."

"Right. And you are the...director. How long have you

been here?"

The doctor's lips soured slightly. "Since eighty-five."

"Ah." Dusty removed his notepad and scribbled something.

The doctor smiled again, this time with the confidence of his position. "A stipulation of bringing me here from Boston."

"Who owns The Rummington Alzheimer's Clinic?" Dusty asked.

"A private trust, run by a board of directors—eight—I believe."

He believes? Oh, give it to us straight doc. I raised an eyebrow to signal Dusty, but once again he ignored me as he continued his questioning.

"Would it be possible for me to get a list of directors?"

Finally. This keeping quiet was driving me nuts. I was drifting around in my chair like a blind man in a wind tunnel.

"Certainly." The doctor leaned over his desk, hit a button on the phone console, and asked someone named Evie to print out a list of the directors. When he sat back, Dusty continued his questioning.

"Would I be right in guessing that the board of directors liked your research and brought you out here to continue?" Dusty said.

"That's correct, yes."

"And what about your theories, exactly, are so different from others?"

"I'm afraid you'd need to know a little about Alzheimer's to understand that."

"Let's pretend I do."

The doctor cleared his throat and puckered his dry lips. He posed his finger tips together forming a pyramid with his hands. "Years ago, I came up with an idea that the brain was compartmentalized, that different parts of the brain are used for different functions. This is a widely held belief these days, and it is a theory that is helping bring about earlier detection of Alzheimer's and creative therapies to ward off dementia."

Dusty glanced at me and even though he didn't shake his head he probably wanted to. "Do these new therapies involve drugs of any kind?"

Bingo.

"They can, but most of my newer research is in the area of early diagnosis. We don't do a lot of drug therapy here. Occasionally, one of the large pharmaceuticals will come up with a magic pill and we will run a supervised test for the FDA, but honestly, there is no magic pill."

"How are these tests handled?" Dusty asked, twirling his pen.

"Blind. My staff never knows who is taking the placebo and who is taking the new drug until the test period is over. I achieve the best results that way."

At the risk of getting slapped back down, I spoke up. "Have any of the tests proved beneficial?"

"Not really, no. What little success we've had has been disappointing. We had something a few years back which looked promising, but once maximum dosage was reached the results quickly petered out."

Dusty took over. "Your research, early diagnosis you said, anything new in that realm?"

"Personally I believe this is the key to understanding the disease." Dr. Rummington sat straighter and rested his hands, fingers still pointed, on the desk blotter. "I'm not the only one working in this area. For example, we now know that learning new things—keeping the brain active—is a deterrent to Alzheimer's. Again, I think this goes back to the idea of the brain being compartmentalized. Other cutting edge research being done at Duke holds the possibility of visualizing the disease in its early stages. Of course, this is still years away."

"Sounds very interesting," Dusty said.

"I can assure you, it is."

Dusty turned to me. "Can you think of anything else?"

I'm sure I would once I'd seen the financials and the Board Members' list, but I was knocked off guard by Dusty's inclusion of me in the process. I shook my head.

"No?" Dusty stood. "We thank you for time, doctor."

"Let me walk you out and I'll get that list for you."

A question popped into my head. "Is there a Mr. or Mrs. Larkin on your board?"

"Larkin? No, I don't believe so." He led us back down the corridor to the main receptionist.

"The clinic smells new, but you've been open since eighty-five?" Dusty asked, taking the brown envelope from Rummington's hand.

"We've only completed a major remodeling of the premises. Mr. Warren wants to attract a more financially sound client base."

Dusty had started to open the envelope, but his head popped up. "Warren, not Mr. Charles Warren?"

"Why yes, Charles Warren. His mother is with us, you know."

The Pizza

We headed south in silence. Dusty hadn't said so, but I imagined he was as discouraged as I. Before my demotion, when I gathered information for stories, I always had a sense when I was getting closer. Even when I was wrong, I was right, because I might not reach the conclusion I thought I was headed for, but I'd reach a conclusion—the story. Here, I sensed none of that. With this investigation, it was as if I was pedaling in pig poop and getting nothing but dirty.

First, there was Tony Amato who was dirty, but probably not a murderer. Next, there was the argument between Haylee and Francine Starling, which could have been regarding Francine's daughter, but was most likely about Francine not wanting Charlotte Warren running the Belvedere Club. And of course, Haylee's ex-boyfriend Gary who says they were sleeping together, but, in my opinion, they weren't. None of this information added up to a Pulitzer-code story, which I knew Haylee was working on. So, if I mixed in the charities—The Auxiliary Aid with Gary's wife on the board, or The Rummington Alzheimer's Clinic with Charles Warren on the board and old Mrs. Warren as a patient—where did that leave me?

Picking my fingernail polish. The more I thought about it, the more I realized a big chunk of information was missing. We were following the Post-It®s, but was that enough?

In Petaluma, Dusty veered off the highway. With tires screeching, we whipped around a hairpin turn and followed a two lane country road into the setting sun. I checked my watch. Forty-five minutes before Doggie Daycare closed its doors.

"Is this a short cut?"

"I'm hungry, thought we should grab a bite." He turned into a parking lot, spinning gravel beneath the wheels. We stopped in front of what looked like a 1950's roadhouse, plunked down in the middle of nowhere. Red neon spelled out "Frankie's."

"This joint has the best pizza in the world. I'm figuring that's the only meal you and I could possibly share."

"Why's that?"

"I'm vegetarian and the way you clog up your body with cigarettes and caffeine, I'm guessing, you aren't."

"Dead on detective. One problem though, Doggie Daycare closes soon and I'm afraid if I left Fifi overnight, there'd be little left of the building come sunup."

Dusty killed the engine and reached for his cell phone. "Let me see what I can do." He pushed two buttons on the cellular—speed dial. He explained the situation using words like "traffic" and "delay," but not once did I hear the word "pizza."

"Huh? Sounds good. Great. I'll call before we arrive." He disconnected and returned the phone to his coat pocket. "Soup's on," he said, getting out of the car.

"What's the deal with Fifi?"

"A deputy went to pick her up. She'll be at the department when we get back."

"You must not like that deputy."

He cracked a sly smile.

Inside, Frankie's Grill was a dive, too. Surprise. Worn wooden floors, red Formica tables, bad lighting, and greasy smells combined to give the restaurant a nasty atmosphere. The current round-shouldered clientele fit right in, most of whom looked as if they'd been sitting in the same spot since Eisenhower was president.

"Do you get an AARP discount?" I asked.

"What do you want? And don't worry—it's all organic." He said over his shoulder. The salty looking guy serving drinks greeted Dusty like an old friend. Then, the scoundrel took a moment to run his eyes down my body in a way that made me feel like I was wearing fig leaves.

The menu was written out on a chalkboard behind the bar, but I had a hard time making out the words. The first three choices were whole grain pizzas, the fourth something with a Barbeque something, and the fifth, a Cesar Salad.

"Triple meat pizza." Pepperoni gave me a bad stomach, but Dusty's vegetarian comment had rubbed me the wrong way, or maybe Dusty rubbed me the wrong way. I was working on the premise that glistening animal fat would make him suffer more than I would.

"Beer?"

"No!" My voice was louder than I'd meant and everyone in the room turned to look at me. "Espresso."

A couple of snorts and a couple of chuckles bubbled from the undertones. I glanced around at the worn faces, all male. Right. If this place had an espresso machine, I was the Queen of England.

Dusty ordered himself a triple cheese pizza with olives and a draft. "How about a soft drink? They're loaded with caffeine."

"Coffee—a double." I resigned myself to drinking some sort of tinted water.

"That Frankie behind the bar?" I asked as we moved to a table by the front window.

Dusty nodded and checked out the basketball game playing on the back television.

"You think Frankie washes his hands?"

He turned back to me, but I don't think he thought I was serious. I was.

I tore a paper napkin from the dispenser and laid it across

my lap. "Frankie like a third-cousin-half-brother kind of relative?"

Dusty laughed. "No relative. I grew up around here. Worked the Petaluma PD for a time."

"PPD," I said. A country bumpkin. "Well, that explains a few things."

"Yeah, like my amiable personality."

"Yo, Dusty," Frankie called.

Dusty went to collect his beer and my coffee. "How can you drink that poison?" He pulled on his beer.

The coffee was amazing. I took another sip to be sure. "Beer makes me burp."

Earlier, we'd brainstormed the connection between Charles Warren and The Rummington Alzheimer's Clinic, but Dusty wasn't as charged up about it as I was. I thought I'd give it another try. "You really think it's a coincidence, Warren and Rummington's?"

"I agree with you that it needs more examination, but come on, it looks pretty innocent. The old lady started the donations when she was still running the Belvedere Club. Now, she's in The Rummington Alzheimer's Clinic and her son wants the best care for her. No big mystery. Hardly motivation for murder." He drew on his beer again. "You're ready to convict the first person that looks suspicious. What's your hurry?"

The warning lights had been flashing for sometime now, but I could hardly tell him about the emotions ready to bury me. I'd been through this before when I'd lost my daughter, but this time around, I had no support system. No Haylee. "You know as well as I do that every day without a suspect leads you that much farther from one."

"Old philosophy, outdated. Now, with forensics, DNA, it takes longer to build a case, but the cases are more airtight."

Frankie delivered our pizzas along with plates and

silverware. Dusty asked about the game on TV while I dug into the first bite. I hadn't realized how hungry I was.

"Umm. This is good, even for organic." I wiped the dripping grease off my lips and took another bite.

"Frankie's is an institution."

"Were you born around here?"

"Here? No. Alaska. My parents were hiding out in a commune. Typical hippie stuff. In seventy-seven, my folks moved down here to Petaluma and started chicken farming. Ugg, chickens. The only animals I'll eat. Pure revenge."

"Any brothers or sisters?" I asked.

"A sister. You?"

I tore off another napkin and wiped my lips, while oil ran down my hand. "Six brothers. And please, no Catholic jokes. I've heard them all."

"Six." He whistled. "Any sisters?"

I shook my head while wiping between my fingers.

"*That explains a few things*." He mimicked. "Like why you come off like a fight promoter all the time dressed in your high heels and what's that, a Gucci jacket?"

"Donna Karan." I started in on my second slice, not sure how to take his remark. "What's with the heels, this is the second time today you've mentioned the shoes. Got a fetish or something?'

"I've never met a reporter, excuse me, photojournalist who wears them, that's all."

"Haylee did."

That shut him up and he returned to his pizza. We ate for a while then he asked, "Married?" His pizza was almost finished while I still had half to go.

"Yep."

His eyebrows about hit the ceiling. He dropped his pizza slice and raised his empty glass in the air, motioning for a refill.

"What? You can't imagine someone wanting a fight promoter for a wife?"

"It's not that, you don't wear a ring, and you've never once mentioned a husband or received a single phone call. Most people refer to a spouse in passing, like my husband says, or ...oh, I don't know. What's his name?"

"Conor."

"Conor Kaleigh. Another Irish. Must be a clan thing."

"Conor Nolan. And we're separated." No need to tell him that I was currently paying a private dick to find the jerk so I could divorce his butt. "Haylee introduced us. He's her second cousin on her mother's side."

While Dusty fetched his second beer, it suddenly dawned on me that I needed to tell my private detective about Haylee. Mourning drew Irish families together. There was a big chance Conor would show for the wake.

"You ever been married?" I'd seen his boat; there wasn't room for a cockroach let alone a wife.

"A long time ago," he said.

"Kids?"

He shook his head. "You?"

"No." The subject made me squirm and I'd had enough friendly conversation for one day.

"Dusty..." I paused. The name again conjured up an image of swirling particles like the cloud his tires had churned up when we spun into Frankie's gravel parking lot. I started to laugh. "Dusty..." In my mind, I pictured him as a swirling mass of matter and it fit perfectly with his controlled yet volatile temperament. I laughed harder.

He pushed the receipt across the table in my direction. "You're on an expense account."

The dust cloud stood. Free pizza at his favorite joint. My laugher faded as I dropped three tens on the check.

Outside, Dusty's cell phone burped. I got in the car to give him some privacy.

"Looks like the charities were the wrong lead to follow," he said, sliding behind the wheel.

Sounds like a break. "Why's that?"

"Amato's dead. Throat slit."

The Company

Tuesday morning, rain gushed over the drain spouts and synthesized into uneven rhythms that made me want to stay crouched beneath the covers. Dusty had called late the previous evening to fill me in on Amato who after making bail had been found dead in his apartment. Today Dusty was interviewing Charles Warren, and I was dying to meet the man whose famous name occupied the final Post-It®.

It would be so easy to believe that Charles was the killer. Haylee was methodical in her research and his name was last in the Post-It® list. Also, he was on the board of The Rummington Alzheimer's Clinic and he was connected to the Belvedere Club through his twin, Charlotte Warren. Plus, he knew Tony Amato. But all these facts were easily explained away and I'd worked with Haylee enough to know she rarely ever finished her Post-It® outlines. Once she found the story it was abandoned so Charles Warren's name at the end could be meaningless.

Dressed in a pair of slacks that I'd had cleaned by the hotel laundry, I wore my cashmere coat and a towel over my head to walk Fifi. Still, I returned drenched. With minutes to spare, I changed into my trusty Donna Karan suit yet again and rushed to the lobby to meet Dusty. In order to ride along, I'd made my standard promise not to say a word, which meant I would have to prep him on the way to be sure he asked the right questions. He wouldn't like my suggestions. One thing I'd learned about Dusty Arkansas was he didn't like taking direction from anyone.

A green and white patrol car sat at the lobby door when I

arrived. Looked like we were going in official capacity, bells and whistles included.

"You must be happy," Dusty said, gesturing to the rain as I slid in.

"A nice change of pace, don't you think? Why the sheriff-mobile?"

"There's a latte in the cup holder. I don't want you to get the shakes in front of the big man."

I'd smelt the coffee before he'd mentioned it. I reached for my prize. My stomach was still queasy from yesterday's pepperoni and I figured a latte would stoke the fire. *Yes*.

At the highway, we continued straight missing the entrance, which was odd since the only way to San Francisco was over the Golden (red) Gate Bridge. Farther down, when we finally did enter 101, I realized why we'd made the sidetrack. Cars were bumper to bumper in gridlock. No one was moving.

Dusty made a grunting sound. "When it rains a whole lot at once, the bay inlets flood at high tide. Some of the inlets are below the highway."

That made no sense to me so I changed the subject. "Where does Amato's death leave us? Who can we rule out?"

"I'm not ready to rule any one out. I'm collecting information. Amato's case is being handled by the San Rafael PD. His mother, the charming creature in the next apartment, said she heard a noise and when she looked out she saw two Asian men running down the hall. She found Tony soon after."

"Asian? That doesn't make sense."

"There's a huge Asian mafia in the Bay Area. Maybe Tony's porn interest were linked or maybe in competition. Like I said last night, his throat was cut from behind whereas Ms. Macklin's was most likely cut from the front."

A pain shot though my stomach, probably the latte. "Not

the same killer," I said, wincing. "I have to tell you this doesn't fit Haylee's Post-It®s."

"We have other theories that don't fit her Post-It®s either like the jealous wife theory or the rebuffed ex-boyfriend theory. I think we can assume the story she was working on probably wasn't what got her killed."

Brake lights lit the road in front of us. We had barely moved. "Should we call Warren's assistant?" I asked.

"I called while I was waiting for you. The north axis was already blocked. Warren said he'd make time for me, although we may have a short wait."

That surprised me. "Wow. CEO of a Fortune One-Hundred and he still can make time for a sheriff's deputy. Must think it's important. Although…he has nothing to do with the Belvedere Club, his wife doesn't even belong. Why would a simple homicide interest him?"

"Ah, because someone is dead. Not all CEOs are cruel heartless animals."

"What planet do you live on?" I took a sip of coffee while wondering if this Buddhist crap hadn't caused a leaky valve in Dusty's brain. "You don't head a Fortune One-Hundred by being Mr. Nice Concerned Citizen. Haven't you heard? It's dog eat dog out there."

"You would know. And why do you keep bringing that camera. You're not taking it inside."

"Habit," I said.

"Hold on." He inched the patrol car to the shoulder and picked up a little speed traveling beside the stalled traffic. Through flapping windshield wipers, drivers launched silent threats our way and more than one car swerved right trying to block our passage until Dusty tapped the overhead lights. I laughed as the drivers, realizing it was an official vehicle, swerved back out of our way. This was more fun than watching an arrest.

By the time we reached Securitec in San Francisco's business district, the rain had almost stopped, but the sky showed no sign of clearing. We parked in an underground garage complete with tire deflation strips and took an elevator to the top floor offices. A pretty young woman, Melanie, greeted us. She looked to be in her late twenties and she informed us, as she led us to Warren's spacious corner office, that she was Mr. Warren's personal assistant.

Charles Warren's facial features were reminiscent of his sister's, but where she looked soft and round, he looked sharp and edged. He also looked shorter, but I couldn't be sure since he didn't rise when we entered. In the middle of a telephone call, he motioned to us while he finished his conversation.

Through the windows behind him, the port of San Francisco panned out before us with a strong pull of the eye to the left toward Coit Tower. Bulbous storm clouds made the white buildings look like popcorn, popping out of the earth. How strange to see a cityscape unmarred by skyscrapers.

When Mr. Warren finished his call, Dusty first introduced himself and introduced me as Haylee's friend.

Looking earnestly into my eyes while he shook my hand, he spoke. "I'm sorry about what happened to your friend."

I swallowed hard. "Thank you." His sincerity echoed his sister's. My Catholic guilt slapped me down for suspecting such a nice man of foul play.

He spoke to Dusty in a direct and concerned manner. "I understand you spoke with Charlotte, was she of any help?"

"Yes, she was. At this point we're collecting information from as many sources as possible."

"No suspects?"

"I'm afraid not."

"What kind of information? What would you like to

know?"

A flock of birds flew past the window, too fast for me to guess at the species. I returned my attention to the interior while Dusty asked the regular questions about the Belvedere Club.

"We're looking for anyone who might have spoken to Ms. Macklin before she was killed," Dusty said.

"Is that how you learned about Tony's illegal activities? Don't look surprised. My sister was afraid she might need a lawyer so she called me."

Dusty perked up. "Why would she need a lawyer?"

"When she learned about Tony's website, she went down to the jail and fired Tony on the spot. He threatened to sue, said he was framed because of the murder."

"Framed. Right." Dusty had his notepad poised. "Do you think she needs a lawyer?"

"Regarding Tony? No. I spoke with a sergeant in the San Rafael Police Department. He told me everything they had on Tony. It sounds like a slam-dunk, not a frame."

"Tony Amato was murdered yesterday," Dusty said without emotion.

Charles's surprise showed in the way he froze in mid-movement. When he had resolved it, he leaned back and cleared his throat. "Is it related to the murder at the club?"

"We're not sure at this point."

Charles started to speak, but was cut off by the ring of his desk phone. He reached over and hit a button, but didn't take the call. "As I mentioned, I don't know much about the Belvedere Club. It's my sister's domain. What I do know is that the club means a lot to its members. It's a retreat for them to enjoy a respite from their hectic lives."

"Husband, kids."

Warren poised his head as if to argue, but didn't.

Dusty pretended to search for something in his notepad,

but I knew after so many interviews that this was a tactic he liked to use. "We also learned that you are on the board of directors of The Rummington Alzheimer's Clinic."

Charles Warren didn't seem fazed. "I'm on many boards. Would you like a list?"

"If you wouldn't mind, but I'm interested in the coincidences. The Belvedere Club donates to The Rummington Alzheimer's Clinic. Your mother is in the clinic. You're on the board of directors. You see the connection?"

"Not coincidences at all. My mother watched both her parents succumb to Alzheimer's. It was devastating for her, especially when they no longer recognized her. She researched the disease, learned everything she could, but ultimately learned nothing that could save them. Once they passed on, she knew there was a big chance that she too would inherit the disease. She liked what she'd read about Dr. Rummington so she did what she was good at. Organized some friends together to buy a clinic and coaxed Dr. Rummington to the West Coast. It wasn't easy, I can tell you, but mother was unstoppable in her day. By the time Dr. Rummington arrived at the clinic, mother was starting to notice subtle changes in her memory. Through the Belvedere Club, she created a charity, securing a financial base to draw the best doctors and care available. Around nineteen eighty-eight, she relinquished her position on the board to me because my sister had the Belvedere Club to run. For the last four years, she's been a patient at Rummington's."

Charles sucked his lower lip and ran his hands through his wavy brown hair. I caught a glimpse of his sorrow before he glanced out the window. He was worried about his mother and, maybe, himself.

Dusty spoke, bringing Charles's focus back to us. "We're collecting financial records from the three charities that the

Belvedere Club supports. We've received a copy from the Auxiliary Aid and we're waiting on a copy from the Catholic charities. Dr. Rummington said that you could provide us with the financial information from the clinic."

"What for?"

"It's routine, we're following the donations made by the Belvedere Club."

"Money's a good motivator for murder."

Dusty's expression remained unchanged. "Why do you say that?"

"Oh come on, I watch television." Charles paused as if waiting for Dusty to agree. "All the clinic stuff is at home. I'll be at the house on Thursday, maybe you could send someone by then. We have nothing to hide. The clinic has been in the red for the past year, but new financing has recently brought it back into the black and the renovation has drawn new interest so it should remain solid for a while."

Dusty stood. "I'll come by personally."

"Good, you can meet my wife, Rebecca."

"I understand your wife and sister don't get along," I said.

Charles Warren smiled. "Not hardly. My sister thinks Rebecca is a money grubbing whore—her words exactly. You see, Rebecca got pregnant while we were dating and Charlotte thinks it was on purpose, to get my money." He stood and pressed down his jacket with his hands. "We have a son and daughter now and we steer clear of Charlotte. I only see her on business matters." He walked around the desk. "This way, please, my assistant will give you my home address."

The Friend

Terrance was chewing my left ear off and Fifi, my right ankle. I shook the dog free and returned my attention to the phone.

"I have a senator caught with his pants down and no one to cover the story. If you want your old job back, you'll get back here, pronto. I mean it Briana, I can't wait another minute. I need a reporter."

"It's not like it hasn't happened before. When are people going to stop worrying about politicians who lie to their wives and start worrying about the ones lying to their country?"

"If you are not in this office by tomorrow morning, you're fired. Clear enough? If you don't want the job, I need to hire someone who does."

I disconnected. Who needed the stupid job anyway? What was I supposed to return to…an office full of young interns, all hoping to replace Haylee? Everyday I'd have to walk by her cubicle while someone else sat at her desk, taking her calls, running her stories. No thanks. And Terrance as editor. I wouldn't have Haylee to argue the fundamentals of grammar. *Communicate in the clearest form possible.*

Fifi lunged for my ankle again and I kicked out, causing her to jump back. She wanted to play. Her idea of play was to cause me great pain and for me to let her.

"Back off, I'm not in the mood."

We strolled out under dark afternoon clouds. It hadn't rained since morning, but it looked as if it might any second. Fifi squatted beside an azalea bush, leaving behind a smelly mess. In my hurry to get her outside, I'd forgotten the baggies. Glancing over my shoulder, I slyly kicked the brown turd under the white blooms. Fifi used my moment of inattention to dash across the lawn. I cursed myself for dropping the leash and barreled off after her, my three-inch heels sinking into the soft earth.

Without a job, how would I feed the stupid dog? Without a job, I'd have no right to Dusty's investigation. What investigation? It was Tuesday, six days since Haylee's death, and not a single solid lead in sight. Would Francine Starling really murder someone over an argument? With her ramrod straight strut, Starling looked like the type to snap, but why did Haylee need a photographer—insisted on it? And where did Tony fit in? The Asian mob would fit the Pulitzer angle, but there was no hint of it anywhere in Haylee's research. My thoughts kept coming back to the circle, Old Mrs. Warren, the Belvedere Club, The Rummington Alzheimer's Clinic, and Charles Warren. *Ring around the roses.*

I gasped for a breath and stopped. I couldn't run any longer; my energy was shot. The best I could hope for was that Fifi's leash would hang on a branch and strangle her. "Fifi, come here! You hunk of insensitivity, I'll stuff you into that drainpipe."

There was a link between the four, the Belvedere Club, Old Mrs. Warren, The Rummington Alzheimer's Clinic, Charles Warren. *A pocket full of posies.* My eyes closed for a second. I wished I could curl up on the lawn and sleep for a decade.

Fifi charged into a neighboring yard and as she squatted near the house, I reached her. The two-tone painted side door swung open and a woman in beige sweats stepped out. "What are you doing? That dog should be on a leash."

I picked up the leash dangling from Fifi's collar. "Charles did it. I know he did. There are no coincidences. His *was* the last Post-It®."

"Get out of my yard. If I see you here again, I'm calling the police. This is private property."

Charles Warren. Board of directors, Securitec. Board of directors, The Rummington's Alzheimer's Clinic. When we reached the hotel room, I was feverish and chilled at the same time. Fifi headed for her water bowl, but I didn't make it farther than the sofa. *Board of directors, board of directors, ashes, ashes.*

I'd forgotten my cell phone and the high pitch beep alerted me that there was a message. With trembling hands, I rubbed my forehead while reading the display. Nadine, Haylee's mom. Without another thought, I returned the call.

"What have you done?" she asked, bursting into tears. "I just spoke to the sheriff. They're keeping Haylee. They won't send her home. You have to make them send her home. She'll never be back by Friday."

"Nadine, I don't know—"

"Why did you let them reopen the investigation? They had that man. Now Haylee won't be home for her own wake. You have to do something."

Dusty hadn't said anything to me about keeping Haylee's body. I didn't know what to say to calm her.

"My poor baby, stuck out there in La La Land," she said, sniffing.

"Technically, that's L.A.. I don't think they La La up here."

"Are you being smart with me young lady?"

"No ma'am. I'm sorry. I'm not feeling very well. I may have rabies."

"Briana."

"Sorry." I knew better than to say more.

"Oh, I guess we can move the wake to Sunday…if you can get them to send her back. That would give you both enough time wouldn't it?"

"Sunday's perfect. I'll speak with Lieutenant Arkansas, Dusty." The name caught my funny bone again and I started to laugh.

"Are you okay, dear? You don't sound like yourself. I'm sorry I snapped at you. This whole mess…." And she was crying again.

Now, I was sniffing. "I'm fine, just caught a chill out walking the dog."

"Aw, poor Fifi. Does she miss Haylee?"

My hand was shaking so much I almost dropped the cellular. "We all do."

Nadine paused, probably checking her own emotions. "The burial will be Monday. A lovely cemetery. Her father and I have reserved two plots right next to her. When are you getting in?"

Busy, the investigation, the charities, the Warrens…Tony. "I'll call you back once I've made my plane reservations."

"That'll be good, hon."

I cut the call and thought about the wake—silly Irish folklore. In days of yore it was believed that fairies—not the ethereal beauties of modern depiction, but sinister winged creatures of the high country—stole human souls for their own use. Wakes were a way of tricking the fairies into believing the person was still alive. They were and are lavish, festive affairs. Once the soul was on its way to heaven, the mourning and burial took place.

If I wasn't mistaken, a couple of fairies were dancing around me at the moment. I didn't see them, but I heard their taunting whispers and the flapping of their wings. I rushed to the bathroom sink and splashed warm water on my face. Next, I threw open the cabinet below and removed the two miniature airline bottles of Wild Turkey. I'd brought them for Haylee as a joke. She'd missed St. Patrick's Day because of her flight out here. It had been almost a year since my last drink. Haylee had forced me to quit. She had bellowed about how I was killing myself and she couldn't live without me. She said that she could live without a lot of things, but not without her best friend. She'd made me promise. *Oh, Haylee.*

She was standing between the sofa and the coffee table. Not really. Not a ghost or a spirit either. But a memory of what I expected her to be. She stood there, slinging her weight to the left, her head cocked mischievously.

And then I knew. My denial was over. I carried the whiskey bottles to the coffee table and sat them before me as I sank into the sofa. Haylee was gone. She was gone, forever. I rubbed my face and felt the fire on my skin. I hadn't solved the case. I'd failed Haylee's mom. I'd failed…Haylee.

The golden bottles twinkled with light. My little gift. They didn't tempt me in the least. My thirst was larger, a bathtub larger.

I picked up the telephone and hit zero for the front desk. Room Service didn't handle food or drink, but the valet said for twenty dollars he'd run down to Safeway and get me a bottle.

"Two. Whisky. Bushmill's. Or…whatever you can find."

The room was like a freezer. I started shaking again. The tears broke free. *It wasn't fair.* Haylee was the survivor. Pain ripped through my chest, deep and searing, as if my heart were being wrenched from my body.

I needed a drink. I glanced again at the tiny bottles. Better than nothing, I reasoned. Left of the table, Fifi stood, her dark eyes boring into my soul.

"Not you too. I know! I've failed! Leave me alone."

A low moan escaped her throat and she raised her head with a question. The horsemen of the apocalypse drew nearer, hooves thundering in my ears, dust rising around me. I was about to be overtaken and I couldn't do anything but lie in wait.

Haylee once told me that animals sensed our weaknesses. Well, Fifi must have sensed mine, because she rushed across the room and started barking.

I wanted to rip my head off. I wanted to rip her head off. "Shut up!" With a thud, I rolled to the carpet, my vision blurred by tears. *Haylee.*

I rolled over, my body wracked with spasms as emotions scorched me from the inside out. *Haylee.* The barking continued, but I no longer cared. Through my own cries, I barely heard it.

I don't know how long I lay there shaking, before the door burst open and Fifi leaped onto my chest. I shoved her off and tried to sit, but fell back to the floor in time to watch her white butt squeeze under the sofa.

A strong pair of arms lifted me and laid me against the soft sofa cushions. Fifi barked again, but the sound was muffled.

"No dogs allowed." The accent was familiar.

"Get me a blanket." Another familiar voice.

The blanket's weight fell over me, but I still couldn't see the face bent before me. "Haylee?"

"Watch her while I call for a doctor."

Fifi barked.

"No dogs allowed."

"Do I need to check the green cards of your staff? That's what I thought. Keep an eye on her."

"Dusty, is that you?" I should have known from the barking. Haylee always said Fifi was very sensitive. *"Haylee?"*

The room melted away. I was alone again. I was headed towards that place of safety, the interior haven I'd searched for and found after Siobhan's death. Fireflies of sound buzzed around me. Through the darkness I saw Haylee, holding Siobhan, my baby girl, in her arms, cooing in her ear.

"Conor, Conor look at that."

"It's Dusty. I'm here with you. Stop hitting me."

"Keep them away." I slapped out, knocking a fairy on its head, sending it into a tailspin. "Keep them off me, they want my soul." I heard myself scream.

"Have you taken something? Pills?"

"I'm so cold. Get back! Tell them I'm not dead. Tell them to leave me alone."

"You're not dying, you're fine. The doctor's here." A strong hand wiped my damp hair from my face. A few minutes later a warm cloth caressed my temple. And, a sharp jolt bore into my arm.

"That should calm her," said someone I didn't recognize.

"Drunk?"

"Don't think so. I don't smell anything. Looks more like shock."

"From what? Is she hurt?"

"Where's Siobhan? Where's Haylee? Haylee!" I called.

"You said her friend just died."

"Almost a week ago."

"Haylee?"

"A week, wow. I'm impressed," said the unfamiliar voice. "She must be a pretty tough nut. Look at it this way, all that strength she's been holding onto for the last week is turning in on her now. She wants to shut down. Keep her warm. I gave her a sedative. She should sleep soon. After a good rest, she'll feel better. If not, call me."

"Conor?"

"It's Dusty. You need anything?"

I tried to sit, but my muscles moved like jelly. "What's wrong with me?" I fell forward and Dusty caught me in his arms. He smelled good, he smelled like strength. He laid me back against the cushions.

"You should sleep."

"I've failed, haven't I? I've disappointed... the quest, it's...."

Sleep came roaring in on a chariot and all else was forgotten.

* * *

The aroma of coffee hovered as my eyes struggled to focus against the daylight. My legs and arms ached as I pushed up on one elbow. Across the room at the dining table, Dusty sat, reading a newspaper. His scalp was shiny, newly shaven. Spots of blood stood out like pox against the pale skin.

I wasn't quite sure what to do. What had I done? How much had he witnessed?

When he saw me move, he stood, an unreadable expression etched in his features. "Morning."

Fifi barked once and he pointed a finger at her. She tucked her pom-pom tail and crawled back under the sofa.

I rubbed crusty sleep from the corners of my eyes. "How long have you been here?"

"I'll get you some coffee."

Ah ha, I wasn't hallucinating—it was coffee I smelled. My gaze fell on the miniature Wild Turkey bottles and I shot to my feet. Halfway to the kitchen, I stopped and grabbed the wall, waiting for the spins to subside.

Dusty held out a steaming mug as I rounded the corner. "You should take it easy. Let's go back to the sofa."

Two empty Bushmill's bottles rested beside the sink, their tops missing.

"Omigod." I pointed. "What are they...?"

Dusty picked up the empty bottles and dropped them in the trash bag.

"I didn't—"

"No, you didn't. I drained them into the sink. Let's go sit, you look unsteady."

He sat beside me on the sofa, placing the mug on the coffee table. "How are you feeling?"

Wiped out. Confused. Worried. Passages started coming back to me, a tornado of images that made little sense. "Omigod."

A strong arm wrapped my shoulder. "Don't cry. It'll be… The hard part's over. You'll be okay."

I wasn't comfortable with him seeing this weakness in me, but I had so much pain pouring from my heart, I couldn't fight it. As if the mug were fine china, I reached for it, but stopped to wipe away tears with the backs of my hands. "What happened to your head?" I touched a red spot and came away with a spec of blood on my index finger. "You're bleeding."

"Only a nick. Buddhist monks shave their heads the night before a full moon. It symbolizes giving up earthly concerns, things like vanity. Since I stopped by from work, I had to use your disposable, hope you don't mind."

Gross. Yuk. "You threw it away, right?" I picked up the coffee and took a sip, haunted by the thought of him shaving his head with my razor. "You don't look like a monk. Don't they wear orange robes or something?"

"I'm not a monk yet, sort of practicing. Maybe one day I'll chuck all this glory and go for it." He reached into his pocket. "Here take these."

In his palm were a large white tablet and a golden egg-shaped pill.

"I don't do drugs."

"They're vitamins, a multi-B and some Omega oils. Something to help get you back into balance."

I snickered. "Life has choked, chewed up, and spit out my heart not once, not twice, not three times, but over and over and over again. You'd think by now I'd be used to it…that I could throw open my arms and say, 'go to it.' But I can't. I can't. Everyone I love dies. I'm like an Irish plague on two legs. And you think…those…those silly little pills are going to balance me?"

He looked me straight in the eyes, but gone was the assuredness he carried on the job. Doubt and discomfort had replaced it and something else that made me uncomfortable—concern.

I scooped the pills from his hand. "Oh, all right. Can't hurt, can it?" I threw them in my mouth and washed them down with two large gulps of coffee. "It just hurts. When does it stop hurting?"

"Maybe never."

"By Jove, you're a comfort." I put the mug down and tried to gain control of my emotions. Taking advantage of the quiet, Fifi wiggled out from under the sofa. She tilted her head up at me, her glossy eyes searching my face…for what?

"I'm alone now, Dusty. My parents are dead. My brothers pretty much stopped talking to me when I fell into the bottle. Siobhan, Haylee, Conor—they were my family. Everyone's gone. They're all gone."

"Others will take their place. It's universal law. Where there's a void, there's something—in this case, someone— waiting to fill it. You aren't alone. You're just sad."

"I've no one who cares about me now. If I died this minute, there'd be no one at my funeral."

"That's not true. I'd be there."

I'm sure his Buddhist philosophy said something about being kind to all creatures great and small, and his generosity was meant to calm me, yet it had the opposite effect. I burrowed into his shoulder and wept.

The Matriarch

Over a light breakfast of fruit and toast, Dusty filled me in on the investigation. I think he was trying to keep my thoughts on something he could control.

"Francine Starling's husband has lawyered her up. We won't get any more about the argument out of her without a subpoena and I'm not sure it matters. So Francine argued with Haylee. If no one can confirm the subject of the dispute it couldn't have been important enough to kill over." He brushed crumbs from the table before continuing. "The murder weapon used on Amato was a drop-point hunting knife with a four-inch blade plus Tony was beaten pretty badly before someone stepped behind him, yanked his head back and stzzzzz." He drew his hand across his throat. "Sorry, maybe you're not ready for this."

"What am I, oatmeal? What you're saying is not the same weapon and maybe not the same killer. Anything else?" I picked up my coffee.

"I saved the best for last," he said. "Your bud, Gary Larkin, he didn't start Larkin Limousines. His wealthy wife bought the company seven years ago. It used to be called California Coaches." He began peeling an apple, removing the skin a section at a time. "I spoke with the previous owner. Seems Mrs. Larkin bought the company for her new husband, Gary, as a wedding present. Her first husband had died the previous spring. I called Larkin's last employer back in New York and got an earful." He cut the apple in half and sliced off a piece.

He offered the piece to me.

"No thanks."

Using the edge of the knife, he popped the slice into his mouth.

"You can talk with your mouth full," I said. "What did the employer have to say?"

He finished chewing before he spoke. "It was another limousine service. The guy said Larkin had a rich girlfriend that was always buying him fancy duds. I assume that was Lenora—wife-to-be. One day the rich girlfriend—Lenora—blows her whistle and Larkin takes off for the West Coast."

"Think she killed her previous husband for a boy-toy?"

"Naw. I looked into it. The old man was twenty years her senior and had been bedridden with a list of aliments for the last two years of their marriage. What is interesting is that the Belvedere Club ladies all swear that Lenora met Larkin through Larkin Limousines."

"Maybe they're lying. I got the feeling that the club's members hold themselves to some weird sort of loyalty. The whole heredity thing. I don't see them dishing dirt on each other. I think that's why no one will tell us what Francine Starling and Haylee argued about and why Francine won't tell us why she wants Charlotte Warren out of the Belvedere Club. They get catty with each other, but they guard the club's secrets to the death." I put down my toast. "We still don't know why Gary Larkin claims he slept with Haylee."

"Well…and you aren't going to like this…" Dusty popped another apple slice in his mouth.

It must be some sort of Buddhist torture technique, saying I'm not going to like it and then chewing an apple wedge for ten minutes. "Do I look like a patient person to you?"

"Hardly." He swallowed. "We compared Haylee's cell phone records with the Larkin household and there were several that corresponded. The first was the Thursday evening after the luncheon, a full week before she was murdered. Looks like during lunch Haylee must have figured out that Lorena's husband was her old pal, Gary. There were several other calls including one the night she died that lasted twelve minutes."

"All that means is she was talking to him. It doesn't mean Haylee was sleeping with him." I finished my coffee wondering why Haylee wouldn't have told me she'd run into him. Had Gary fallen into his old role as informant, supplying Haylee with dirt on members of the Belvedere Club?

* * *

After breakfast Dusty drove me and Fifi to a new hotel. Earlier, management had silently slipped a note under my door, stating that the hotel didn't allow dogs and checkout was at noon.

I tossed my knapsack on the back seat next to the dog. "You knew about Fifi. Why did you ask the manager to let you in?"

"Because unlike you, I can't pick locks."

"What's wrong with knocking?"

"I knocked, but you were howling like a wolf caught in a leg trap and the full moon isn't until tonight. I can't wait to see what kind of creature you morph into later." He reached forward and fiddled with the police scanner. "Someone had to let me in. The manager was the only one with keys. Besides, you'll like the Best Western. It has a bigger pool and they allow pets, if that's what you call that thing."

"You never told me what brought you to the hotel in the first place."

"I was down in Belvedere, going over the case with their sergeant—"

"Ah, the one back from vacation."

"Exactly." He tapped the steering wheel. "I realized there's one person all this drama revolves around and we haven't spoken with her yet."

"The mother—old Mrs. Warren."

He glanced my way. "You bounce back fast. I'd like to talk with the old woman."

"If she can talk." I hadn't bounced back as well as he thought. My head was pounding. My thoughts kept getting jumbled causing confusion. But I paid attention. I forced myself.

"Right. If. I called yesterday and spoke with her nurse, a Ms. Peters. She said Mrs. Warren has bad days and good days, mostly bad. You've had a rough time, maybe you aren't up to it."

Truth was, my soul felt shot through with buckshot. And with no job, there was no story. Officially, I had no right to ride along during the investigation. But this was an invitation. Sort of. And a chance I wouldn't have again once Dusty learned that I had been fired from *The Dispatch*. "I feel great, but this time you pay for the pizza."

Was I mistaken or did he look relieved?

We tucked Fifi into her new home, which was much smaller than the suite we'd vacated. For one thing, there were no separated rooms. The living room doubled as a bedroom, the bed folded into the wall. The kitchen was a stove and fridge along the back wall separated from the living room by a four-foot counter. Two stools at the counter served as the eating area.

I tried to find a spot where Fifi would be comfortable until I returned.

Dusty wanted to get on the road. "I'm sure the dog's fine, let's go. Whoa, drop the camera bag."

Even after two cups of coffee, the previous night remained pretty much a mystery except for a few strange visions replaying in my mind. I thanked God that I hadn't taken a drink, but I had no other explanation for the blackout. Neither Dusty nor the doctor had mentioned "psychotic break," which was the buzz word after I'd lost Siobhan. I'd never agreed with that diagnosis either. I thought of it more as a bender that lasted a year too long; a bender that I might not have survived if not for Haylee.

Dusty could probably fill in some of the missing pieces, but because of his disturbingly doting behavior, I found myself uncomfortable with asking. Instead, the only voices inside the car as we headed north this time were those coming in over the police scanner. I listened to the spewing codes. Some of the more universal ones, I knew, but others were more difficult to decipher. Ten-One was "receiving poorly," used often and the most obvious. Next was Code Four, which Dusty said meant "No further assistance needed." When he figured out my game, he reached over and turned the scanner down to where it wasn't discernable to the untrained ear.

Party pooper. "So is 'Dusty' a nickname?" I closed my mind, warding off the whimsical images that flared up when I thought about his bizarre name. "What's your real name?"

"Dusty."

I wasn't going to laugh. I bit my bottom lip to make sure. "Come on. Your parents actually named you Dusty Arkansas?"

"They had a sense of humor."

I snickered. "I guess so. What's your sister's name? Hilly?"

"Rocky."

I snorted, trying to stifle a laugh. "No really."

He grinned.

"Who would do that to a kid? I guess they really do have a sense of humor." A sadistic one, I wanted to add, but wasn't about to bring on his temper by insulting his folks.

"Did I mention we lived in a commune? You should have heard some of the other kids' names—Cord, Ramrod, Tulip.

How many dates do you think poor Ramrod gets now that he's all grown up?"

I laughed freely. Names were such an ordeal with my family, every one researched not just for its meaning, but for the good or bad luck it might have given a previous bearer.

"My name is a derivative of Brian," I said. "It means powerful."

"That you are."

I couldn't tell if he was mocking me or not, but chose not to spoil the moment by dwelling on it. Instead, I turned my thoughts to The Rummington Alzheimer's Clinic. There was a name. The current Mrs. Warren was another Amanda, named no doubt after the Belvedere Club's founder, Mrs. Amanda Weathersby. Mrs. Warren's mother had been a Charlotte also. A lot of egotism within the lineage. Dusty had stolen the Post-It®s, but not before I had committed each square to memory.

"We'll reach the clinic in about fifteen minutes. Do you need another coffee before we go in?"

"Okay, enough. What's with you and the coffee? All you did was complain about it—the caffeine, being wired, false energy, etcetera, etcetera—now, you can't pour it down me fast enough."

"I'm a little slow. I didn't understand before," he said.

Oh, geez. What had I said last night? I was almost afraid to find out. "Understand what?"

But Dusty remained silent, his eyes on the road.

"Now, you clam up. What? Un-der-stand what?"

Still no answer.

Irish anger was often compared to a steam cooker; it builds and builds until something blows. I felt the boil. "Give me a clue." I held up my palms, waving them. "Did I cut myself and bleed latte?"

"The cigarettes, the coffee. I didn't get it. Now...I get it, okay. Leave it alone."

"Are you messing with me? Because I'm really not in the mood." I shook my hands in the air to push my point.

"You're an alcoholic."

My heart stopped. My hands dropped to my lap. I closed my eyes and a loud ringing filled my ears.

"Are you okay? Oh... Hey, can you hear me?"

I turned and looked at him with a calm I didn't know I possessed. "I'm fine." He, on the other hand, looked dreadfully pale. "How about you?"

"Sorry. I guess I probably shouldn't have said anything."

"I'm an alcoholic. So are a good portion of my relatives and... coworkers, a few neighbors, and the guy at the Stop and Save. No biggie."

"If you say so."

I clenched my fist. "Oh, don't give me that crap. I don't need your pity."

"Pity! How about understanding?" He turned the car right between the brick pillars and into the drive leading to The Rummington Alzheimer's Clinic.

"What's to understand? I'm not drinking now." But I sure wanted to. Oh, dear Lord I wanted to. "I drink the occasional coffee because I like to drink the occasional coffee. I smoke because I like to smoke."

He stopped the car so fast the tires squealed. "Good. Enough of your heartbreak. We're here."

We both hit the clinic steps like storm troopers, each shoving through the door at the same time, making entry almost impossible. Dusty grunted and I cursed as we squeezed through the doorframe without yielding to the other.

A startled receptionist watched our theatrics.

"We're here to see Mrs. Warren," Dusty announced.

The receptionist called for a young nurse, who, with her

squeaky white shoes, led us through the building opposite the offices. As we stepped into a sun-filled communal room, I paused while Dusty and the nurse continued across the floor. A herd of wheelchairs filled the space, many holding men and women with slack jaws and vacant eyes. Ages varied from person to person, the oldest looking quite ancient, the youngest about Dusty's age, mid-thirties or so. The more animated patients moved freely about the room able to look into their future.

A chill sent goose bumps over my flesh, a sensation the Irish attribute to someone walking over our graves, but it wasn't *my* grave I was thinking about. To my right, a woman sat flexing and releasing her fingers like she was scratching an invisible itch. Ahead, a man danced, stooped over an imaginary partner, his slippers gliding across the Linoleum.

A heaviness filled my heart.

Across the room near a large picture window, Dusty and the nurse stood beside another wheelchair. Dusty caught my eye and in a brief moment communicated that he was as disturbed as I by what he saw. I joined him as the nurse was introducing Mrs. Warren.

Her wheelchair was facing the window, her gaze was locked on the horizon. Not the eccentric picture I expected. With knotted hands she picked at the shawl covering her legs. Instead of the designer duds her daughter sported, Mrs. Warren wore a heavy woven sweater buttoned to her neck.

Dusty greeted her, but she showed no sign of having heard him. He spoke again, louder.

"I'm afraid Mrs. Warren's not doing well today." The nurse patted Mrs. Warren's back. "It's been somewhat traumatic, well, with her nurse, Ms. Peters, and everything."

Dusty crossed his arms. "Where is Ms. Peters? I spoke with her yesterday on the phone and she assured me she'd be here for my visit. She told me Mrs. Warren was more coherent in the mornings."

Confusion wrinkled the young woman's forehead. "You are the police, right?"

"Marin County Sheriff's Department."

"Marin?" Tears welled in the nurse's eyes, accentuating their clear blue color. She brought a hand to her mouth and sniffed.

Dusty shifted his weight, leaning back, away.

I could stand by and wait out the misunderstanding—if that was what it was—or I could break my vow of silence.

"Sheriff Arkansas didn't mean to upset you. Would you like to sit?" I dragged one of the few plastic chairs over to Mrs. Warren's wheelchair and the young nurse lowered herself into it, knees and ankles primly locked.

With fingers covering her mouth and tears streaming down her cheeks, she spoke. "I'm sorry. I guess you haven't heard…I thought they called the police… They did call the police…I mean…."

The hair on the back of my neck rose and by the way Dusty took a step closer, he must have had the same sensation.

I pulled over another chair and sat at an angle to the young woman, our knees almost touching. "Tell us what happened."

Dusty gripped the back of my chair.

"Emily…I mean Mrs. Warren's nurse, Ms. Peters…I call her Emily…she's…ah, Ms. Peters has passed on." The woman bowed her head and sniffed into her hands. Mrs. Warren's chin dropped to her chest.

I felt one of those knots in my throat that comes from dealing with too many emotions at once.

"Oh, I'm sorry," the young nurse said as she leaped up. "I'll be right back."

A long deep silence followed the nurse's departure. When I finally had the strength to move, I turned to Dusty and asked, "Dead or murdered?"

Holding a tissue, the nurse dashed back in. She went to sit, but was moving to fast and tipped the plastic chair, losing her balance. I grabbed the back of the chair keeping the nurse from going over. She settled and wiped at her eyes.

Dusty gestured me out of my chair and sat before her. "What happened to Ms. Peters? It's important."

She sniffed again. "They said it was a robbery. Last night."

"Here?" Dusty asked.

She blew into the tissue and shook her head. "Her apartment."

"Did she live nearby?"

The nurse nodded.

"We need to speak with the Santa Rosa police," Dusty said to the young woman, but I knew he was speaking to me. He stood. "Sorry we upset you." He faced Mrs. Warren. "Sorry for your loss."

Mrs. Warren didn't react. It was impossible to know if she heard or understood. The nurse lifted Mrs. Warren's chin so she could see us, but she pulled away and went back to staring out the window as if we weren't there.

"Wait." I reached into my handbag and took out the photo of Haylee. I showed it to the nurse. "Have you ever seen this woman here?"

She dabbed her eyes with a clean tissue and palmed the photo. She studied the image, wanting to help, but in the end, shook her head, her shoulders sagging. I took the photo and held it under Mrs. Warren's blank stare, but if she saw it, she didn't let on. I waited another minute, watching her and wondering about the disease.

Some research I'd read said that with Alzheimer's the fantasy part of the brain didn't switch off to allow the brain back into rational thought. Sort of like being locked in a dream. If so, I could only hope it was a pleasant dream.

The Police Station

A Homicide detective named Vetter, with biceps the size of my head, verified Dusty's credentials and told me I would have to wait outside in the reception area. No reporters allowed.

Dusty stood up for me and I tell you, the earth moved. He assured Vetter that I wasn't investigating a story, but was a team member in a homicide investigation.

A team member!

Vetter looked at me like I was something that had washed up from the sewer. He glanced back at Dusty with an expression that said what he didn't have the guts to say.

"She can sit in, but I reserve the right to withhold anything I deem necessary." His voice had a nasal quality, probably because his nose looked to have been broken more than once. At the bridge, it slanted slightly left like my brother Kevin's who'd broken his during a street fight.

Dusty agreed to his terms.

I didn't. "Like what?"

"Like anything I don't want the press to get a hold of." He shoved a thick bicep in my direction.

I shoved a scrawny one in his.

He tossed a gray file folder on the conference table and drew up a chair. Dusty and I sat.

Without opening the folder he began. "Emily Peters was killed in the parking garage of her apartment building. Location, downtown Santa Rosa. Our timeline puts the homicide at about nine p.m., the time she was getting home from work, allowing for a short stop at the grocery. Her shift ended at six but she stayed on until seven-thirty." He fingered the folder. "We believe the perp followed her either from The Rummington Alzheimer's Clinic or from Safeway because another couple arrived in the garage minutes before Peters and didn't see any cars that didn't belong or anyone hanging about. It's a fifty-two car garage."

He opened the folder, letting the cover drop to the table. Separating the photos from the paperwork, he handed Dusty a series of eight-by-tens. "Peters was stabbed several times in the upper chest and her throat was cut."

Dusty flipped through the crime photos without passing them to me.

"Are you going to let me see?" I asked him.

"Don't think so."

"Trust me, I've seen worse."

He handed the photos back to Vetter. "Detective Vetter doesn't want you to see these."

Vetter took a minute to catch on, but when he did, he agreed with Dusty. "No way." He laid the photos in the folder and slammed the cover closed, posing his hands on top as if he thought I was going to fight him for them.

"You said, throat cut?" I looked at Dusty. "Similar to Haylee?"

His nod was almost imperceptible. I drew in a deep breath, trying to remember Haylee's photos, but they were erased from my memory like a computer disk wiped clean. I knew better than to dwell on it. "Do you think—"

"I do." He turned back to Vetter. "You should have received something on a homicide in Marin County last Thursday morning. We sent out a flyer for information on similar cases."

"Must not have had a hit. When we don't have a hit, those things get filed." Vetter rubbed his two day old beard, his whiskers sounding like sandpaper on glass.

Dusty's hand went automatically to his smooth scalp.

"You have a hit now."

"Hold it a minute." Vetter stood and picked up the folder. "Better take this with me," he said, scowling at me. He left, the folder pressed to his chest.

Dusty fingered his head as if looking for a nub he'd missed. "You remember looking at Ms. Macklin's photos."

No. I nodded.

"These are almost identical. Nothing at all like Tony Amato's."

"Same killer."

"Something you said: up close, face and chest, the jab-slash pattern denoting personal anger. You remember?" he asked.

No. I nodded again, wondering why everything was coming up blank. Maybe it was the headache. It wasn't like me to forget the details of a case, especially one this important.

"I thought you were right, but after seeing these photos something else struck me. I'll have to speak with the coroner or someone who knows more about the human body than I do, but this isn't a coincidence."

His eyes glassed over as he looked inward. I had no idea where he was going with this.

"The chest incisions looked, well, if someone wanted to stab someone in the chest, wouldn't he aim for the heart, the center of the chest?" He touched his chest as he spoke. "All the wounds were to the side. At first I thought it was because of the struggle, but two victims, both with puncture wounds to the side, plus an identical carotid slice."

"Fill me in here," I said. "I didn't see the photos, I haven't a clue."

"It looks like the killer was aiming for a lung or major artery, some type of injury to slow the victim down. Afterward, the carotid cut was to assure death. It looks more technical than emotional."

"A health professional. Someone who'd studied the body. Rummington!"

"Whoa. Talk about jumping to conclusions," he said.

"You have to admit it looks suspicious."

"Do you know how many health professionals are in Marin alone? We have a long way to go to narrow the database."

Vetter returned, reading the flyer as he entered. "Huh, a reporter." He looked at me, and then Dusty. "Doesn't say anything about a robbery. This was a robbery. Handbag, wallet, a bag of Cheetos, according to the sales slip." He continued reading. "Throat cut with a knife, extreme pressure applied. Weapon, sharp four to five-inch blade, probably a kitchen knife."

Again he lifted his eyes from the paper. "Looks right with the knife, but I don't have the autopsy yet, maybe by morning. Doc's going to write it up and fax it to me this evening. You thinking serial?"

"Serial, no, but there is a link."

"Are you going to tell me how this Peters woman ties into your case?"

Dusty filled him in on the Belvedere Club, the Warrens, and Haylee's story, leaving out the three components of a Pulitzer, but mentioning that Haylee thought she was on to something. "Would it be possible for us to see the crime scene?" he asked.

Vetter's biceps seemed to be bulging a little less. "No problem, I'll drive you over."

Maybe he and Dusty were bonding. Maybe Vetter was getting too attached.

"How about the victim's apartment?" Dusty said.

"I've got people going through it now. If the S.I. guys are through, you can have a look."

"She was Mrs. Warren's nurse," Dusty said to Vetter. "That links her to our case even if the MOs weren't exactly the same. We need to look for some other connection to the Warrens or the Belvedere Club."

* * *

During the short ride across town, Dusty called Dr. Rummington and asked whether Ms. Peters had any connection with the Belvedere Club's charity.

When he clicked off, he swiveled around so he could see me in the rear hunched behind the seat grid like a criminal. "Dr. Rummington confirmed that Ms. Peters was Mrs. Warren's private nurse, hired by the family three years ago. No connection to the charity, none that he knew of, but he mentioned Peters spent a lot of time with the family. Trips, holidays, stuff like that."

"Maybe he's lying," I said.

Dusty frowned. "The charity was begun in the eighties. Peters has only been on the scene three years."

Vetter parked across from the garage's entrance, which was blocked off with a thick linked chain. He led us inside. Of the four structural pillars at the garage's center, two were cordoned with red police tape which was anchored by a fluorescent orange cone. The triangular area encompassed a chalk outline and the huge rusty stain lay next to it. Deemed a crime scene by the Santa Rosa Police, the garage was currently carless, making it harder to visualize what had actually happened. Detective Vetter walked us through what he believed happened.

"The victim pulled up here, parked. These two cars on each side of hers belong to neighbors. She got out, walked around here to the trunk, probably for the grocery bags. The perp came through the entrance there, up behind her. The victim must have heard the approach because she turned, receiving the first jab into her chest." Vetter leaned over the tape to point out blood spatter confirming the first forward attack.

"She fell back against the trunk and—kicking out—received a cut to her knee." He raised his right knee. "Next came the second jab." He stabbed out with a pretend knife. "The third. Here the victim slides to the ground, instinctively rolling away from the perp." He stepped back as if watching an invisible falling body.

"Here, the perp yanked the victim's hair, pulled her head up and zowie, the throat."

And zowie my stomach. I ran for the exit, barely reaching the outside hedge before spewing toast across the narrow leaves. I'd seen plenty of crime scenes, and that had never happened to me.

"You okay?"

Dusty's strong hands were on my arms as I dug through my handbag for something to wipe my mouth on.

"Sorry. I usually have a camera lens to buffer me," I said.

"You've been through a lot these last few days. You're entitled."

Now, that just pissed me off. "It has nothing to do with—"

"Vetter's letting us see the apartment, you coming?"

I spit into the bushes, wiped my lips on a used tissue. "Think I'm up to it?" My mouth tasted like overcooked three-day-old gravy.

Dusty didn't answer and I didn't turn around. "I need a cigarette. I'll meet you up there."

"Here, take these." He shoved a pair of plastic gloves into my hand. "Second floor, the door will be open."

I fumbled for a cigarette, my hands a little shaky. Alone, I drew in a mouthful of nicotine and was blanketed by its calming properties. I drew in a second mouthful.

Waddling down the sidewalk, came a man with two stomachs separated by a leather belt. A Chihuahua was tied to the leash in his hand. The Chihuahua's gray muzzle mirrored the man's gray beard. The dog stopped four feet from where I stood to do its stinky business. I met the man's nasty scowl and sneered back.

"Hey, you can't smoke here," he said.

I was outside, in the great American wilderness. Well, urban wilderness. But, just in case, I turned to see if there were any No Smoking signs posted on the garage like the ones I'd seen in the hotel's parking lot.

"Excuse me."

"This is California. You can't smoke here."

I drew in a long drag and blew it out slowly. "I have a gun."

The man scurried away, the Chihuahua trotting like a quarter horse to keep up. I stubbed the cigarette out against the garage and carried it to the dumpster inside without ever casting an eye towards the crime scene.

The Nurse

Emily Peters had lived in a corner apartment overlooking the complex's most popular feature, the Lavender Garden. The apartment was still clean even with police personnel trampling through, which meant the apartment had probably started out immaculate. As a general rule neat freaks worried me. In today's modern society of working, shopping, exercising, volunteering, learning, praying, socializing, looking the best, smelling the best, who had time to clean house? The other option—a cleaning woman. People with cleaning women, I related to. My father had employed cleaning women of every nationality. With seven kids to pick up after, none stayed too long. The only one I remembered was a Portuguese woman named Beatriz. She liked to read, mostly my school books, especially history, and she was always asking questions about English grammar. *"Why do you say, he is cold and not he has cold?"* I often credit her for my love of language.

"Cleaning woman?" I offered up.

"I'll look into it," Vetter said, noticing my presence. "Hey, you don't touch anything. I don't have your prints on file."

I held up my hands, covered with the plastic gloves Dusty had given me. Vetter ignored me, scanning the room as if it were the first time he'd seen it.

Right of the entrance, an ebony commode leaned against the wall. On top stood several birthday cards, opened at an angle. The last birthday Emily would ever see. Without touching the cards, I peeked at the inscriptions. *Love Mom and Dad. Happy Birthday sis, love Allie. Happy Birthday, Mike.*

"There's a card here from someone named Mike."

Vetter opened his notepad. "Another nurse from the clinic."

"A boyfriend?"

Vetter didn't like answering me. He looked at Dusty to see if he wanted the information.

"Well?"

"Naw, the guy's gay. They were just friends. Had dinner once a week, did some hiking, that sort of thing."

I tried again. "How old was she?"

Vetter looked at Dusty and then at his notepad. "Just turned thirty-two. Nursing school, Boise State U. Divorced. Ex lives in Montana." He looked up. "We're still trying to track him down. No known enemies." He flipped the book closed and stuffed it in his coat pocket.

The sofa was American Traditional; the type found in every suburban home on the East Coast, boxy, printed, and unoriginal. A copy of Frances Mayes's *Under the Tuscan Sun* was lying on the coffee table, a copper bookmark stuck a third of the way through. Peters died without knowing the ending. Sometimes it paid to see the movie.

The kitchen was the same size as the bedroom and rather spacious for the apartment's design. I opened the refrigerator and found the usual suspects: milk, butter, lettuce, and cheese. I remembered that she'd been on her way home from the grocery. I could see why.

"No wine in the fridge," I said.

Dusty offered me a bemused expression. He continued rummaging through her desk.

I walked over to him. "Rummington's from back East and the Warrens are Californian. Who recommended Peters for the job? Also," I stuck my nose in the air and drew in a deep breath. "No pets."

"Right, like those cigarettes you suck on haven't burnt

your nasal passages to a crisp. Leave the sniffing to the dogs."

Ah, the mean Dusty. Wasn't he adorable? "There's no dog or cat food in the fridge and no water bowls anywhere, and not an animal hair in the room unless you count Vetter's mop."

Vetter wagged a fist at us. "Hey, don't draw me into your scrap." He picked up a picture frame.

Dusty wanted to add something, but held back. Instead he asked the detective about the bills. "There's a phone bill here, have you checked it out? What about her bank account, any unusual deposits or withdrawals?"

"We had no reason to check that stuff. The case looked like your standard robbery." He held up two fingers, "I'll look into it."

"That's the money," Dusty said, turning to me. "What about drugs?"

Surprising both of us, another detective leaving the bedroom answered. "Standard medicine cabinet: aspirin, vitamin B complex, vitamin C, Trimox—an antibiotic, Naproxen—an anti-inflammatory, and Percodan. Band-aids, Neosporin, toothpaste, waxed floss and Listerine."

"Percodan's addictive," I said.

Vetter cocked his head at me. "You know a doctor or nurse who doesn't have Percodan in their home?" he asked, as if I was a third grader.

I had a sister-in-law who was a registered nurse. I could call and see if that urban legend was true. "As for the third component," I said, turning back to Dusty. "The closet is mostly white uniforms, one party dress. The sexiest panty in her drawers was a black lace number, not even a thong. If she's sleeping with someone, I hope they're blind."

Vetter was curious now; I think the "T" word got his attention. "Hey, why do you care what kind of panties she wore? Is there something you aren't telling me?"

Dusty answered. "Like you, we're looking for clues, connections, and so far I don't see anything that raises an eyebrow. Looks like Ms. Peters lived a fairly straightforward, if not boring life, but I'll be interested in the bank information. If you give me a copy of the phone bill, I'll run the numbers for you."

"It's my case, Lieutenant, I'll get back to you."

A wariness crept into Dusty's face. "Look Vetter, no one's trying to steal your thunder. My case, your case, they're linked and we need to work together before this person kills again. When I get back, I'll fax you everything I have. I'd appreciate it if you did the same."

* * *

"There's a connection with the Warrens. I'm sure this time," I said as we reentered the highway, heading back to Marin County.

"This time?"

With a big splash, Dusty dove back into his giving-me-a-hard-time mode and as much as I preferred it over his condescending-and-pitying mode, he was starting to get on my nerves. "Are you denying it?"

"Oh, there's a connection," he said.

"Damn straight. What are you thinking about? The photos?"

Dusty's expression didn't change, which was validation enough for me. Time to brainstorm.

"What kind of person uses a knife to kill?" I asked.

"Someone who doesn't have access to a gun."

"Come on, guns are easier to get than CDs. Whip up the Internet, add one credit card number, and voilà. Even I have one."

Dusty's bald head whipped so fast in my direction I heard a whistle of air.

"You're kidding? *You* own a gun?"

"Sort of. Haylee took it away from me, but I own it."

He turned back to the road. "At least someone had some sense. No doubt about it, we need stricter gun control."

"It's a Constitutional issue," I said, throwing my chin out.

"So I've heard. Don't tell me you're a Republican on top of everything else."

What did that mean?

"Ah no, you are, aren't you?" He pulled the Sentra over on the shoulder and stopped. "Get out! Get out of this car, right now."

Cars flew by at high speeds, shaking the Sentra. A familiar shame settled over me. I heard Haylee's taunting above the roar of the traffic. She was always on me to register to vote. But issues needed to be researched, not just taken as opinions. Candidates' voting records needed to be reviewed because everyone knew candidates lied, but what they voted on told what they really supported. And I never found the time for all the research. If an issue *really* struck me, I did the research. I spread the word. I promised to register to vote. But I never did.

"You're a filthy Republican—what *is* wrong with you?"

One of those whiny Democrats. Figured, Buddhist, Democrat—different shoe, same foot. "Have you read the Republican Oath lately?"

"Are you joking? Who cares about a stupid Oath? Certainly not Republicans. History has proven them to be nothing but liars and cheats. You're a journalist, for goodness sake."

"Once you whiny Democrats get off your soapbox and do something, then maybe we can have a discussion." *Said the woman not registered to vote.*

"Do something? Do something! Like lie to the American people? Like pour all of our national resources into an unnecessary war? Like cheat the voting public?" He grabbed the steering wheel until his knuckles looked like they were going to pop. He sat very still, his face the color of cherry Kool-Aid. After a minute or two, he took a deep breath, and another.

I had a good retort to his last statement, but honestly, I was afraid to open my mouth, afraid he might sock me one, afraid I'd be walking the fifty miles back to my hotel.

He drew his palms together into prayer position and poised his lips on his fingertips. "We better stop before one of us pulls a gun."

"And let's notice which one of us has a gun strapped to his belt," I said.

"Don't think I won't use it if you don't shut up."

Did that make him a Democrat who believed in the death penalty? I didn't ask. God had given me an "off" switch. I sometimes forgot when to use it, but luckily this wasn't one of those times. Dusty had his eyes closed and was doing some funky breathing thing, or else…he was hyperventilating.

"Should I call a doctor, or next of kin?"

He continued as if I hadn't spoken.

After what seemed eternity, we pulled back into traffic. I was still a passenger and determined to keep it that way until we reached Marin County. I began brainstorming what we'd learned about Peters and tried to fit each piece into a mold with Haylee's murder. After a few miles, I'd completely forgotten Dusty was angry with me. "Could the killer be a woman?" I asked.

"Could be a baboon if it was strong enough." His voice was civil, but not friendly. "I read Vetter's crime report. A couple had just gone up the stairwell when Peters arrived. They believe that if she'd screamed, they'd have heard her. Why didn't she scream?"

I thought about it. "Maybe she didn't have time."

"Vetter said she struggled. I think she knew her attacker," he said. "The more I think about it I'm convinced that the first wounds were to bring the victim down, end a struggle, or even prevent a struggle. And then the final slash." He looked across the seat at me.

"I know how Haylee died, you showed me *those* photos."

"The slash was a sure thing, cut an artery. A jab between the eyes would be just as effective or to the heart."

"The heart is harder to find and the blade was small, wasn't it?"

Dusty nodded. "And if you were a medical student, you'd know that. Why was Haylee at the Belvedere Club so early? What did she want you to photograph?"

"We've gone over this. Hey, isn't that the exit for Frankie's?"

"You're hungry?"

"Starved." I tapped my belly for effect. "Besides, I think better on a full stomach."

"I'm sick of pizza," he said.

"No, you're sick of me. It's not the same thing."

The traffic slowed to around fifteen miles per hour. Dusty huffed at the cars because he didn't want to huff at me.

"Can't we call a truce?" I asked.

He didn't say anything for a moment, and finally, "You like Mexican? Not that Mexican-American crap either, I mean the real thing."

"Is salsa and chips the real thing?"

He gave me a pitiful tilt of the head. My cell phone rang, cutting further discussion of culinary delights. It was Terrance.

My heart leaped. Did it mean I was still pulling in a paycheck? He really did value me. Not Terrance. He was probably calling to gloat about my new replacement.

"Where are you?" His standard line.

"Cal-i-for-nia." Hopefully, he'd get it this time. "I've got great news too. There's been another homicide and it looks like it's linked to Haylee's."

"A serial killer?"

"Probably not. We're back to thinking there's a connection somehow with the story Haylee was working on."

"What's the connection?"

"Don't know yet. I'm with Du…, ah, Lieutenant Arkansas. We're going over the details." Feeling excited that I might actually have my job back, I winked at Dusty.

"How many times do I have to tell you, I need you back here! Senator Robins has just declared she's a lesbian. The husband has agreed to an interview. Who am I going to send?"

"My guess would be, ah, one of your political reporters."

"They're all covering the crime beat. I mean it this time, Kaleigh, if you aren't in my office at sunrise tomorrow morning, you're fired."

"You already fired me. You can't fire me again. This is a bigger story than some senator's pussy-whipped husband. When are you going to see that?" I clicked off before he could say another word. I was already resigned to finding another job.

"You're fired?" Dusty asked.

Cell phones. Everybody's listening. "Apparently not. He wants me to continue for now, but I don't have much time left. I'm starving."

He reached across the dashboard and switched on a siren. Two lanes of cars parted like the Red Sea and the Sentra picked up speed.

What a life.

The Dinner

Dusty dropped me at the Best Western so I could walk Fifi. The plan was to meet at his boat afterwards, but when I tried to leave Fifi, she started barking. The rapid fired yelps carried down the corridor to where I waited by the elevators. After a full three and half minutes she didn't stop. I foresaw getting thrown out of yet another hotel and who knew when my company credit card would be rescinded, if it hadn't been already.

I threw open the door. "Okay, you can come." I grabbed the leash and hooked it on her collar, her little legs trembling with anticipation. "You'll have to stay in the car and you can bark until your tongue turns blue, no discussion." Like a quarter horse she trotted beside me to the parking lot. It was uncanny how she picked out my car from all the other cars.

We found Dusty on deck, both hands extended over his head, palms pressed together and with one leg bent and his foot pressed into the thigh of his standing leg. He looked like a fleshy radio tower.

"Searching for other galaxies?"

Fifi barked.

"Oh, you." He lowered his arms and stretched the bare foot into the strappy sandal loitering beside him. "Vrksasana, Tree pose." He bent to hook the sandal. "With you in a minute." He had changed out of his business slacks and golf shirt and was back in his uniform of choice, Jesus sandals and jeans. He wore his cotton shirt loose, the tails hanging. He pointed at Fifi. "What's with you-know-who?"

"She wouldn't shut up. I had to bring her along. Does the restaurant allow dogs?"

"Yeah, but I doubt they'll allow that. You can tie it up outside. If you're lucky, it'll get stolen." He looked down at my feet. "I thought you were going to wear comfortable shoes."

I glanced at the Steve Madden sling backs. "These *are* the lowest heels I have."

"You can't walk in those things?"

"Unless we're headed for Australia, I'll manage. And what about you, aren't you afraid you'll trip over all those straps?"

The sun was setting behind the mountains that protected San Rafael from the ocean breezes. The evening—I was told—was unseasonably warm. I wore a blazer because it was all I had available, but back home I would have chosen something lighter like a sweater set.

We walked along the dock to where it dead-ended into a sidewalk. The sidewalk led us along several marinas, the sour smell of algae following like BO.

Dusty scanned the boats as we passed. I kept an eye on Fifi, worried her sniffing would lead her over the edge. And no, I wasn't going into the filthy, mucky water after her. Haylee would have to forgive me.

At the end of the marinas our path led behind, rather than in front, of a Mediterranean-styled strip mall.

Dusty pointed across the water to another row of boats. "That's where we're headed. But since you can't swim we have to walk the long way around."

"What makes you think I can't swim?"

"East Coast, snooty shoes. Can you?"

"It's what…twelve feet to the other side. Don't you have a dinghy or something?"

"That dog is not going in my dinghy."

"Are you kidding, twelve feet? I'll throw her across."

"I'd like to see that." He kept walking. "Wow. Look at

that sky. Feel that energy. It's so clear. Do you feel it? Very cosmic, don't you think? Regenerative."

Yeah, right, and I'm Mahatma Gandhi. I pointed to the rear of the strip mall and the gray supply doors, where store names were stenciled in white. "Any stores there good for shopping? My two-day wardrobe is looking a little shabby after a week."

"You'll do better across the highway from where you're staying. There's an all-purpose mall there," he said still gazing at the sky.

For all-purpose clothes? Who was this guy?

The sidewalk curved, leading us over a small bridge where we had a clear view down the marinas. "Cheapest real estate in Marin County," Dusty said, holding his hand out. His face glowed with the secret he was sharing, telling me I was allowed, not necessarily into the inner circle, but a step closer to his private realm. It was a male moment and I understood that because I'd been raised with six brothers, but I couldn't stop the female in me from thinking, so what? Who wants to live on a boat?

We walked down a service road just yards from highway 101. Wind splashed our faces from the cars rushing northward on the highway. The traffic noise made it difficult to carry on a conversation.

"Detective Vetter called. Cause of death, asphyxiation, same as Haylee."

"No surprise there."

"This is an investigation. The facts are important, not the guesses."

"I get snippy too when I'm hungry. How much farther?" I asked.

"Feet hurt?"

Fifi went the long way around a sign post, tangling her leash. "Stomach." I patted my belly. "Did he have any other *facts* to relate, like who killed Peters? Fifi, come here." I shortened the leash.

"He spoke with her bank, no large withdrawals. Regular deposits signed by Rebecca Warren, Charles' wife, probably paychecks. My guys have finished with the financial statements from all three charities. Not a single inconsistency."

"Fifi!" I tugged the leash. "That in itself is odd."

"Okay, there are a few problems, some questionable petty cash stuff, but nothing major, nothing worth killing over. Also, Amato's mother has identified mug shots of the two Asians she saw leaving Amato's apartment. They're linked to a Chinese gang, a few priors. San Rafael PD is looking into the connection."

We turned into another boat dock that ran perpendicular to the service road and 101. The traffic noise died down to a level where we didn't have to yell. Ethnic restaurants—Thai, Vietnamese, Italian—lined the building across from the dock's parking lot.

"Oh, forgot to tell you, we're releasing Haylee's body tomorrow. She'll be flown home in the morning."

I stopped mid-stride and covered my face with my hands, which wasn't as easy as it sounds because Fifi's leash was on my wrist and she didn't want to stop. I closed my eyes and remembered last night's phone call from Haylee's mom.

Dusty stepped forward and laid a hand on my shoulder. "I'm sorry. Did I say something wrong? I didn't mean to upset you. I thought you would want to know."

I peeked up from my fingers. "No. I'm fine, I'm trying to remember something from yesterday. Haylee's mother called, she was angry—that's a little strong—she was upset. She thought my investigation had held up Haylee's release."

"Your investigation? That's a good one." He looked away for a moment then back at me. "Maybe you should call her."

"Have you spoken to her already?" I asked as we started walking again.

"Yeah. I had the message when I got back to the boat, I called her directly."

After tying Fifi to a lamp post, we went in the empty restaurant with a Mexican flag draped across the front windows.

Without looking at a menu, Dusty ordered for both of us, a long list of Spanish. I didn't recognize a single plate, but figured they would all be meatless.

"Somewhere in all that gibberish, you added my chips, right?"

Dusty drew his index finger to his temple and teasingly pretended to be thinking.

"Drink?" The waiter's English was clearly limited and he made the gesture of holding a glass and bringing to his lips.

"I'll take a beer, no on second thought..." Dusty looked across the table.

"Take the beer, I don't care. I'll have an iced tea."

"Don't want to tempt you," he said.

I flicked something hard and white off the table. "A bottle of Jameson's might tempt me. Beer isn't worth the pain, literally."

He ordered a Mexican beer and waited for the waiter to leave. "You in AA?"

"You have a girlfriend?"

"Why are you changing the subject?"

"Do monks have sex?"

After the shock waned from his face, it hardened up. "So you aren't in AA. Getting help is not a bad thing, you know."

This was not my conversation of choice, but I understood his curiosity and I owed him an explanation about last night. If only there was one. "I'm not much of a joiner, or real good with excuses. I'm more the do or die type. It's the way I was raised. I promised Haylee I'd stop, and I have. I'm not real sure...I don't remember...what tore me down last night, but I thank you for being there."

"Drinking. Is that how you earned your demotion to photojournalist?"

He had ignored my gratitude, which I expected. Dusty was a man uncomfortable with emotion. "Where are we going with this? You want to psychoanalyze me? Scary proposition during the best of times."

"Oh, I agree. No, just making conversation so you don't chew off my arm before the food gets here."

"Fine, let's talk about you. What made you want to be a sheriff?" Seemed like a safe enough question.

The waiter returned, covering the tabletop with a paper tablecloth. He set a basket of chips in the center and added a bowl of salsa, with lots of jalapeños. Before leaving he mumbled something in Spanish and Dusty's eyes followed him to the back of the room.

The waiter quickly returned, placing Dusty's beer on a coaster and my ice tea on the paper tablecloth. I took a sip of tea, chuckling to myself. People were far more uncomfortable with an alcoholic who didn't drink, than I was with fighting the urge for a drink. After a year, the urge was intermittent. Sometimes, I thought I could have a drink without wanting six. But I also knew that was where the danger hid, so I never took that first drink. Last night was different. I'd caved into the urge and ordered two bottles, but I hadn't really expected today to dawn. I'd expected to lock myself in grief and never face reality again.

Across the table, Dusty sipped his beer. He was watching me in a way that made me uncomfortable. I repeated my question. "You were saying...why you wanted to become a sheriff. You liked the uniforms? The authority? The macho-macho?"

He set the beer down, his hand resting around it. "Gee, I don't know, it was a long time ago."

"Bull. My dad said a man always remembers what made him want to join the force."

Tension clamped his jaw. Now, he was evading me, which made me even more eager to know what he didn't want to say. To my surprise, he shrugged and spoke, the complete one-eighty I'd seen before.

"My folks were from the anti-war era. Vietnam, I mean. Keep forgetting about this other mess we're in. They met in an Ashram in Alaska. That's where I was born. When Jimmy Carter pardoned the draft dodgers, they migrated southward, stopping for a time in Washington and Oregon before landing up in Petaluma."

The way he was staring over my shoulder told me that this wasn't going to be an "I always loved the sirens" kind of story and even though I was curious, I was starting to feel bad for asking.

"During the time we were on the road, the police treated my folks like dirt. We were thrown out of a couple of towns, once my father wasn't even allowed to go back and pick up his pay. We ate wild blackberries for a week. You can imagine, going from the safe environment of the commune to being hated and ostracized. The kid that I was saw only the prejudice against those who were different. It ate at me." He paused as if self-editing, then continued.

"Once we were settled in Petaluma, it took years before we were accepted by our neighbors. Luckily for my parents and I guess, me and my sister, there were other outcasts living in the area. Petaluma was a true melting pot back in those days. The outcasts hung together, creating a sub-society, sort of a support network. Anyway, I joined the force because it seemed like the way to stop the prejudice." He shook his head. "Boy, was I naive."

The waiter arrived with our food, and while he set several plates on the table, I thought about how Dusty was still different from the pack. He made it a point—the shaved Buddhist head, the Jesus sandals—to stand out. How much of his efforts reflected who he really was, and how much was simply a method for testing those around him? I didn't yet know.

"In English—what's all this stuff?"

Dusty pointed at each dish and said what it was and what was in it. "Cheese tamales. Chile rellenos stuffed with chiles and cheddar. Frijoles, beans with spinach. And especially for you, a chicken enchilada." He pointed to a green pepper in a red sauce. "This here's a killer—nothing like it back East. It's hot enough to burn a hole through your tongue. I suggest you steer clear."

I don't know if it was his expression or the tone of his voice, but he was obviously challenging me and I wasn't about to back down. I plunged my fork into the green mound and ripped off a piece.

The taste was pungent. "What do you mean? This isn't hooooooo…ah." I grabbed my tea and guzzled the whole glass.

Dusty's face turned red with laughter. He grabbed the edge of the table and threw his head back as if his enjoyment needed more room. So carefree, he looked like a different person.

For an instant, with his face so full of humor, I had the urge to lean across the table and kiss him. I snatched a chicken enchilada instead and wrote off the feeling as lingering insanity.

Hunger overtook us and we dug in, cutting and chopping and chewing without another word. Our whole meal passed in slurpy silence, only becoming awkward when a few bites remained. Dusty broke the rhythm by ordering a second beer and another iced tea for me.

"Your folks still alive?" he asked.

"No. Yours?"

"Oh, sorry, I was going for light. Yeah, mine are both in Petaluma, still as crazy as ever."

Another silence. I'd had blind dates more comfortable than this. Whatever had happened last night had put us in a different playing field, one I wasn't at ease with.

I said, "My mom's been dead most of my life. She gave out after child number seven, my brother Mel. My father fell off the roof trying to clear away ice. He was drunk." I saw Dusty's surprise. "Your typical Irish family full of kids and drunks."

"I wasn't thinking that at all."

"Actually, I'm the only one who followed my father into the bottle. For the moment, that is. There's still hope for a couple of my brothers."

"Did your marriage failing have anything to do with that?"

Okay, enough of this buddy-buddy crap. I scraped my plate clean with the last chip and drew a sip of the tea. I wiped my hands and lips on the paper napkin.

Outside, Fifi was barking. I looked around and noticed the restaurant was still empty. Since we'd arrived, the only other clientele was a couple who had dropped by for take-out.

"We should have saved something for the dog."

Dusty looked the empty plates over. "Like what?"

"I don't know, a jalapeño or something."

That got a laugh. Haylee would have liked it, too. Tomorrow would be a week, a week without Haylee. "Tomorrow's Thursday, still going to Charles Warren's house?" I asked.

"That's the plan. Hopefully, no one's called him about Peters and I'll get to see his face when I break the news of her death. This last homicide makes me think we've stirred something up. I'm getting real suspicious about The Rummington Alzheimer's Clinic, I'm beginning to think you're right."

I couldn't help but smile. For all my lying and backstabbing, he was starting to see the value of my input, I wondered if honesty might be easier.

Pulling a few bills from his wallet, Dusty held them up. "My treat." He stood. The waiter appeared and they exchanged a few last words in Spanish.

Dusty slid his hand to the small of my back as if to lead me out. Omigod, that date feeling again.

The Psychic

Tired of barking, Fifi had collapsed at the base of the pole. She lay still as I untied her, undoubtedly looking for sympathy. Evening had settled in, dropping the temperature to where I was glad I had brought the blazer. Headlights from the 101 lit our way as we returned along the stores and car dealerships, now closed and silent.

Instead of taking the path behind the strip mall, we followed the sidewalk around the front. I didn't know if the detour was intentional or recreational until we approached Dusty's marina where, just before reaching the harbor, we veered off to the right. Dusty said he had someone he wanted me to meet.

As we walked along the potholed road, I noticed several houses were weather-beaten and in various stages of disrepair. To the left, set back off the road behind huge bougainvillea bushes was an apartment building that I hadn't seen when driving by. A few cars were parked under the streetlamps near the main axis, San Pedro. Farther along vagrants started appearing like weeds through cracked cement, a few at first, and then too many to count.

After we passed the apartment house on the left, the harbor came into view and I spotted Dusty's boat wedged between larger sailboats. This was the road leading to the point of land that I'd noticed from the dock. Sure enough, the larger apartment buildings soon appeared to the right, the illuminated windows adding a halo to the bay.

All along the road open fires were being used for cooking while fires in trash drums were warming the heavily clad population. Fried fish was the dinner of choice, that, and corn. Food odors mingled with the permanent algae stench wafting in from the marina, but as we got more entrenched in the homeless camps, there was a new smell, that of soiled clothing. The mix was nauseating.

I wondered about this mysterious person Dusty wanted me to meet. Another step towards his inner circle.

The *dung-dung* of the *Law and Order* trailer stirred the soup of Spanish and Latin music coming from the larger apartment buildings. But here on the street the landscape belonged to those living out of cardboard boxes and shopping carts. Dusty greeted a few by name. Others eyed Fifi and licked their chops.

Lying across a cement barrier, a grungy character in a torn overcoat and knit cap reached out a gloved hand to Fifi. She jumped away, wrapping the leash around my legs and causing me to trip.

"Wanted to pet her, is all," the man said.

"She's shy."

A younger man sailed by us on rollerblades. Shirtless, his skin was red and cracked and oozing a clear liquid that gleamed when hit by the firelight.

I untangled and picked Fifi up, not because I wanted to, but because Haylee would want me to. As we drew nearer the end of the road, another man with a long beard approached me and held out a brown paper bag.

"I'll trade you for the dog," he said.

Two hundred or so bottle caps filled the bag, different colors with bright logos. I could make a necklace. Or perhaps, a picture frame. I looked at Fifi. What could I make with her?

Hum. "A good offer, but I better not."

He wandered away, unfazed by my refusal.

"Is this necessary?" I asked, putting Fifi back down. She whined.

Dusty pointed. "There she is." He popped two fingers in his mouth and whistled. "Being Irish, you're going to love this."

Three old women, pushing overstuffed shopping carts, were headed in our direction. The carts' wheels thundered over the wooden planks and leaped onto the asphalt like a stampede of stallions.

"I bet." What did bag ladies have to do with being Irish? We're so misunderstood.

The nickel chrome glistened beneath the moonlight. *The Witches of Eastwick: The Return*, I thought as they neared, carts rattling, hair flying, determination ruling their gait.

"Star, over here," Dusty called.

The carts bore down on us, circling, and rushing past with an urgency that was spellbinding. In the whirlwind of movement, one woman hung back. Her skin was alabaster, marred only by a single sooty handprint on her cheek. White dreadlocks hung down her back with wild threads poking out in all directions. Shorter than I, she wore layer upon layer of clothing, culminating in an unbuttoned wool coat the color of fine Bordeaux. Her hands were covered in a pair of torn pink leather gloves, the fingertips cut out. A sleeping bag, an upholstered pillow, and several brown paper bags overflowing with clothing, lined the shopping cart with the stench of decay.

I stepped backwards. Fifi joined me.

"How time flies," the woman said to Dusty in a voice that sounded like a melodic whisper.

"Evening, Starlight. I want you to meet someone." Dusty took my hand and rested it in the woman's pink glove. He introduced me. "She's helping me with a case."

Up close, I saw what had startled me before. Her eyes had no irises or pupils and looked like a pair of milky quartz crystals, but she appeared to be looking directly at me.

"The alpha and omega," she said, running her fingers over my palm.

"Starlight is a seer," Dusty said.

"A what?"

"You know, a psychic. I thought she might point us in the right direction in this case. We need some help, wouldn't you say?"

The Mexican food had burned up his brain, or at the very least, short-circuited the wiring. Starlight couldn't see a thing, visually or any other way. I waved my free hand before her face to see if she would react and darn if she didn't follow the movement.

"If seeing is believing," she said. A smile curled her cracked lips.

I turned to Dusty. "Why does she talk like that?"

"It's riddles," he answered.

"It's clichés."

Starlight snorted. "A little learning is a dangerous thing."

I pulled my hand away. She gave me the creeps. Even Fifi had backed up and was pulling at the leash.

Taking charge of the cart, Dusty led Starlight to the concrete wall and lowered her down like a glass statue. He sat beside her.

"We're hunting a killer, Star. Someone who has already killed two women."

Sounded like he'd already discounted Tony's involvement. Could we do that just because Tony's killer appeared to be different from the one who killed Haylee and Emily Peters?

Without a word, Starlight took Dusty's hands and held them together for what seemed like an eternity. Tired of standing, I shuffled upwind and sat on her other side. Fifi curled at my feet and closed her eyes. When I'd just about given up on a miraculous prediction, the old woman spoke her words of wisdom.

"Two strings to one's bow." She dropped his hands and turned, facing over her shoulder. Obviously, she wasn't looking at the boats, but maybe the breeze from the bay felt refreshing on her skin.

The reflective expression on Dusty's face was priceless. He actually believed this woman had given him a piece of the puzzle. *Two strings to one's bow.* Please!

Before I had time to stand, Starlight shifted her weight and grabbed my hands. I shot Dusty a silent plea. *Get her off me.*

"Childhood is the kingdom where no one dies."

She couldn't have hit harder with her fist. Dropping Fifi's leash and forcing myself to my feet, I sucked in air. How had she known? I threw my head over the concrete wall and gave up my dinner to the bay, the spices burning on their way up. Great. Twice in one day. What was happening to me?

Dusty rushed to my side to keep me from falling. "What is it? What does it mean?"

I wiped my mouth on the sleeve of my blazer and reached in the pocket for the paper towel I'd brought to pick up Fifi's poo. The old woman sat idly on the wall. Her head drifted innocently around as if she were in her own little world, but she'd hurt me and she'd meant to—I had no doubt. "Spicy food, I think it's disagreeing with me. I better head back to the hotel. You stay, I'll be fine."

"No, no, I'm finished here. Hold on," Dusty said.

He leaned over Star and thanked her, kissing her sooty cheek. He told her he'd see her soon. I started walking, the smell of stagnant water lodged in my nostrils. It was an improvement; dead fish beat the old woman's smell flat out.

Childhood is the kingdom where no one dies. The bitch.

"Wait up," Dusty called.

He drew up beside me and picked up Fifi's leash, which

I'd let trail behind. "That's twice in one day. Maybe you should see a doctor."

It was a mystery to me, too. I rarely got sick, only when I was drunk or pregnant, neither of which fit the equation. "I'm still shaky from last night. I'm fine now, just need some sleep."

We walked a little farther in silence.

"Two strings to one bow; what do you think it means?" He'd already distorted the phrase to his liking.

"One's…one's bow. Not the same thing," I said. "You don't seriously think it's a clue."

"I do. I know it's crazy, but she's helped me on other cases. She helped us find a kidnapped girl once, hidden in a house in Mill Valley."

"She helped you solve a case with clichés?"

"I always thought they were riddles, but yeah, with clichés. Two strings—could be two murders. One bow—one killer, or the reverse. If the homicides are linked and we're sure they are, maybe it's two killers for one crime."

"Again it's *one's*, possessive not the number. And where does Tony fit in?"

"I'm not sure he does, but let's look at it. Two murderers—one that killed Amato and one that killed the women," he said.

Fifi barked at the sky. "For once, Fifi and I agree. This is nuts. You're nuts."

"I thought you Irish believed in seers and all that prophesying stuff? What about the fairies and the leprechauns?"

"When was the last time you saw a leprechaun? I rest my case." prophesying

"Apparently, you saw some fairies last night."

"I did?" *Really*? I couldn't remember, but that was crazy because fairies didn't show themselves to living beings.

"Two strings to one bow. Two, two…the twins!"

I had to admit he was getting me interested. "Okay, I'll play along. The twins being the two strings, what is the one's bow—possessive not numerical—not one crime, there were two crimes, two women, two cities, two police departments. What about the Larkins, husband and wife, Haylee being the one's bow?"

"And why Peters?" he asked.

Why indeed? We reached my rental car and after removing her leash, I opened the door, allowing Fifi to jump in.

"How's your stomach? You still look a little greenish. Sure it wasn't what Star said?" He looked at me in a way that made me think he knew things he shouldn't. He was certain Star had ruffled me. "Want to stay on the boat tonight? There's room."

I slid into the driver's seat. "Tempting, but Fifi doesn't eat tofu."

He held the door open against his hip. "You promise me you aren't going to do anything stupid."

"Like take a drink?"

"Like take anything," he said.

I realized that he thought the meaning of Star's other prophesy was about me taking my life. "Not before I see the two strings again."

The Injury

For the first time in a week, I slept like a normal person, which is to say without night tremors, nightmares, or insomnia. When my feet hit the floor I had energy—real energy not that wired craziness I'd been pumping through my veins for the last seven days. The world seemed different too, shifted somehow. And I knew, the way one does when facing a profound revelation, that I'd survived. To test my theory, I thought of Haylee—her silly laugh, her infectious enthusiasm—and as tears welled beneath my eyelids, I realized that I wasn't going to break apart. Yes, I missed her. I'd miss her for the rest of my life, but I'd learn to live with it as I had learned to live with so much other loss in my life. Indeed, if there was a thread holding me together, it was the thread of death.

I dressed in a hurry, fed and walked Fifi, and under another sunny sky, drove to the courthouse to meet Dusty. He was waiting in the parking lot and after exchanging a few tart remarks, we headed out.

From San Rafael, we passed through the quaint town of San Anselmo, blooming with antiques shops and themed boutiques. It reminded me of the weekend communities laced between Boston and New York City.

On the west side of the county, the community of Ross was home to the more affluent Marin County residents with large homes and gated estates. The surrounding ancient oaks and redwoods were so tall they blocked out most of the revitalizing light, making moss the town's mascot. Judging from the size of the estates, these people could afford sunlamps, or arc lamps, or trips to Tahiti when the undergrowth grew too claustrophobic as it was now in the residential streets.

We arrived at Warren's home and a housekeeper directed us to a side garage where Charles Warren was working on a cracked chair. By working, I mean that he was mostly staring at it, his head tilted with curiosity. Poised across a router table, the wooden leg looked severely damaged and you would think Warren could afford to replace the whole thing. He wiggled the broken piece this way and that while we looked on. Finally, Dusty spoke.

"Hope we aren't disturbing you."

Charles whipped around as if he'd been caught with his secretary between his legs. "My, you're out early."

"You know what they say, the early bird catches the worm."

Another cliché. Omigod, it's contagious. I covered my mouth to keep from being infected.

The phrase appeared to confuse Warren, who always looked slightly confused anyway. "Well, then."

"Charles darling?" The tinny voice sounded like a buzz saw on high speed. The woman attached to it was extremely thin, that emaciated look that some women over forty thought made them look younger, but actually added years. Wearing a strappy pair of Jimmy Choo's, she was an inch or two taller than Charles. The shoes didn't quite match the cotton yoga pants, but that was the point. "I'm off. Yoga, darling." She flicked blond strands, bleached past their prime, and smiled. The teeth were capped, the blue contacts tinted, giving her turquoise eyes.

Charles introduced her. Rebecca. She was slow to react, but when she did, she did it with grace. One-hundred-percent phony. Pure grace came from the heart, anything else was effort. I've never understood what men saw in this sort of woman, maybe a mate as insecure as they were.

"Mrs. Warren, just one question before you go," Dusty said. He introduced me as Haylee's friend. "It regarding Emily Peters—"

Rebecca interrupted. "Dr. Rummington called us. We're listed as her emergency contact."

"In that case, the Santa Rosa police will want to speak with you later, but I was wondering about several monthly checks signed by you made out to Ms. Peters."

"I sign her paychecks. I take care of all the household expenses." She rested her hand on her husband's arm. "Charles dear is so busy with that company of his, aren't you darling." Before he could answer she asked why Dusty wanted to know.

"We're looking into the link between her murder and the one at the Belvedere Club."

Rebecca Warren looked surprised. "Link? I didn't know the woman who was killed at the Belvedere Club, but Emily was like family. We often take Charles's mother with us when we travel and as her nurse, Emily always comes along."

"I understand from Charlotte that you don't belong to the Belvedere Club," Dusty said.

Rebecca's hand dropped from her husband and she took a step back. "I suppose you spoke with Charlotte?" Her voice sounded like a scream she was trying to control. The control fooled no one.

Charles, without a change of expression, appeared to cower away from her. When Charles had said that he and his wife steered clear of Charlotte, it must have been the understatement of the year. This woman had hate flaring from her pupils.

"We're interviewing everyone who may have come in contact with the victims."

"I see. If you don't have any other questions, I need to

run." She glanced at her husband. "Charles, you'll be here when I return." It wasn't a question, but a command.

She stomped off down the driveway, her heels hitting the pavement so hard I waited for one to snap.

"How handy are you with a hammer?" Charles asked Dusty.

"Handy enough to know you need some type of glue to fix that. A nail won't do the trick."

"Of course." Charles sounded guilty for not knowing that. He reached for the chair with both hands.

"Do you know of anyone who might have wanted to kill Emily Peters?" Dusty asked.

Charles turned, almost dropping the chair, the splintered piece slicing through the meaty part between his right thumb and forefinger. When he pulled his injury away from the wood, the chair clanged to the ground. "Ouch." He stuffed the bleeding hand into his mouth.

Dusty leaned over and picked up the chair, placing it on the work table.

"Look what I've done," Charles said, examining the wound. He looked like he might cry.

My mothering instinct kicked in. I took the hand, turned it over, and checked the depth of the incision. Deep, but not deep enough for stitches. His drama was a bit too much. "You should rinse it."

"Of course."

We followed Charles through a rear door and into the kitchen. Painted peach and green, the room's ceiling was high with a skylight cut in the center. Charles stuck his hand under a faucet and hollered like a three-year-old when the cold water splashed over the cut. Dusty tore off several paper towels from a stainless steel stand on the countertop.

Warren thanked him, and pressed the wad of paper onto the bleeding wound. "To answer your question, ouch, Dr.

Rummington told me it was a robbery gone wrong. It's still bleeding."

If we were ever going to get past his injury, the baby had to be pacified. "Where do you keep your Band-Aids?" I asked.

"Oh, good idea. I'm not sure. Maybe the upstairs closet."

I motioned to the hallway. "Do you mind?"

"Please. And bring Mercurochrome too. Thanks."

Guess he didn't know that Mercurochrome had been outlawed by the Food and Drug Administration back in the late nineties due to an unfounded fear of mercury poisoning. I climbed the wide spiral staircase to the vast honeycomb of rooms. The linen closet was next to a bathroom the size of my hotel suite, and it was stocked with an impressive inventory of medical supplies, including the forbidden Mercurochrome which still had two years of use, according to the date stamp.

After grabbing what I needed, I took a few minutes to scour through the other rooms. Their daughter's room was a pink and purple menagerie of stripes and florals, shiny and furry toys, overstuffed and over-organized. Two shelves of Madame Alexander Dolls looked like they'd never been touched. The furniture was antique white with a surprising lack of knickknacks. Their son's room was just as neat although the army green motif was less distracting. I assumed the double closet doors hid the noticeably lacking toys and games, but I didn't want to get caught going through them. Snooping was bad enough.

As I left the son's bedroom, I collided with the housekeeper whom we'd met on arrival. She didn't look pleased. She lashed out in Spanish, at least I think it was Spanish since I didn't hang around. I held up my stash of Band-Aids and made for the stairs.

The kitchen was empty when I returned as were the living

room and dining room. I heard Dusty's low voice, but I couldn't get a bearing on where it was coming from. "Hello, yo?"

"In here," Dusty said.

That was clear enough. The echo led me down a beige corridor filled with oil paintings, and into a lightly furnished office. On a black lacquered set of file cabinets, a fax machine was spooling pages off. They fell to the floor and curled in on themselves. No one but me seemed to notice.

On the other side of the room, Dusty and Charles Warren stood beside his desk, Dusty reading from a stack of papers stapled together, and Warren holding his hand out for me to dress his wound. Unbelievable. I crossed the room and set up shop on the edge of the desktop.

I removed the bloody paper towel and dropped it into a black metal trashcan. I opened the Mercurochrome. From the corner of my eye, I saw Dusty bend over and remove the bloody paper towel from the trash and stuff it in his coat pocket.

"Ouch."

"Hold still, you're worse than a kid," I snapped.

"I have a low threshold for pain."

Privileged people. I wanted to smack him and say, *toughen up*. Instead, I asked something I'd been wondering. "Are you going to hire someone to replace Ms. Peters?" I slathered mercurochrome across his palm and up his thumb.

Warren hissed and looked over his pinkish injury as if he was studying a new product. "We'll have to, won't we? I'm not ready to think about that yet, Emily was family. She was always around here."

Again, he looked like he was going to cry. "I'm sorry for your loss," I said unable to come up with anything more original. That phrase was starting to sound trite. "I didn't realize you were that close."

"You heard my wife, Emily Peters has been taking care of mother for years. Mother's very upset. They're having trouble getting her to eat. I'm planning to drive up this afternoon. By the way, when can we reopen the Belvedere?"

And just like that, Warren was back in business mode. He was easier to take that way.

Dusty looked up from the pages he was perusing. "We?" he asked. "I understood you had nothing to do with the club."

Good going Dusty. I hadn't even picked up on that little "we" pronoun. Those are the kind of things that hit me long after an interview, leaving me to beat my brains out with recriminations.

"Charlotte has been calling me incessantly. She wants to get a cleanup crew in there as soon as possible. It's so upsetting and now, with poor Emily murdered."

Charles stiffened as I rolled the second Band-Aid across the injury. He turned the hand back and forth to get a good look while listening to Dusty.

"A detective from Santa Rosa is visiting the Belvedere Club today to see if we overlooked something. Afterwards, I'll speak with the evidence lab, but it's just a matter of days. Have you found a new chef?"

Charles lost interest in his hand. "Santa Rosa? Do you think the two murders are linked?"

"Two women killed in the same manner, both connected, however remotely, to your family."

"My family? That's not possible. Who would want to harm sweet Emily?" His voice trailed off, leaving the question in the air, but he must have sensed as much because he quickly added, "Dr. Rummington said it was a robbery."

"There's new evidence," Dusty said, putting down the papers and taking out his notepad. "Where were you Tuesday night?"

"You aren't serious. Me? I'm a suspect? Why would I kill

Emily? I depended on her." He dropped into the executive chair behind the desk, the only chair in the room. Besides the desk and filing cabinets, the room lacked any semblance of personality. Totally utilitarian and quite different from Charles' office at Securitec with its bold paintings and sensual colors.

"By elimination of your whereabouts, we won't have to suspect you," Dusty said.

"Oh, right, everyone's a suspect, right? Let's see, Tuesday night. Well, I would have been at the office. What time?"

"Between eight and ten."

"I'd have to check my calendar, but I usually leave the office around eight. If traffic is good that puts me here around half-past. The guard at the front desk would have the exact time I left."

"I'll check with him," Dusty said. "And your wife, can she verify you were home afterwards?"

He drew out his agreement.

"You seem hesitant."

"Well, there was one night she was out with her girlfriends, someone's birthday or something. I don't remember what night that was, but I always kiss the children before they go to bed."

"What about the housekeeper?" I asked, remembering the hulking woman upstairs.

"She would have left by that hour, but if it was the night my wife was out there was a baby-sitter."

"And you have a number for this baby-sitter?" Dusty asked, writing something on his notepad.

"My wife does."

"I'll verify everything. Thank you for being so helpful and for these, too." Dusty slid aside some papers and picked up a brown envelope, waving it like a trophy. He started for the doorway. "I'd like to speak with your sister again, but when I called this morning no one was home. Do you know a good time to reach her?"

"Charlotte's out of town. She doesn't know about Emily yet. I thought I'd wait till she returned before giving her the bad news. Tomorrow, she gets back tomorrow. You should try her in the afternoon. By then, I'll have had time to break the news to her."

Warren walked us to the entrance. I saw the housekeeper watching from the upstairs banister. She didn't look happy.

* * *

"Depending on traffic, it takes over an hour to get to Santa Rosa from San Francisco. His alibi will be easy to check." Dusty said as we drove back to the courthouse. "A man that busy has to make calls, or have some type of electronic trace like cell phones, pagers."

"Busy? He looked busy to you while he stared at the chair as if willing it to fix itself."

"Not all men are good with their hands, don't be such a stereotype. What about the wife?"

"Ooooo, that spooky anorexic thing," I said.

Dusty cast me a glance that was unreadable.

"What? Why the look? Don't tell me you didn't notice?"

"I doubt you weigh an ounce more," he said.

"I'm shorter, besides I lost a lot during my alcoholic phase and I haven't put...oh wait, could she be an alcoholic?"

He turned off the police radio. "Does it matter?"

"You just like her because she does yoga."

"Think Charles could be our man?"

"The big baby? He's a man used to being taken care of. Cutting someone's throat is way too physical. The blood alone would do him in and speaking of blood, I saw you swipe the paper towel."

"Free DNA. Never know when it might come in handy."

"But legally, can you use it?"

Dusty fell silent and I figured he wasn't thinking about the paper towel, but about everything he'd seen in the last hour. The case needed some serious brainstorming.

"You want to hang out tonight? Review the case?" I asked.

"Can't, I have plans."

"Oh right, you have a personal life."

He glanced across the seat. "You'll be okay?"

A surge of anger swallowed my words. He'd helped me out *once*. I had a terrible, horrible moment and now he thought I needed a babysitter night and day. It was a bit much.

He misunderstood my silence. "I guess I can always cancel. It's not that big a deal."

"I just remembered, Terrance wants me to write up the case as it is so far. He wants to run a portion Sunday with a side about Haylee." I'm not sure why I chose to lie instead of confronting him about his condescending attitude. Maybe I was afraid he couldn't handle my anger.

That meant we'd never truly be friends.

The Diagram

Terrance hadn't called since Wednesday. A two day absence could only mean one thing—I needed to send out resumes. This morning I'd taken Fifi for so long a walk that she'd refused to walk back and I had had to carry her. Now, I was staring at the walls. The moss green was some designer's answer to lithium. Actually, years ago I'd read that hospital psych wards were painted this exact lifeless color. Maybe I should repaint them.

I was obsessing again, but with good reason. Haylee's wake had been moved to Sunday, her funeral, Monday. I had two days left to find out who would want to kill a rising young reporter from D.C.. Half a dozen deputies from two counties were working the case and still not so much as a suspect. I needed to think, I needed to brainstorm, but first I needed to calm down so I could focus.

I logged onto the Internet and searched for a paint store in the vicinity. Remembering my last hotel room, I chose a banana-yellow from the online swatches and scribbled down the store's address.

Who paints a hotel room? Well, I'd already asked myself that. Painting was the activity—repetitive strokes—to focus my thoughts much like writing used to be when I was a journalist. The activity would help me forget that Haylee was going into the ground on Monday.

Grabbing my handbag and Marin County map, I had started for the door when the phone rang. It was Dusty. He'd finally reached Charlotte Warren and wanted to know if I wanted to go with him for a visit later. I glanced at the sad walls. The painting would have to wait.

"What are you doing right now?" he asked.

"Looking at paint swatches."

"Why did I ask? Listen, I've diagramed all the evidence we've collected from the Post-It®s right up to Peters' autopsy info. I've been going over it and going over it and I can't find a link to your Pulitzer angle unless Peters was sleeping with Warren. That would cover your 'sex' and 'money' theory, wouldn't it? I've pulled phone records on his cell, home, and office and if they were an item it's pretty well hidden. There are calls from his mother's phone each week, which might have been made by Peters, but nothing to her apartment since the first of the year."

"I doubt a man cheating on his wife would have excited Haylee enough to call for a photographer, unless, of course, it was the President. Plus, it's a pretty lame reason to kill someone."

"Happens all the time," he said. "A man like Warren is important enough to like things on his terms. Here's an idea; maybe Warren was having an affair with Rummington, that's different, and oh so San Fran." His voice rose in a bad effeminate imitation.

"That would be a little on the weird side."

"Weird, I'll give you weird. This morning I had some pea brain climb a power line because, according to his girlfriend, he was afraid the squirrel on the wire would electrocute itself."

"Dumb. Is he okay?"

"Dead. Electrocuted. And the squirrel too. The screwy thing is, if he hadn't climbed up there the squirrel probably would have been all right."

This beat painting any day.

He continued. "Why don't you drive over and take a look at this diagram, maybe something will jump out at you, something that might have jumped out at Macklin. No pun intended."

Police humor. "Not funny."

"You coming?"

"I'll stop at Peet's first. Want anything?"

Part of me was flattered he thought I might add to the investigation, but another part, the more rational part, figured he was trying to keep me occupied so I wouldn't slit my wrists. Haylee used to be like that, too. Why did everyone think I was suicidal? Fact was, I'd never, ever thought about taking my life, let alone planned it, and the Lord knew I had plenty of reasons, especially these last few years. Granted, my behavior was sometimes self-destructive, but hey, everyone has bad days.

* * *

Normally, diagramming crime scenes wasn't how I worked, but if it was, I would have diagrammed this one differently. Dusty's method followed the collection of evidence plus the one or two things that were linked, like Amato's and Peters' murder, death causing the fork from the main line of Haylee's murder. He was rereading Peters' case file while I and two other deputies stared at the corkboard of thumbtacks, red and green strings, envelopes, photos and other assorted info. It made no sense to me, but I wanted to help so I read along with the others while fighting the urge to rearrange the information. But, as previously mentioned, straight teeth replaced patience in my genetic makeup. I jumped up and went to the board.

"Anyone mind if I rearrange a few things?"

"Mann, you took the photo?" Dusty asked. Mann nodded. "Good. Go to it, that's why you're here."

In case of earthquake or other natural disaster, sergeant Mann had photographed the diagram's order. I started reworking the material based on the model from Haylee's Post-It®s. They were tacked to another board at the far end of the conference room. That was the method she'd used to come across whatever had gotten her killed, and I was sure it would work for me unless her death had nothing to do with her research, a theory that kept rearing up for lack of hard evidence.

I unpinned a printout of credit card charges. "What is this?"

Dusty glanced over and then back to the file he'd been reading. He didn't want to answer me. I started reading through the charges. A few I recognized.

"Why do you have a copy of Haylee's credit card?" I read down to the last entry. It was for an Italian restaurant near her hotel. The date was hours before she had died. The amount, whoa, expensive unless she wasn't dining alone. "Who did she dine with?"

"Larkin," Dusty said.

"Gary? I thought he was at a fundraiser."

"The wife." Dusty put down the file. "I didn't tell you because you are so intent on this Pulitzer theory. You might as well know, one thing we were working on was that the wife asked for the meeting, put something in Macklin's food, and later murdered her."

"Why at the Belvedere Club?"

"Doesn't matter. The tox screen was clean—there weren't any drugs in Macklin's system. Maybe the wife used the club as a way to get Macklin someplace private. Maybe she promised Macklin some dirt and Macklin fell for it."

"Where does Peters fit in?" I asked.

"That's the piece we can't figure."

I continued my layout, removing everything that didn't relate to Haylee's research and tacking it on the right side of the board. Tying in Peters' homicide was tricky because it had nothing to do with Haylee's research, unless Haylee had met Peters when she interviewed the matriarch. I laid it all out that way—all connecting to old Mrs. Warren.

Finished, I returned to my chair and read the grouping again. Read and reread. Nothing. The point at which Emily Peters' death intruded bothered me. I went to the board and removed it. I sat back down. Dusty had put down the file folder and was looking the board over.

I replayed my last phone conversation with Haylee. Her voice was already fading from my memory. "Stupid dog," I said.

Dusty picked up a juice bottle and waited for me to reiterate.

"Fifi, she knows, I'm sure she does."

He swallowed a sip of juice. "Maybe we can beat it out of her."

"Haylee told that dog everything. Isn't there some fancy lab at Stanford that can extract a dog's brainwaves?"

"In Fifi's case, they'd have very little to work with."

I pointed to the corkboard. "It's here. I know it is, but we don't see it because we haven't investigated something deep enough. What can it be? The illegals, the charities, the clinic? What?"

"Two strings to one's bow."

"Oh, please."

"Hey, it's worked before." Dusty repeated the phrase several times while pacing before the board and pointing steps out with the juice bottle.

I had to admit it was more than coincidental that we were working with twins, but I'd never admit that out loud. I'd looked up the cliché earlier on the Internet and learned it was from "to have two strings to one's bow" mostly referring to a woman having two suitors. Had Larkin really been sleeping with Haylee? I would have known. If Rummington or Warren had made a pass, she would have called straight away. That was how it was with us.

Could Dusty be right? Was all this about infidelity? Rummington and Charlotte? Larkin and Haylee? Rummington, Warren, and …Peters. But who cares? No matter how I put it together, it didn't fit with the Pulitzer code.

"Can we put it back the way it was?" Sergeant Mann asked.

"No," I said. "This was Haylee's research. This is the correct order."

"Photograph it," Dusty said, tapping the board with his finger.

Mann picked up a Canon from the conference table. "More stuff links the other way."

"No, it doesn't!"

Mann shot three pictures and printed them out. As soon as they were laid in front of me, he started to rearrange the information on the board.

I stared at the images lying side-by-side. Something was tickling my brain cells. I stared harder, but to little avail. "Hmm."

"What?" Dusty peered over my shoulder.

I pointed to the images. "This is the right configuration. There's something there and it's centered on the Warrens, including mama."

"Come on, the woman's barely conscious."

"It's there Dusty, everything connects."

A tall slender woman entered the room and handed Dusty a fax. "Hold up Mann." He raised a hand while reading. "We have a new configuration. Remove references to Amato's murder and the Asian mob."

I reached for the fax, but he wouldn't give it up. "What's that?"

"San Rafael has one of the two men who did Amato in custody," he said. "Turns out his last name matches one of

Amato's female tenants. It was a sister. Looks like Amato's murder was a revenge killing. Go on, put the board back your way, but leave the stuff on the Larkins at the end."

The Coincidence

It was nearly seven p.m. when we pulled up to Charlotte's home. Again I was surprised when she answered the door herself. Maybe this was the new chic. West Coast *laissez-faire*.

"Lieutenant and Ms. Kaleigh." She greeted us as sweetly as the first time, but as I shook her gloved hand, I thought she looked uneasy.

Dressed in a vintage Christian Dior suit, she led us into the same sitting room as before, but the fluffy curtains were drawn, creating a cozier atmosphere. Across the room in the chimney a fire burned, adding a burnt edge to the antique odor.

Dusty started right in on the questions we'd worked out during the ride over. "Was your mother following any experimental treatment at The Rummington Alzheimer's Clinic?"

"Experimental?" Charlotte paused. "I wasn't aware of any experimental treatments going on at the clinic. My brother's on the board of directors and—"

"I was just wondering. Sometimes drug companies test new drug therapies right before FDA approval comes through. I was wondering if The Rummington Alzheimer's Clinic was one of the private clinics licensed to test any such drugs."

"Oh, dear, I have no idea. You should ask my brother. I can tell you that no one uses my mother as a guinea pig without asking me and no one has asked. I understand mother wasn't her best when you went by." Emotion filled her face, her eyes watered and her chin vibrated. "Of course...she had just lost Emily. She has her good days and bad days."

"I'm sorry about Ms. Peters. Were you close?" Dusty said.

"She was like a daughter." Charlotte pulled a clean tissue from her pocket and dabbed her eyes. "I'm sorry, I haven't offered you anything. The help leaves at five and I'm on my own. I believe I can manage a cup of tea if you would like."

"Don't bother, we're fine," Dusty said without consulting me. "Can you tell me anything about Ms. Peters' private life? Did she have a boyfriend, someone she saw regularly?"

"She had friends she saw regularly. I don't know any names, but she spoke of different people she spent time with. She was starting to be interested in men again. She'd mentioned that she'd like to start dating again." She dabbed at her eyes. "She'd come to us out of a terrible divorce. She complained that she didn't know where to meet men. There weren't many prospects where she worked. Are you investigating her death also?"

"We think the two homicides are linked. Learning about Ms. Peters might give us an idea of who might have killed Ms. Macklin. Is there anyone Ms. Peters had a problem with?"

"Oh, dear, no. Emily was so kind, a jewel, really. I don't think I ever heard her use a cross word."

I wondered if her ex-husband would agree.

Charlotte stifled back a yawn using her left hand to cover her mouth. "I'm sorry, I'm a little tired from my trip."

"One or two more questions and we'll be on our way," Dusty said. "Where did you go, by the way?"

"Santa Barbara. To visit friends."

"Fly?"

Charlotte paused. "Drove. Am I a suspect?"

"Not at all, just call me curious. Can your friends verify your whereabouts Tuesday night?"

Charlotte frowned. "Is that necessary?" Without waiting

for a reply, she said, "Yes, of course. It's a little embarrassing, you understand."

Dusty continued. "Did Ms. Peters get on with Dr. Rummington?"

"As far as I know. She was privately employed by the family, their only contact would be over mother's treatment. If Emily disagreed with any treatment, I'm sure she would have spoken with us."

Unless she was killed first, I thought. What if Haylee had stumbled on to an immoral or questionable treatment or an euthanasia plan? She was murdered to shut her up. Peters might have been murdered because she was witness to said treatment or...because she was going to go to the family. If it was euthanasia, who's to say it wasn't the family's decision? I had to ask. "Had Ms. Peters ever mentioned anything to you about the doctor's treatments, anything she might have disagreed on?"

"Her death had nothing to do with the clinic, I can assure you. If anything about mother's treatment bothered her, she would have come straight to us. She was family."

Dusty took over the questioning. "If not at the clinic, can you think of anyone who would want to harm her? Her ex for example."

"He's remarried. I don't think they've had contact in the last year." Her voice sounded tense. "I can't understand why you think this had anything to do with what happened to Ms. Macklin."

Dusty stood. "Thank you for your time. I'll be in touch."

"Ah." I looked at Dusty for permission. "Just one more question, something that's been bothering me. It's probably not relevant, but why are you designated as Acting President? Your mother handed over her membership so doesn't that make you President of the Belvedere Club?"

Charlotte stood also. "That was my idea. You see, Mother

did so much for the club, she should be president until she dies. Out of respect. The ladies agreed with me. President, Acting President, Grande Dame, they're just titles, after all."

There was no handshaking as we left, but when Charlotte reached for the door, I thought I saw the outline of a bandage through her beige gloves. The door closed before we were off the steps, which left me no time to catch a second glance.

"Did you notice a spec of blood on her glove?" I asked as we crossed the street to the car. "She had a bandage in the same spot as Charles."

"They're identical twins."

"Tell me you're joking. Identical twins are identical, not boy and girl."

Dusty started around the car. "I think we need to speak with the Larkins next."

But I'd snagged a thought and couldn't let it go. "Maybe they aren't twins at all. Omigod. What if…no…." Even I couldn't believe what I was thinking.

Dusty stopped. "What if, what?"

He would never believe me. "What if they're the same person?"

"Tell me *you're* joking. They barely look alike."

"Holy…" My mind was racing. "Annette Vaughan, one of the Belvedere ladies, said something. She said Charlotte was different, had choices none of the other women had. Why would that be? And it would answer why Francine Starling doesn't think Charlotte belongs in the Belvedere Club."

I opened the car door, but found my thoughts taking off in a whole new direction. "Have you ever heard of Kevyn Aucoin? He's a makeup artist who makes people up to look like celebrities. For a charity event, he once made up Haylee to look Hillary Clinton. With enough pancake foundation you are working with a clean slate. You can make anyone look like anyone."

Dusty wasn't buying it. He put the key in the ignition.

I sat. "Don't start the engine. I want to think this through. If Charles and Charlotte are the same person, who benefits? The trust says the Belvedere Club must pass to female heir."

"It would have passed to Charles' daughter. It stays in the family. The man hardly has to parade around in a dress to keep it."

"Unless he likes to parade around in a dress," I said.

"The man is a CEO of a Fortune One-Hundred."

"I've heard it said that J. Edgar Hoover was a cross-dresser."

"Wasn't he a Republican?"

I leaned forward and looked back at the house. "I'm not going to fight with you."

Dusty's glance followed mine as the lamp over the front door went dark. The only remaining illumination was an indirect source through the upstairs left window. Several feet ahead of us, a streetlamp burst on, bringing me back from my runaway imagination.

"You think she can see us sitting here?" I asked.

"Why? You want to go back inside?"

"I want to see if she leaves. If *he* goes home."

Dusty twitched in his seat. "I've had my suspicions, but now I'm sure. You're not right. Were you dropped on your head at birth?"

"I love it when you talk dirty." I removed my cell phone from my handbag. "Give me Charles Warren's home number."

A sour grunt puffed from Dusty's nose, but he opened his notepad and found the number. As he read it off, I punched it in. The phone rang twice before Mrs. Warren answered. I introduced myself and asked to speak to her husband. After listening to her response, I hung up, and bit back a smile.

"He's not home yet. Surprise, surprise. Do you know

why? He's up there," I pointed. "Taking off his makeup, all two inches of it."

"He said he stays at the office until eight. Here, call this number." He read off Securitec's phone number.

"Reception's closed. There's only a recorded message. Do you have a direct line?"

"No." Dusty rubbed his bald scalp and checked his watch. "I've nothing planned. How long you want to wait?"

I was excited now. "CEO of a security firm abundant with government contacts, Fortune One-Hundred, leading a double life, running a posh woman's club, yes, this might explain 'Pulitzer.' We're on to something. Also, think about it. Charles' name on the Post-It®—there wasn't a separate Post-It® for Charlotte. Her name was scribbled at the bottom of Charles's."

"You honestly think he killed Macklin to shut her up?"

I had to admit, the man didn't strike me as a killer, but his alter ego? Possibly. "I think you need a search warrant. I bet we'll find a bloody, forest-green Chanel suit in that house."

"What are you talking about?" he asked.

"You found forest-green material under Haylee's nail and Charlotte only wears designer."

"Right, and what proof am I going to use to obtain such a search warrant? I think this woman is actually Charles Warren of Securitec, your Honor. Why sir, because he has a cut on his hand." He crossed his arms and grunted.

"We need to access the birth records. Aren't they registered at the courthouse?"

"Friday night. Records is closed until Monday morning. That is, if they were born in Marin. We aren't even sure of that."

"He. If he was born in Marin County." I leaned back and closed my eyes, wondering if there was another way to find out about the so-called twins.

* * *

Roughly two hours passed before the upstairs light went out. Dusty's complaining had run its course and we had sunk back into our seats to wait it out.

"I need a cigarette," I said.

"Call Warren's home number again. I bet he's there."

I knew he wasn't, but I whipped out my cell phone. Mrs. Warren answered and apologized for not having told Warren to phone me back. When I asked to speak with him, she said he'd fallen asleep, reading to their son. She was lying. I said that it was urgent and asked if she wouldn't mind waking him.

A few minutes later, a groggy Charles Warren came on the line.

"Mr. Warren." I looked to Dusty for inspiration. His smirk didn't help. "I'm sorry to bother you at home, but could you tell me again where you were on Tuesday evening between seven and nine?"

There was a long yawn. "I believe I was at work. You'll need to check with the security guard for the exact hour I left. He'll have it in the ledger."

I disconnected, and closed the phone. "Ok, he's home. Maybe the light's on a timer."

"We've been right here. No one has left the house. Good try, Sherlock. Plus, I've already verified his alibi with the security guard. He signed out at eight-seventeen. He wouldn't have had time to drive all the way to Santa Rosa and kill Peters."

"The guard works for him. He would put whatever time in that ledger that he was told to put."

"Maybe so, but I checked the ledger for two weeks running and it was consistent with the time Warren usually left the office."

"Two strings to one's bow. Two sides to one man." I

remembered another one, although Chinese. I'd seen the symbol carved into a plaque on Dusty's boat. "Yin, Yang. Feminine, Masculine."

"How did he get home so fast? The light went off and he was already in Ross—teleportation, maybe. Securitec isn't that advanced."

"You're the lieutenant, I don't have all the answers, but it fits with Haylee's research. Maybe Warren didn't do the killings himself. With his millions, he can afford to hire someone."

"I'll verify with the guard what time Warren left this evening."

"I need a cigarette." Without waiting, I hopped out of the car and walked under the streetlamp to light one up. Dusty joined me. "I have another idea." I pulled my pick case out of my handbag. "Why don't we go in and take a look around?"

Dusty turned his back to me. "I didn't hear that."

"Take a walk. I'll tell you everything I find."

"And if you find Charlotte Warren, whose ass will burn?"

"Plead innocence."

He whipped around and grabbed the pick case out of my hand. "Breaking and entering is a crime. There's no way I'll be a party to what you're planning. I'll hang onto these too, in case you get any more stupid ideas. Get in the car."

"That house is empty. I don't know how he left, but he did." I trudged up the incline after him. "Charlotte wears enough pancake makeup to hide a hyena. Why? Have you noticed any scarring, any deformity?"

Dusty threw open his car door and shoved my picks in a side pocket. "We're not breaking the law." He got in. "We'll follow channels."

Sliding in, I felt deflated. "There's one big problem with your way. You won't be able to talk to the guard before Monday."

"Is that too late?"

"For me it is."

Haylee's funeral was Monday. I had a reservation on a red-eye flight Saturday night. "Two women are dead. What if a third is out there about to be slain to hide this secret? You're taking the weekend off?"

He started the car and did a U-turn in front of Charlotte's house. I had to find another way to get information on the twins. Did Annette Vaughan or any of the other Belvedere ladies know the truth? Even so, if someone validated what I believed about Charles, it wasn't proof he killed Haylee. Not enough for a search warrant. "Do you have a printer at the office?" I looked over Dusty's pinstripe suit. It hung on him like a wet towel on a rack. "Do you have a change of clothes at the office?"

"I have some jeans in my trunk. Why?"

"Are they clean?"

"Of course, they're clean. I'm not a nine-to-fiver. I always carry a change of clothes. What crazy idea do you have spinning in that thing you call a brain?"

The Clue

At nine-thirty, when we reached the Sheriff's Department, it felt ominous. The building looked like a brightly lit umbrella, protecting us from the darkness looming beyond the arched windows. Only two cubicles were occupied, plus the uniformed officer at the front dealing with an upset Mexican woman. Dusty mentioned that the other deputies were probably on rounds. He led me to a computer terminal where I logged onto the Belvedere's website. Enlarging Charlotte Warren's picture, I sent it to the printer while Dusty went to change clothes. He returned from the locker room, wearing a Hawaiian button down shirt, a gray windbreaker, the jeans, and the famous Jesus sandals.

"Yummy," I said focused on his feet.

He glanced down. "At least these are comfortable."

"Don't your feet get cold?"

"If they do I put on socks." He pulled a pair of white athletic socks out of the windbreaker's pocket.

I wanted to cry. He looked like he belonged on Fort Lauderdale's beach with a Margarita in each hand, but at least he didn't look like a lieutenant.

"Where are we going? Or do I want to know?"

"I've printed two pictures of Charlotte Warren from the Belvedere's website. And I've printed a list of cross-dressing clubs in the area. As you can see, there's only one in Marin County, in Tiburon. The rest, I'm afraid, are in San Francisco."

Dusty laughed, not a belly laugh, but a sarcastic sort of chuckle. "You aren't serious. I've had enough of this cockamamie idea of yours. It's late, I'm going home."

"Whoa." This took me aback. I didn't know how to respond. Maybe he wasn't as dedicated as I'd thought.

"Warren's at home," he said. "You spoke to him." He dropped into a rolling chair at another computer station, propelling the chair back against the wall and propping his feet on the edge of the desk. "What do you hope to find in any of those clubs?"

"Someone who might recognize Charlotte. If Charles likes to dress in women's clothing, I assure you he doesn't just stand around gawking at himself in the mirror. He goes out. He wants others to admire him. Maybe it's a dead-end, but don't we have to check it out like any other lead."

"First we need to prove Charles is Charlotte," he said.

"Well, if Charlotte frequents cross-dressing clubs, there's a pretty good chance, don't you think?"

He grunted. "And if not, we've wasted our evening. I've other things to do with my time."

A heaviness permeated the room like dense San Francisco fog. Neither of us dared speak. His behavior was so unexpected I didn't know how to take it.

Dusty's cell phone rang.

I half-listened to his side of the conversation while deciding that I would visit the cross-dressing clubs on my own.

"That was Mann," he said, tapping the cell phone. "With a real lead. He's at S.I.S. and they've identified a substance found at the Belvedere Club. It was talc, a fine ground, like the powder found on surgical gloves."

"Peters."

"You think Peters killed your friend? What motive?"

"Peters had access to surgical gloves from the clinic. Maybe she was protecting Warren, or in some misguided way, the old woman."

"Who then killed Peters? It doesn't fit the crimes, but I

should call Detective Vetter and see if they found any talc or surgical gloves at Peters' crime scene. You know, anyone can buy them at a pharmacy. It's not really relevant. Anyone who watches TV knows to wear gloves and we already know the crimes were premeditated. Yesterday I showed the coroner both sets of photographs and he, too, believes the same person did both victims. The incisions were too similar in execution."

"Back to your medical personnel theory?" I said.

"The coroner thinks so. He agrees with me, said the killer was trying to puncture a lung, probably to stop the struggle and that the carotid, death, was the actual goal."

"Disarm and death."

"With as little trouble as possible, but both women struggled. The attack wasn't as easy as the killer had planned. If we find a suspect, there may even be some physical damage that would give him away. What? You're looking thoughtful, did I say something?"

"Thinking about Warren again. Did you see what a baby he was when he cut himself? It's hard to imagine him in a bloody struggle."

Dusty was still holding his cell phone like he wanted to call someone. "I think you're right. Warren's not our guy. Let's call it a night."

"Not on your life," I snapped. "I'm checking out these clubs with or without you. Maybe Charlotte isn't such a wimp."

"According to you—they are the same person." He dropped his feet to the floor and went to work on the cell phone's keypad. "Hold up. Let me pass this on to Detective Vetter. I'll drive you. I'm not going in, but I'll ride along in case you need back up."

"Back up—they're cross-dressing clubs. I can handle it myself. Go home, get some sleep."

"Excuse me. As far as I know, this is still my investigation and you don't wear a badge."

"With that half-ass attitude of yours, you'll just reject anything I find out."

"Good. It's settled. I'll drive."

While he called Vetter, I walked down the hall to the conference room trying to figure a way to leave him behind. The diagramed crime information was back to Mann's liking, incorrect as it was. I went straight to Haylee's Post-It®s, scanning them, and applying what I now suspected to each yellow square. When I reached the last Post-It®, the one I'd always thought was out of place, the one with Charles Warren's name and date of birth, my theory made perfect sense.

A few minutes later, Dusty saddled up beside me. "See anything new?"

"There." I tapped the last square. "I told you, Haylee was methodical. It can't be any clearer. Even to one with your limited detecting skills."

"Why didn't you see it earlier, Einstein?"

"I did, but I *interpreted* it incorrectly. Haylee *had* finished her research. Warren's name is in last spot. Of the Post-It®s you found in Haylee's trash, was there one with Charlotte's name on it?"

Dusty walked to the other corkboard and read the crinkled squares. "No, not here."

"She had finished her research. Maybe even left it as a clue for me since she had changed rooms at the hotel. She knew it was an explosive story. She was meeting someone at the Belvedere Club to confirm her suspicions and she wanted photos as witness."

"Back up. She changed rooms? Are you sure?" he asked.

I barely had time to react before Dusty tore into me.

"Why don't I have that information?" He looked back at

the corkboard. "I thought you were through holding back."

"What's the big deal?"

"The big deal? Her phone records! That's the big deal. We've gone over her cell and there were only two calls from her room—to you and your editor. How had she set up that meeting?"

"Oh, you're right," I said.

"You think? Do you know the original room number? I can get it from—"

"Two-ten."

He removed his cell phone and punched in a two-digit code number. Someone's Friday night was about to be ruined.

Why had Haylee changed rooms? Someone knew her room number. If someone had contacted her with information… This was potentially a break. But what had always bothered me was why did she go to the Belvedere Club alone if she felt that she was in danger? Haylee wasn't reckless. Either she hadn't thought she was in danger (had she'd changed rooms for another reason?) or she'd expected me to arrive before the meeting.

Dusty closed his cell and put it back in his pocket. "Mann's going to be a busy guy tonight. Good thing he's separated, his wife would have hated this." He crossed the room. "Who do you think Haylee was meeting?"

"Peters maybe. But whoever it was tricked her. If my plane hadn't been delayed…"

"You can hardly think you would have made a difference. If someone wanted her out of the way, they would have done it with or without you around. The only thing you could have done was get yourself killed."

"Let me ask you—other than feeling threatened, why else would she change rooms?"

"The simple answer? The telly didn't work. Or maybe too

many people knew where she was. How did she work? When Haylee gave out contact numbers did she usually include a hotel?"

"She may have, sure. Remember, in the beginning, Haylee thought this story was a fluff piece on women's clubs," I said, rubbing my forehead. "We don't know at what point that changed."

"Maybe Amato threatened her after she snooped around his building. Maybe she was trying to ditch that Larkin guy."

"She wasn't sleeping with Gary!"

We both turned back to the board. I realized we would never know why she had changed rooms, we could only move forward.

"So who was she meeting?"

The Wild Side

Tiburon lay across the water from Belvedere. In the way that Belvedere looked like old money, Tiburon looked like new. Trying to recreate a picturesque old port, the town planners had ended up with a cheap facsimile: pristine streets, brightly lit sidewalks, and old-fashioned storefronts that looked more like a Hollywood movie set than a functioning town center. Perhaps that was the reason why, on a warm Friday evening, the sidewalks were empty despite the relatively early hour. Of course, if I had the view most of these folks had from their hillside homes, I doubt I'd come to town either.

Dusty pulled into a red zone and killed the engine. "I'll wait for you here. No need for me to go in."

"Afraid you'll get your butt pinched?"

"Hmm. I'd like someone to try."

"Ooooh, Mr. Tough guy." I winked before shutting the door.

Our first solid lead and he was being a jerk. I wondered if it was because it was my idea.

I walked along restaurant row, my heels clicking on the red-brick sidewalk. "Petticoat Junction" was cradled between a Vietnamese restaurant and another pub proclaiming home-style cooking, whatever that meant. I grabbed the door handle and was a little surprised when it opened.

Loud rock-and-roll assaulted me, and I tensed as I stepped inside. I don't know what I expected, but from the sterile outside, something a little more sedate. Strobe lights flashed pinks and blues across the room, pulsing to the voice of Mick Jagger. My eyes took a moment to adjust to the darkened interior. By the door, a man with a handlebar mustache and butterfly tattoo on his arm announced there was a ten dollar cover charge, which included one drink.

"Can I pay five and skip the drink?"

He held up ten fingers. "Ten dollars."

I handed a bill over and he stamped my hand with a curvaceous Betty Boop image. The bar was the most visible area with a halo of white light falling from the ceiling. I shoved my way through the dancers until I reached it.

To my right, a couple was trying to flag down the bartender. They were snipping at each other about their failure to draw attention to themselves. The shorter one looked like Jayne Mansfield at an age she never reached. The taller one looked like a female Freddie Krueger. I offered them my drink coupon as Eric Clapton's *Layla* burst from the speakers.

Freddie thanked me and said something about Clapton, which I didn't hear but agreed with anyway. My brothers were big Clapton fans and I could recognize the music, but other than that I was at a loss. Jayne snagged the bartender and asked me if I wanted anything.

"No and yes." I wagged the bartender away with my finger and pulled out Charlotte's photo. I waited for Jayne to give their order. I handed him the photo. "Ever see her around here?"

"You a cop?" Jayne asked.

I shook my head. "Looking for a friend."

"You a private dick?" They both laughed at Jayne's joke.

"You look like that actress, what's-her-name?" Freddie said, taking the picture from Jayne. "Is that a De la Renta?" he asked, pointing at Charlotte's image.

I leaned over the photograph. "Not sure, check the cuffs."

"I think so, check the buttons," Jayne said, fingering the photo.

"Might be, she can afford it," I said.

"She wouldn't hang in here. Look around. She'd go to one of the fancier joints in the city."

My eyes had adjusted a little better so I glanced around the interior. The crowd was less upscale and more the wash-and-wear variety. I pulled out my list of clubs. "Any of these?"

"Let's see." Freddie ran his red nail down the list. "Oh, Queen Judy's, very TG friendly. Mimi's. Oh, there. The Brick House, very she-she. A fashion show every night. If I could afford the wardrobe, I'd go there."

The bartender returned with two colorful umbrella drinks and the duo toasted themselves.

"Could I ask you another question, one maybe a little more personal?" I said.

"Here's where it gets interesting," Freddie said with a smile.

Jayne concurred. "Shoot, sweetheart."

"What type of man likes to dress in women's clothes?"

"What type of man doesn't?" Jayne asked.

"Why don't you ask your friend?" Freddie said.

"I will, when I find her."

Jayne's hand fanned out across the dancing crowd. "All types. Take your pick."

I studied the gyrating crowd of men: tall slender ones in formfitting knit dresses, heavier ones in slinky gowns, older ones in dress slacks and gold lamé sandals, and younger ones in bustiers and jeans. There was even a man with a full brown beard wearing a wrap dress and matching pumps. Some were gaudy, others well-groomed. A few were ethnic, but for the most part, the crowd was white American. I wondered if this was true for the cross-dressing community at large or only in Marin.

"Dana, over there in blue, has won the Best Legs

competition three years running." With a heavily jeweled finger, Jayne pointed to a sexy dancer in blue chiffon. "Babette can tango like nobody's business."

We watched Babette's partner trying to keep up with her and the annoyance on her face when the partner went left instead of right.

Although I was having a pretty good time, I saw little reason to stay and chat without a positive ID on Charlotte. I reread the San Francisco address for the "Brick House". Dusty was going to blow a fuse, but if it came down to it, I had my own car. I wasn't waiting until Monday for confirmation on what I now felt sure of. I thanked Jayne and Freddie and headed out.

The Brick House

Dusty appeared deep in thought as I approached the Sentra. He flinched when I opened the door and slid in.

"That was quick. Can we go home now?"

"I have another address. It's in San Francisco. You driving or am I?"

"You're determined, I'll give you that. It's past eleven. Look, I'll go talk to Charles in the morning."

"He'll deny it. We need a positive ID before you confront him."

Without a word, he burned rubber out of the parking space and took the southern ramp onto 101. Just before we reached the Golden (red) Gate Bridge he spoke.

"This is insane."

I watched him drive through the toll plaza. The pass on his windshield beep-beeped.

"I can't believe you aren't excited," I said. "This is the first break we've had."

"Break? We're driving all over creation in the middle of the night because *maybe* some guy likes to dress in women's clothing."

"Not some guy—Charles Warren."

He whipped right four lanes at a speed that had me grabbing the door handle. The tires squealed around the entrance to Nineteenth Avenue.

I made the sign of the cross and said a silent prayer to St. Michael, the archangel, also the patron saint of Police officers because if we crashed and Dusty lived, I figured I would too.

"While you were changing clothes, I did a little research

on the Internet," I said, hoping to capture his interest. "Cross-dressers don't consider themselves gay, although sometimes they turn out to be transsexuals. Many live heterosexual lifestyles."

"You said Divisadero? We'll take Geary," he said, his voice flat. Suddenly, he hit the brakes and threw us against our seat belts.

I caught my breath, wondering what I'd said wrong, when I saw the tail of an orange cat scamper behind a parked car.

"An interesting detail," he said, driving on. "It would fit Warren's double lifestyle. Bet his mother made him dress up when he was little. She needed a daughter, didn't she? But what does he get out of it now? I need a motivation."

"Satisfying whatever propels him to want to dress in women's clothes."

"No. How about it's his way of holding on to the trust until his daughter is old enough to inherit The Belvedere Club. With Mrs. Warren hospitalized, there'd be no one from the family to run it for years."

There was always a possibility he was right, but I didn't think so. From what I'd learned, Charlotte Warren was at the Belvedere Club every Thursday. Would that be the case if Charles only wanted to control the trust? I kept my mouth shut though, because Dusty was more comfortable with his explanation.

Spelled out in fuchsia neon, the "Brick House" was easy to spot. Dusty let out a long, slow hiss between his teeth then parallel parked within view of the club. The neighborhood was the antithesis of Tiburon. Night gates locked in boutiques, sealing their wares. Spray paint spelled out gang names and symbols while up at the corner, loiterers passed a brown paper bag and made remarks to pedestrians that drew too close. This was the perfect location to hide a swank cross-dressing club, *hide* being the key word.

He killed the engine.

I reached for the door handle. "This club might take a little longer. I'll be back as soon as I can."

The air was crisp and I pulled my jacket tighter at the collar. Walking up the sidewalk, I felt more comfortable than I had in Tiburon. These people, I knew. These people, I recognized. They lived in Every City, USA.

Suddenly, I sensed rather than heard someone drawing up behind me. My fist clenched instinctively and I turned. Dusty was closing in.

"Shut up," he said, halting beside me. "Buddhism stresses intuitive learning."

What did that mean? Did he want to intuitively learn why men dressed in women's clothing? Or maybe he wanted to intuitively stop being a prick. "I'm not sure I understand what you're saying here."

He started to speak, but before he got a word out a homeless man approached with an extended hand. To my surprise, Dusty dug into his jeans' pocket and pulled out several quarters, which he dropped into the open palm.

At the "Brick House's" entrance I asked again if he really wanted to enter. Dusty reached for the door, motioning me inside.

The cover was twenty dollars. Dusty still believed that I was on an expense account and this wasn't the time to educate him. I handed over a fifty and tucked the change into my wallet. "You'll get the drinks."

"I'm on duty."

"Good excuse."

The "Brick House" was more than a step up in class; it was a whole staircase. The music was Chopin, at a comfortable level. Dim lighting replaced the "Petticoat's" busy strobes, and a stained-glass lamp hung over each polished pine table. A black lacquered Baby Grand occupied center stage. Floral curtains shut out the neighborhood and the bar at the back looked more like one found in private homes, small and portable. Overall, the look was pastel and tastefully feminine.

"This place gives me the creeps," Dusty said, leaning over my shoulder.

Everyone was seated at a table. The bar didn't invite stragglers which made mixing a challenge. The room appeared to be divided into a social side and a quiet side. We took a seat on the social side. Dusty glanced around before pulling out his chair. Once seated, he arched his back and puffed out his chest.

"You can go back to the car, if you want," I said, having had enough of his bravado.

"Really?" he snapped.

I shook my head while sniffing the tempting odor of carbohydrates. I noticed several couples were eating. "Hungry?"

Dusty gestured toward the rear. "There's a buffet."

My watch read eleven-fifteen. I'd never sleep if I ate this late, besides, I wasn't hungry, but we couldn't just sit and stare. "How are we going to do this? We need to mingle, but the club is mingle-proof."

Couples were drinking and chatting at their private tables, although at one point or another, everyone in the room had checked us out. This wasn't an environment where one slipped in unnoticed.

"You're the reporter, pretend you're working on a story."

"I am working on a story."

"Funny. I thought you were working on a homicide case."

"It's the story part that paid your entrance fee, macho..." I refrained from saying *monkey boy*.

Our waiter turned out to be a man, in men's clothing. "Do you need menus or is this to go?" He gripped two menus like he wanted to hit us over the head.

"A couple of cokes," Dusty said.

"I'll bet you're big tippers too," the waiter said, turning back towards the bar.

Dusty tapped the tabletop with his fingers. "What did he say?" He looked at his watch.

"That's good. Keep looking at your watch. It makes it appear like we're waiting for someone."

"As opposed to sitting here like idiots with some stuck-up waiter making fun of us," he said.

"Tell me about your wife?"

"Are you really trying to piss me off?"

That killed conversation. Silently, we waited for our waiter to return with our drinks. When he did, Dusty couldn't wait any longer. He whipped out his copy of Charlotte's photo and handed it to the guy. "Have you seen her in here recently?"

The waiter looked at Dusty, and then at me. He dropped the photo on the table without so much as glancing at it and shook his head.

"Subtle." Afraid he might have frightened off any future contact, I spoke louder. "Be careful, people might think you're a cop."

A hand fell gently on my shoulder before a woman appeared at my side. "But he is a cop, honey" she said softly into my ear. Her voice was laden with a testosterone.

"No. Why do you say that?" Innocence wasn't my strong point.

"Takes one to know one." She/he stretched a hand out. "Gracie, S.F.P.D.. This here's Ruthie."

A shorter African-American woman/man stepped up beside Gracie, looking more feminine than broad-shouldered Gracie.

Dusty broke his silence. "You a cop too?"

"No, I work at City Hall," Ruthie said.

"Would you ladies like to join us?" I asked.

Dusty cleared his throat and shot me a menacing glare.

"Someone has to save you," Gracie said. "But would you mind moving to our table? My taffeta catches on these wood chairs."

We grabbed our cokes and followed them to a larger table with floral-cushioned rattan chairs.

Dusty sat beside Gracie. He/she was wearing a strapless pearl-colored gown and her biceps looked as cut and hard as a weightlifter's.

"You undercover?" Dusty asked her.

Gracie winked at me across the table. "You need me to be?"

"Yeah."

"Then I'm undercover."

Dusty introduced himself using his departmental credentials. He pulled out Charlotte's photo and handed it to Gracie. Gracie passed it to Ruthie. Neither recognized Charlotte or her name.

Dusty checked his watch.

"You don't need to do that any more," I said. "We've made contact."

"Do what?"

Gracie chimed in. "You two stand out in here like nuns at an orgy. Want me to pass the photo around?"

Dusty propped his elbows on the table, clenching his hands. "That'd be great, thanks."

Gracie set off with Charlotte's photo. Ruthie sipped her pink drink while across the table, Dusty tapped the tabletop with his fingers.

"Ruthie," I said, leaning on the table. "Are you gay?"

"Yes, I am." She held her glass in the air as if to toast herself, before taking another sip.

"So, you're a transsexual?" Dusty asked.

"No. Cross-dressing makes me feel softer. That's all it is for me. I consider myself gay. Predominately, I live a gay lifestyle."

"A gay cop," Dusty said, looking over the heads for Gracie.

"Gracie's not gay," Ruthie said. "At least he doesn't think so. It's one of our big debates."

Gracie slid into her chair. "Not this again. No, I'm not gay. I have a wife and three kids. Not all cross-dressers are gay. Most of the women in here aren't gay."

Ruthie spoke up. "Or they haven't realized it yet."

"That's Ruthie's philosophy; we're all closet gays. Personally, I think I was a woman in a past life."

Dusty moaned.

I had to laugh at Dusty's discomfort. "Don't Buddhists believe in past lives?"

Gracie continued teasing Dusty as she fawned. "I was born like this. For as long as I can remember, I've always loved to dress up. I had three sisters and I would get evil when they could wear cute dresses with big bows and I had to wear dull, boring pants. When no one was around, I used to steal their clothes."

"Do the other cops know about this?" Dusty asked. His tone gave away his opinion.

"I don't broadcast it. They'd probably feel the same as you."

I saw the tension building between the two, but felt powerless to stop it. Dusty's resistance was hard to understand. His hands were clutched together on the table, the pose he struck when trying to quiet his anger. What about cross-dressing bothered him so much? Or was it the gay aspect?

"How about your wife? Does she know?" I asked Gracie.

"Sure. We go on cross-dressing cruises together." She held up her left arm displaying a series of jewel encrusted bracelets. "She lent me these for the evening."

Dusty rubbed his face and scalp. "Shit."

"Hey, don't judge me. Wear a pair of women's panties under your uniform one day, I dare you. If it doesn't excite you, nothing will."

"You're more perverted than the ones you put in jail." His tone was humorous, but the words had the bite he intended.

Gracie stood and slammed Charlotte's photo on the table. "I don't have to take that!" She stomped off towards the restrooms with everyone in the room watching us.

"Good going, Buddha." I went after Gracie, leaving Dusty to fend for himself with Ruthie.

When I reached the restrooms I found a Little Boys room and a Little Girls room. I took a shot and entered the Little Girls room. Gracie was at the mirror, applying lipstick.

"Sorry about my friend, this is all new territory for him."

"Oh, I'm used to men like that, I work in San Francisco, after all. For some reason the heteros are terrified of the gay men in this city. I see it on the job everyday. And when someone like me comes along, riding the dividing line. Well..." She/he waved at her image in the mirror. "Don't worry about the theatrics. They were more for fun than anything else." She/he clicked her handbag shut. "One of my girls knows your lady. Says she drinks Strawberry Daiquiris. Says she hasn't been around for a month or so. You want to talk with her?"

"You're the cop. Was she sure it was Charlotte?"

"Positive I.D.. Said she sometimes buys a round for everyone. Oh, she calls herself Amanda, though, not Charlotte."

Amanda, Charles's mother's name. Interesting. "You have some lipstick on your teeth. Here let me show you a trick for that. After applying the lipstick, stick your index finger in your mouth like this. Wrap your lips around it and pull. It takes off the excess."

"Luscious."

I thought of Haylee and all the feminine tricks she'd taught me. "My best friend showed me that. You know, I would like to speak with this woman if she wouldn't mind."

I followed Gracie to a table of four well-dressed men/women, all in designer duds. From what I'd seen these ladies were the *crème de la crème*. Gracie introduced me to the one called Wilma. His/her eyebrows were tweezed pencil thin to accent a beautiful pair of almond eyes.

"Gracie tells me you recognize this woman." I laid my copy of Charlotte's photo on the table.

"I can even tell you what she was wearing the last time I saw her. A blue and white Nicole Miller dress."

"Ever seen her in forest-green?" I asked.

Wilma made a face.

"Never mind. When was the last time you saw her?"

"It was in here, back about a month or so." She turned to her companion and asked, "When was it that Lulu was playing?" Wilma turned back to me. "Our friend Lulu plays the piano here sometimes. I know, it was Valentine's Day." She turned back to her companion. "It was Valentine's Day."

"I believe you're right," the companion said.

"And you're sure this is the woman you saw? And she called herself Amanda?"

"Positive. Is she a bank robber?"

I forced a laugh. "Not at all. But she may be a cross-dresser." I gave her a comical smile. "Thanks for your help."

Gracie and I headed back to our table. "Thanks for helping, Gracie. We may have just found a killer."

Dusty was finishing his Coke while sharing a friendly conversation about the Oakland A's with Ruthie.

"Thanks," I said to Ruthie, letting him know I appreciated the subject change to something Dusty was more comfortable with. "I need to get the old guy home. He needs his beauty sleep."

"Know how that goes." Ruthie puffed her curls.

Ruthie shook Dusty's hand, manly style, and he and Gracie butted fist. "Hey, what's the definition of a cross-dresser?" Gracie asked.

Dusty grunted.

"A man who likes to eat, drink, and be Mary."

Dusty chuckled and butted Gracie's fist a second time.

"Knock 'em dead, Lieutenant," Gracie said.

As we returned to the car, I shared Wilma's information. Dusty didn't seem surprised.

"Something Ruthie said made me realize it was possible for Warren to lead a secret life, even to kill to keep it a secret."

"Ruthie? Why Ruthie? Gracie fits the pattern, heterosexual, husband, father."

"Gracie's a cop. He's probably undercover."

I snickered. "If that'll help you sleep at night."

The Intruder

When I reached the hotel room a little after midnight, Fifi was clawing at the door. As much as I didn't want to, I was going to have to walk her one last time. What I had originally seen as a flaw in evolution I now saw as genius in a divine plan. Were we walking our pets or were they walking us?

Tonight, I didn't need walking. I needed to fire up the Internet and learn more about cross-dressing before we went to confront Charles Warren in the morning. Dusty figured Charles's wife, Rebecca, didn't know about her husband's fetish and he hoped to pressure Charles by interviewing him at home. After what Gracie had said about his wife taking cruises with him, I thought there was a good chance Rebecca knew all about her husband's double life.

I allowed Fifi two squats and a jaunt around the parking lot before we headed back to the room. If it was up to her, she would wiz on every tire out there. Luckily, it wasn't up to her. She moaned and curled next to me on the sofa while I strolled the information highway. By two a.m., my eyes blurred under the strain and I switched off the computer and slid it under the sofa. Fifi didn't budge.

I pulled the bed down from the wall and within minutes of hitting the pillow, was following a snaking train into dreamland. Consciousness blended into unconsciousness so smoothly that when Fifi's bark jarred me awake some time later, I sat up dazed and confused and slightly trembling.

Then, I heard the click of the door shutting. My head shot towards the sound and fear took my breath. I reached for the lamp.

"Who's there?"

At the base of the door Fifi yapped and danced, her aggression propelling her forward, her fear forcing her backwards. Otherwise, the room looked empty.

"Dusty?"

Someone in the next room banged on the wall behind the bed. Ignoring them, I checked the door handle. It was locked. In my rush to get on the computer, I had forgotten to latch the chain. Behind me, Fifi continued barking. I ran to the bathroom window and scanned the parking lot to see if I saw anyone sprinting to a car. No one.

"Good dog," I cooed. "Good dog." I picked her up and she gargled a growl. We walked around the room, looking to see if my intruder had left me a gift like a bomb or rattlesnake. Nothing obvious. "Good dog." I opened the refrigerator and spooned the rest of the dog food into her bowl. She deserved a reward. She might have saved my carotid artery.

With shaky hands, I dug through my handbag for my cell phone. The battery was dead. I picked up the hotel phone and punched in Dusty's private number.

"It's four a.m., you're going to die," he mumbled.

"You'll have to wait in line."

"You? Can't this wait?"

"Someone broke into my room. While I was in it." He knew as well as I did robbers waited until you were gone. That left rapist and murderers or someone that wished you harm.

His voice shifted gears, not a trace of sleep left in it. "Keep the door locked, I'll be right there."

He must have slept in his clothes because in less than ten minutes he was banging at my door.

"Show me some I.D.," I joked as he pushed his way in.

He circled the room, looking for I don't know what, but something none-the-less. "Talk to me," he said.

"I was asleep. Fifi started barking and the person fled. I

think she saved my life."

He turned towards the dog. "What's wrong with her?"

Fifi was lying on her side and moaning. Her food bowl was licked sparkling clean.

"I gave her a reward, the rest of the dog food."

Dusty held up the twenty-two ounce can. "You gave her all this?"

"She wasn't supposed to eat it all at once." I knelt beside her and tried to lift her head, but she snapped at me.

"It's a walking garbage can and you fed her twice her body weight."

"Should I walk her?" I asked.

"That'll work. She'll probably explode." He took his notepad from his coat pocket. "Did you see anything?"

"Maybe the door shutting, it happened so fast. By the time I was on my feet, the corridor was empty. I checked the parking lot, but nothing. I looked around here and called you."

"Looks like we've upset someone. We'll need to move you again."

"Can't. Terrance won't pay any more of my expenses. I'm on a red-eye flight out tonight. Haylee's wake is tomorrow."

"Fine, pack up, I'm not leaving you here."

* * *

Twenty minutes later, under a receding moon, I was trailing Dusty's Sentra north to the Lowrie Yacht Harbor. We had used a blanket as a hammock to carry Fifi to the car. She moaned the whole time and had only switched to heavy snoring in the last few minutes. Parking on the street behind Dusty, I got out and started unloading the trunk.

"I suppose you want me to leave the dog in the car," I said as Dusty picked up my knapsack and camera case.

He leaned over the trunk to peer into the rear seat. "Guess she can't do much damage like that. You think you can carry her, or you want me to come back?"

I looked at Fifi's distended belly and wondered what he'd do if she upchucked on his schooner. But I kept my thoughts to myself and wrapped the blanket edges around my hand. "I have her." Fifi moaned as the blanket lifted her weight off the seat. Each time the blanket bounced against my leg, she snarled. I gently lowered her down on the deck. "She'll be fine out here."

"After what happened, I don't want you to get it in your head that she's some kind of guard dog," he said.

"Hey, Fifi Brindacier, *string of steel*. She saved my life."

"She surprised your intruder. The next time, your attacker will be prepared with poisoned meat. Don't let your guard down."

Next time?

"From now until you board that plane tonight, you need to be extra vigilant. You shouldn't be alone. We have to assume that whoever killed Haylee Macklin and Emily Peters has you in his sight."

He led me along the cabin, dropping my bags beside the potted orange trees. The cabin was actually two cabins split by a passage way. He reached in his pocket for the keys. "I have two beds, they're separated by the companion way." He removed the lock and slid back a panel over the forward cabin, opening the doorway. He picked up my bags and climbed down a ladder. "Hope that will do."

At the bottom of the ladder we turned left into the sleeping quarters. A single-size bed lined the wall to my left, a double-size to my right. The double was unmade, the sheets balled at the bottom. Both beds were raised with a series of drawers beneath. Dusty tossed my bags on the single mattress.

"Try to get some sleep before we head over to Charles Warren's house. The toilet's through there." He pointed to a door in the narrow passageway.

"I'm good. Hope you don't snore."

He squeezed by me and back up the stairs. "All locked down," he said when he returned. "Climb on up."

He hoisted himself onto his bunk and I did the same with a little less grace. He switched off the overhead lamp and a dense darkness fell over us. I never knew claustrophobia had a smell, but it was something like fungus, moisture, and oil fumes stirred together.

I scooted under the blanket and wondered about the dry scraping noise coming from below. "What's that noise?"

"I don't hear anything."

"That scratching. Can't you hear it?"

"Oh. Barnacles."

Well that was logical. What the hell were barnacles? Did they bite? I was about to ask when I heard his breathing deepen. I glanced around, eyes wide yet filled by a darkness so dense it felt like an isolation tank. I wondered if the barnacles were getting nearer—they sounded nearer.

The Morning

By eight a.m., Fifi hadn't moved so much as a paw. She'd fallen into a gentle slumber, breathing through her mouth, her little pink tongue dangling to the side. Dusty attached her leash and looped it around a cleat in case she awoke while we were gone.

Two of Dusty's deputies had questioned the employees at the Best Western. They'd passed around photos of Charles and Charlotte. No one recognized either of them or had noticed anything odd around four a.m., except for the one guest who'd called the front desk complaining about a barking dog.

I needed a strong brew. I'd already had a cigarette on the dock while Dusty prepared his "green" breakfast of yogurt, vitamins, and some grass he'd cut from a flowerbox and thrown in—wheatgrass he called it. Wheatgrass, crabgrass, all the same to me.

The shower on the boat consisted of a faucet in the ceiling of the closet size bathroom and a drain in the floor. From my point of view, neither hygienic nor comfortable, so we'd carried a change of clothes to the Sheriff's Department and showered in the locker rooms.

Once I was clean and humming with one and a half lattes down, I was finally able to focus on the corkboard and the all the crime info pinned in the wrong order.

Dusty ended his call. He moseyed to the board. "Mann couldn't get the phone records last night, but he's gone to the phone company to pick them up. We'll have them by afternoon."

"Don't put too much stock in the phone records," I said.

"She had to arrange the meeting somehow."

"If it was a meeting. What if she and I were to lay in wait for someone or something that I could catch on camera?"

"Like what? The only person likely to show was Tony when he came for the cooler." He scratched his shiny scalp while looking the board over. "Where does Emily Peters fit in?"

"We know that Haylee investigated each charity. Since Peters was Amanda Warren's private nurse, Haylee must have spoken with her."

I tried to imagine that conversation. "Haylee would have visited Mrs. Warren same as we did. After all, she was doing a story on the Belvedere Club. She would have wanted to speak with the head of the club, or at the very least, see the woman's condition for herself. Haylee was thorough."

Had old Mrs. Warren been lucid during her visit? No way to know. "Perhaps Haylee mentioned Charlotte, or a daughter, and Emily Peters corrected her. Or, what if Peters knew about the cross-dressing? Warren said she was like family."

"Any way you turn it, I don't see Warren as a cold blooded killer," Dusty said, rubbing his baldness. "Crime of passion like Haylee, okay. She was going to expose him, but to stalk Peters and kill her. I could be wrong, but from what I've seen of the man, it's difficult to fathom."

"In his society, money buys anything. Maybe he did Haylee and hired someone to cover up his 'crime of passion.' Maybe he knew that if Peters let his secret slip once, she might let it slip again. She was a liability."

"We won't know until we speak with the man," he said. He picked up the receiver and punched in Warren's home number. He spoke with someone other than Charles.

He turned back to me. "The wife. Charles left for Santa Rosa about fifteen minutes ago." He slapped the tabletop.

"Don't tell me, we just missed him."

"I missed him. Briana, this time I have to do it by the book. He's a potential murderer. If he breaks, things could get out of hand and I don't want anything to go down that his lawyer can later use against us. You understand what I'm saying?"

"He's not going to break."

Dusty was flipping through his notepad at lightning speed. "Let's just say that I don't think he's that strong of character. When faced with what we know, he might confess."

"What do you know?" I asked. "The man has a secret. You don't even have enough for a search warrant. You need to tie him to the crime—time and place. He's not going to crack, certainly not today."

With one hand leaning on the conference table, he punched another number into the telephone. "Sorry, but you have to sit this one out." He turned his attention to the phone. "Detective Vetter, please." He covered the mouthpiece and spoke again. "I got reamed out by the San Rafael Police Chief when we brought Amato into custody. He wanted to know what a reporter was doing there before the police. I lied, told him you were already on the premises, had called in the suspicion. Santa Rosa's a different county. I can't risk breaking the rules again. And yeah, I know it's not fair after all your help."

Vetter came on and he went back to his phone conversation, relaying the whole cross-dressing angle.

The cross-dressing motive was only a suspicion until we had concrete evidence. Contrary to Dusty, I didn't see Charles Warren, a man with a staff of lawyers on call, confessing to murder. I didn't see him confessing to jaywalking. No doubt a search warrant for Charlotte's house would reveal enough to prove Warren's double life, but would it prove that he was at the Belvedere Club when

Haylee died? Until a search warrant was granted, Dusty had nil. By confronting Charles about the cross-dressing, he was giving Warren a heads-up, he'd have time to destroy any trace—designer rags included.

Dusty hung-up in a hurry. "Vetter's going over to The Rummington Alzheimer's Clinic. He'll wait for me there and if necessary, retain Warren. With any luck, I'll make an arrest today and you can catch an earlier flight home." He pulled a key ring from his pants pocket and flipped it to me. "Keys to the boat. You'll be safe there. I'll call you to let you know what's going on. Detective Vetter might make the first arrest. It would be better if Charles is tried up there. Impartial jury and all."

I shook my hands at him. "He won't confess. He has more lawyers on staff than you've got hairs on your chinny-chin-chin."

"You know, I researched Securitec, too," Dusty said. "And I've been thinking about Charles. I think the pretty boy got lucky. Seventy percent of his business is with the airlines, twenty with the government, and a mere ten with the private sector. He happened to have a security company when the country was suddenly forced to think about security."

"It's called foresight, not luck," I said. "Your problem is, you can't believe a man who dresses in women's clothes can be anything but a sissy. You better wise up."

He reached for his jacket that was lying across a chair. "I'll call you when I've spoken with the nutcase."

The Lane

Lowrie Harbor was buzzing with weekend sailors, warriors of the high seas and gentle trade winds, toting coolers and lawn chairs from their shiny SUVs. Fifi was sitting in the cockpit when I reached the schooner and a wallet-size poop was resting beside her. She barked once when she spotted me.

"Hungry?" I looked at the poop. "Is your stomach that big?" I untied her and dropped my bag on a dirty blue cushion beside the helm.

We walked to the end of the pier where Fifi squatted and let loose a flow that could have sunk the Titanic. When she finished, she lay across the planks like she did when she was tired of walking. "You've got to be kidding? You need the exercise."

She remained on her belly, big chocolate eyes watching me. She had saved my life. I reached down to pick her up. "We're going home tonight and things are about to change. Got that?" I carried her back to the boat and unlocked the cabin. Everything looked as it should be. Dusty had made the two bunks, fluffed the pillows, and cleaned up his breakfast dishes. He was going to make some lucky woman a nice wife one day.

I didn't find any paper towels, but I did find a ratty tee shirt that in my opinion needed to be thrown out. Using the shirt, I scooped up the poop and carried it down the dock to a trash barrel where Dusty wasn't likely to see it in case the shirt turned out to be his favorite.

I couldn't fathom that there was a cable to hook up my computer. There wasn't even a phone line, but I searched anyway determined to waste my time. On the other side of the galley, a bank of cushions circled a large table. From the stack of bills and police files, I figured this was Dusty's home office. I looked for something that might connect to a computer, but an extension cord was all I found. Without the Internet, I was at a loss. My bags were packed and ready for the flight. Fifi had been added to my ticket. I had nothing to read and the only book in sight was *The Yoga Sutras of Patanjali*. No thanks.

On deck, Fifi spread out beneath a ray of sunlight, her belly having shrunk slightly. I lit a cigarette, sat, and propped my feet up, listening to the weekend sailors talk the talk without ever leaving port. I thought about Haylee's notebook and the murder weapon and the forest-green fuzz found under her nails. Even the best criminals made mistakes. Was there still a chance of recovering something?

Charlotte and Charles. How did Charles get back to his home without Dusty and I seeing him leave the mansion? An underground passage? Wouldn't a secret life require a secret entrance? Too many questions remained for me to believe we'd found the killer. Some needed to be eliminated.

On the other hand, Haylee's notes drew a straight line to Charles. And if one could believe it, Starlight's prophesy—two strings to one's bow—pointed in the same direction. Two people of one personality. Could a dead woman and a blind woman be wrong?

The one thing that bugged me the most was Gary Larkin. Why had he lied about sleeping with Haylee and why had his wife, Lenora, dined with Haylee the night she died? I had my suspicions about Lenora Larkin, but Gary's lie didn't fit in anyway I turned it.

I had to answer some of these questions before getting on that plane tonight. I owed Haylee's mom something. Stubbing out the cigarette and dropping it into the lemon tree pot, I rose with the bud of a idea pulsing through my brain.

Because he thought I was on my way out of town, Dusty had returned my picks this morning. I transferred them and my notebook from my camera case to my handbag and retied Fifi to the cleat.

In the rental car, I pulled out my Marin County map and studied the oblong shape of Belvedere Island. I'd "X-ed" the location for the Belvedere Club. From there I looked for Gary Larkin's street. One main road circled the entire island, offering two possibilities on and off. Inland, a string of twisting smaller roads connected to the main road, which changed names several times before linking with Tiburon. And there it was, walking distance from the Belvedere Club.

Weekend traffic was light, and being one of the few vehicles not draped with bicycles, boats, surf boards, or wind sails, I reached Belvedere in twenty minutes. The main road led up the mountain to the Belvedere Club. I bore left, away from the club and up an incline. The Larkin's house was a red brick colonial style accented with lots of boxwoods. There wasn't a gate only two stone pillars delineating the empty driveway.

I rang the bell and crossed my fingers that Gary was home. After a long pause, he answered the door, wearing jeans and a San Francisco Giants tee shirt.

"Briana, I didn't know you were still in town."

As he showed me inside, I noticed his feet were bare.

"I'm leaving tonight. I just had one more question for you."

He stopped, the door not yet closed. "My wife doesn't want me answering any more questions without a lawyer present. Sorry."

"Why's that?"

He shrugged.

"That's okay, but since I'm here why don't you show me

around. The house looks beautiful. Do you have one of those bay views?"

"Only from the front bedroom. We're on the wrong side of the road." He closed the door and led me into the house. "The good thing about this side is we're cut off from the wind. We like sitting outside and the wind can drive you nuts in the evenings."

The corridor opened into a brightly lit great room with two walls of floor-to-ceiling windows. Matching sectional sofas faced each other around a marble coffee table. Newspapers were strewn across the table and one end of one sofa.

"Have the police found who murdered Haylee?" he asked.

"They have a suspect. Something should hit the papers in a day or so."

"Great! I hope he gets the death penalty. It is a he isn't it?"

"I can't really talk about it," I said.

"Right." He motioned around. "So this is our main room." The stuff hanging on the walls are things we've picked up on our travels. Lenora loves to travel."

The walls were covered with colorful masks from Venetian to African to the Commedia dell' Arte.

"They're beautiful."

"Yeah, Lenora has good taste. So was it someone from the club? Can you tell me that much?" He walked to the back wall and opened a sliding glass door.

"I'm not free to talk about it. But maybe now you can tell me why you lied about you and Haylee sleeping together."

His sheepish grin told me I was right.

He turned back to the open doorway. "Come see the garden. I just love the back."

I followed him outside. "Come on Gary. I know Haylee wouldn't have slept with a married man. What was the point of lying?"

"There's a Koi pond over there with a little fountain," he said, pointing.

"This is me, not the police. I know you didn't have anything to do with the murder so why taint Haylee's memory? She was a friend."

He hung his head and shoulders, but soon picked himself up and continued. "I picked out the flagstone."

"Talk to me."

"Gee Briana, it was Lenora's idea. She knew the police would trace the phone records."

That Lenora was always thinking. "An affaire would explain why you spoke so much," I said. But I figured the truth was more that Haylee had been badgering him for information. "You let something slip, didn't you?"

Again the sheepish grin.

"Am I interrupting?"

I turned to find whom I assumed was Lenora Larkin coming through the doorway. She was my height with the build and coloring of an avid tennis player. Her face bore a stoic expression, natural or Botox—I couldn't say. She extended a slender hand. "I don't believe we've met."

I introduced myself. Her grip was painfully strong.

Gary jumped in. "This is Haylee's friend, the one I mentioned. She says the police have a suspect in Haylee's murder."

Lenora's lips showed the slightest twitch of surprise. "Is that true?"

"It is. Even so, the police will still need to know why you dined with Haylee that evening."

"You what?" Gary asked. "I thought you—"

"Ssst. What have I told you?"

Gary took a step back.

I didn't like this woman or the way she was treating my

friend. "Maybe you should go call your lawyers. The police should have a subpoena by this evening," I said.

She huffed. "It's Saturday. Judges aren't available. I think you should leave."

"For your information, it's a capital case. Judges are available. And I'm here to see Gary, I believe it's his house, too."

For the first time she looked shaken. I could see her thoughts racing ahead and knew this was my moment to strike. "Look, you aren't a suspect. I know why you went to see Haylee. Confirm it and I'll pass it on to the lead investigator. You might never have to speak to the police."

Lenora shot Gary a look filled with accusation.

"I didn't say anything, I swear."

"He's telling the truth," I said. "I figured it out on my own."

Lenora propped a hand on her hip. "And just what is it you've figured out?"

The morning sun was heating us up and I realized I'd forgotten my sunscreen, again. "Can we go inside?" I stepped through the doorway without waiting for an answer. Lenora and Gary followed.

"You met Haylee to give her information about Charlotte. She'd badgered Gary, must have threatened to reveal something about his past if he didn't give her something on the Belvedere Club." Gary's frozen frown transmitted that I was on the right track.

He focused on his wife. "Is that true?" he asked her.

Lenora turned to leave. I stepped to block her passage. "What you told Haylee isn't important. It'll only help the police build their case."

"That blond was nasty, threatened to tell everyone at the club details about our relationship, details that I've kept private." Lenora's voice was filled with venom.

For an instant I wondered if she could have killed Haylee. "So you told her about…" Did I dare say it? "Charles?"

She didn't move. Gary was unreadable. He stepped up and put an arm around his wife. "Briana, I think you should leave."

Back at my car I thought about what I'd learned. No confirmation that Lenora had told Haylee about Charles's double life, but the lack of response was confirmation itself. It made sense. Haylee had manipulated Gary into giving her something on the Belvedere Club's members, but Lenora stepped in—apparently, like she always did—and took care of Haylee's threats by giving her a bigger piece of gossip: Charlotte. In exchange for this information, Lenora demanded Haylee's silence regarding Gary's low income past.

As I turned the corner and passed the Belvedere Club, I wondered if I could find Charlotte's house. I continued around until it became Beach. The road narrowed and offered cutoffs for off-road parking. I pulled over and got out to set my bearings.

Charlotte's house was on the hill, stately and overseeing everything below. I got back in the car and drove past her mansion until the road started its decline. I wanted to park out of sight, but couldn't locate another cutoff. Finally, with the town center in sight, I pulled into a public lot and hiked a quarter mile back up the hill.

Judging from the curve in the road, I was almost directly behind Charlotte's house when female laughter caught my attention. I crossed the road to listen. There, built into the mountain, was a set of stairs, a wooden rail to one side. At first I assumed it led to a private home until I noticed a hardwood plaque hanging from a post with the name Strawberry Lane carved into it.

I'd read about the lanes when Terrance had sent me

Haylee's initial research on the island. Supposedly, they had
been built to allow those living at higher altitudes to access
the beachfront and the merchants without having to round the
mountain. Nowadays, they were used mostly by joggers. I
didn't remember how many there were, but that wasn't
important because if my calculations were correct, this lane
was the only one that mattered. Charles's secret way in and
out.

I started up the steps, watching my feet rather than the
steep incline. A group of women, the source of the laughter,
passed me coming down. They weren't jogging, but they
weren't out of breath either. Winded, I stopped about
halfway up and took a minute to quell my heart rate. Coming
down looked easier. I continued. At the top, I doubled over
and waited for my circulation to restart and the tingling in my
fingertips to stop.

Cattycorner from the back of Charlotte's house, the path
split in three directions. A weathered redwood fence backed
Charlotte's property, connecting with fences of neighboring
homes. The gate's rusted lock was a problem. Towering
eucalyptus trees blocked most of the sun, but not so much
that I couldn't read the deadbolt's brand name.

Dropping my handbag, I squatted to dig through my picks,
looking for a tension wrench and something to extend it into
the keyway. I checked over my shoulder before going to
work, but because of the hill's slope, I was invisible to the
houses. I was only exposed to those who came along the
path.

The rusted tumblers took a bit of strength to align, but
after about three minutes, I pushed my way into an urban
jungle of lush, exotic plants. Tree ferns, palms, Cannas, and
bamboo. There were flowering lilies and other blossoms as
big as my head.

A nauseously sweet smell swirled around me as did a

swarm of fruit flies. A fine mist hissed from an invisible watering source, clouding the air and condensing on my skin. The mist was warm and cold at the same time.

A flagstone path wove across the moist earth, creating a backwards "S" curve towards a barely visible back porch. Somewhere along the way I lost the flies.

As I approached the back porch, the mist cleared and a ray of sunlight struck my face. I looked up, letting the light warm me. My damp clothes clung, restricting me as if they were a size too small. I considered removing my jacket, but when I stepped onto the porch a loud alarm rang, startling me. Three feet from the door, my only option was a quick retreat. Taking the flagstones back would expose me to the upper floors of the mansion, plus windows of the house on the left. I dove through a clump of bamboo, and my Ferragamo heels bore into the earth like a drill bit.

When the alarm finally went silent, my heart was pounding against my chest almost as loud. I scrunched behind a pineapple palm and waited. Upstairs, a window banged open and a woman leaned over the ledge. "Who's out there?" The voice was strained, but I recognized it.

Slowly, tilting my head so as not to disturb the branches hiding me, I caught sight of Charles Warren in full wig and partial makeup. I didn't see what he was wearing, but I'd bet it didn't come from Sears.

The man ran a security company. I should have been more careful. On the other hand, he was supposed to be in Santa Rosa. I was a bit curious as to what Dusty would find when he reached Rummington's Clinic. Out of left field a strange thought flew into my mind. Was it possible Charles had a twin brother who was masquerading as a twin sister?

No way. Why not? Too weird even for me. But it would explain why Dusty didn't see Charles as a killer. One child raised as a girl, another raised as a boy. Crazier things have happened. We had to get those birth certificates.

Something wiggled by my foot and I leaped up, leaving my shoes planted in the ground. Mud squished through my toes as I burst through the bamboo, back into the sunlight. Had the porch launched the alarm, or had the flagstones? Confused about where I should step, and what was living beneath the palms, I rapidly glanced about the tangled flora.

Above, the window remained open, but Charles was no longer in sight. Through the mist and jungle I couldn't see the gate, but I couldn't see much of anything else, including my shoes, which I had to find. I squatted near the pineapple palm, realizing that Charles, or whoever he was, might be heading down the stairs toward the back door at this very instant. I shoved aside my fear of reptiles, gritted my teeth, and reached into the leaves, tapping the ground. I landed on one shoe, and then the other. Grabbing them both, I started to rise.

A knock sounded behind me, and a click, but I didn't turn to look. Instead, I dashed to the flagstone path and let it lead me back to the gate. The stones were cold and wet. I slipped twice while holding my shoes weapon ready should a reptilian dare to cross my escape route. So intense was my search for life that I almost plowed head first into the fence. Sidestepping to the gate, I threw it open, but as freedom loomed, a voice called from behind.

I didn't turn. I didn't stop. Two other women had trusted him, not me.

The Magazine

When I was safely off the island and out from under the watchful house on the hill, I pulled into a gas station and got out to walk around. My knees had been bouncing so hard from fright it had been difficult to press the accelerator. Standing wasn't much better. I called Dusty's cell phone twice, but kept getting his voicemail. Rummington's clinic had a strict cell phone policy. Posters hung every twenty feet stated something about resuscitation equipment. No doubt the same sort of bull the airlines used regarding navigational equipment.

The way I saw it, when it was your time, it was your time, phone call or no. I tried Dusty again and got voicemail. That meant he was still at Rummington's clinic with his phone switched off.

I wondered what to do next. My feet were soaked, my pumps mud encrusted. Returning to the boat was my best option, but I needed to know if Charles had really gone to the clinic. Back to Dusty.

I asked the attendant for the key to the ladies room and went in to clean up. With only cold water working, I wiped down the leather pumps and held them under the air blower used for hand drying. The task calmed my nerves and I tried Dusty's cell again.

With a lot of determination I managed to shove my bare feet into the damp shoes. But now walking was even more painful and I felt the tickle of blisters waiting to form. I returned to the rental car and fired it up. One thing I knew for sure was that Charlotte was a man, whether that meant Charles or another brother remained to be seen. Monday, the birth certificates would clear the confusion. I mulled this over, wondering why the Sheriff's Department didn't have access to Records when it was closed. It was only a database. Another option occurred to me.

Charles was either in Santa Rosa or back at Beach Street, which meant he wasn't at home in Ross. If I caught up with his wife, she could confirm—or deny—whether or not there was a twin brother. Genius. Sometimes I surprised myself.

I pulled out of the gas station and headed towards the highway. I needed clean clothes, but Dusty's boat was in the wrong direction and I had no way of knowing how long I had before Charles would head home. I'd already spent ten minutes or so in the service station. I didn't want to waste any more time.

Traffic off Sir Francis Drake Boulevard was heavy, slowing at the Bon Air Shopping Center. I followed the green signs to Ross while wondering if Charles and Charlotte were the same person, would Charles' wife know? My Internet research had turned up an equal split of wives who knew and those who didn't. But if she didn't, did I want to be the one to inform her? If Charles had already killed to keep his secret, I might be putting her life in danger.

Better still, maybe Mrs. Warren would be out shopping, or socializing, or whatever corporate wives did on weekends, and I could let myself in and snoop around. I still had my picks, and this time I'd expect an alarm.

After parking in front of the house, I plugged my cell phone charger into the lighter and I tried Dusty's phone again. Still voicemail. I left a message telling him to meet me at the boat if Charles hadn't shown at the clinic. If he had shown, we'd know there really was another twin.

Rebecca Warren was home. She answered the door with her cell phone pressed to her ear. One eyebrow shot up when she saw me and I wondered if she remembered me from our brief meeting.

"I have company, I'll call you back, dear." She switched off the phone and directed her attention to me. "Hello." Simple, sweet, and leaving me to explain myself.

"Mrs. Warren," I held out my hand. "We met a few days ago when I came by with Lieutenant Arkansas to visit your husband."

"You're with the Sheriff's Department?"

I was tempted to say yes, and let the poop fly, but I owed Dusty more than that. "I've been working with the Sheriff's Department, but I'm actually a journalist with the *District Dispatch* out of D.C.. I was wondering if I could ask you a few questions about your sister-in-law, Charlotte Warren."

Her eyes opened a little wider, her brow wrinkled. I remembered her anger the last time Dusty had mentioned Charlotte. "Come in." She stepped aside to allow me room to pass.

She led me into a living room with Early American furniture and an oriental rug, but before offering me a seat she had a change of heart. "Why don't we go to the back," she said, returning to the corridor. "It's more comfortable."

Indeed, the backroom clashed styles with the rest of the house. Cozy, overstuffed sofas sat perpendicular to each other on a mismatched area rug banked by the same Italian tiles that filled the entranceway. The missing toys from upstairs were piled in bright colored plastic containers stacked along the wall. A doll house, the size of one of the sofas, filled one full corner of the room; it was a replica of the house we were in.

The main wall sported a custom built home theatre, while framed family photos competed for space on the other walls. I stepped up to the photos. The quality wasn't bad for snapshots. They were mostly of Charles and the kids...actually...they were all of Charles with the kids. I glanced from wall to wall. There wasn't a single photo of Rebecca in sight.

"I don't see any pictures of you," I said.

"I hate to have my picture taken."

I could believe that. Spontaneity for her required a stylist and manicurist at the very least.

She stayed in the doorway as if she were afraid of me. "Would you like something to drink?"

I put on my friendliest smile, hoping to ease her anxiety. I had questions that required her cooperation. "I'm fine, thank you. I don't want to take up much of your time. I know you're a busy mother." Right. She was a Barbie doll who probably didn't know the first thing about parenting, which reminded me… "Are the children here?" Not cool to say anything about cross-dressing with little ears listening.

She looked tense. "Do you need to speak with them as well? They've never met Charlotte."

Never met their aunt? "No. I wanted to be sure we weren't overheard."

That reply seemed to relax her. "They're at their tutoring lesson." She glanced at a diamond encrusted Rolex watch attached to her wrist. "I need to leave soon to pick them up; what would you like to ask?" Her smile was pressed so tightly to her teeth, I thought they might pop out.

"I understand from your husband that you and your sister-in-law don't get along. In fact, I think when we interviewed her she compared you to a fish monger."

The smile strained the lips like elastic bands pulled not quite past their stretching point. "She did? She said that?"

"Yes." I opened my notebook and found the quote. "Her exact words were 'you had the manners of a fish monger'." At moments like these, I've found silence to be the best fuse. My gaze traveled back to the family photos, both kids dark-haired and fair-skinned. The girl wore a spattering of freckles across the nose. One photo in particular grabbed my attention. It was of the son, wrestling with Charles in a grassy patch. Charles looked like any other doting father, nothing effeminate frozen in the moment.

I thought about the room, its coziness, and wondered about the dichotomy. Upstairs, I remembered from my last visit, was so pristine and ordered as if photographed from a catalog, yet here, so comfortable and inviting. It meant something, said something, but about whom? Rebecca? Charles?

Rebecca still hadn't replied. I checked her face, but she appeared to be thinking of something that had nothing to do with me. My eyes dropped to a stack of magazines on an end table. I reached for one. RN Magazine. The mailing label read Emily Peters, her address in Santa Rosa printed below.

"Didn't my lovely sister-in-law tell you I was a nurse before I was a fish monger?" The voice startled me, yet held all the venom I expected.

"She didn't," I said. "In fact, I had the impression…well, never mind." What did I think? Could Charles have learned his deadly strokes from a magazine? "Your husband cut his hand the other morning; your medicine cabinet was well stocked."

"That was you." The fake niceness had fallen off the earth, followed by the smile. "He should have had stitches; now he's going to have a scar."

"Sorry. I'm not a nurse." Dusty's words came to mind… *a healthcare professional.*

"Obviously. What do you want to know about that vulgar woman?" She took the magazine from my hands.

But not before the cover image switched something on in my brain: a healthcare professional, her hatred of Charlotte. What did that mean if Charlotte was her husband and what did it mean that her husband—as Charlotte—had accused her of marrying him for his money? I needed to keep her talking. "The name on the magazines—"

"My mother-in-law's nurse, Emily Peters. She gave them to me when she finished reading them. Now, I'll have to…no…wait, would you excuse me a minute? I need to make a phone call."

Now? "Of course, but how did you come to hire Ms. Peters? Who recommended her?"

Her stick legs had carried her halfway across the room before she turned to answer. "I went to nursing school with Emily's mother."

She left the room, and I realized that she'd never really commented on the sister-in-law, although her demeanor had morphed from phony sweetness to bitchy mad. If she knew about the cross-dressing, she knew the fish monger comment had actually come from Charles. If someone else was masquerading as Charlotte and she didn't get along with him, shouldn't she have expected a nasty comment and wouldn't she retaliate with one of her own? And…there was the matching hand injury on Charles and Charlotte.

Her phone conversation filtered in from the kitchen, angry words spaced with pauses. I concentrated, but only managed to pick up a word or two and nothing that made sense. My guess was that she was speaking with Charles. With that much anger came familiarity. So where was he? The mansion or Santa Rosa? I needed to call Dusty.

Digging through my handbag, I panicked when I didn't find my cell. I had left it to charge in the car. Time was slipping by and I wanted to be out of the house when Charles returned. I decided I would come right out and tell her that I knew Charles didn't have a sister. What could it hurt? First, I would ask who was dressing up as Charlotte Warren. Direct, but effective. I'd come for answers, not to spare feelings.

But what if she and Charles had done the murders

together? It was possible. Charles was too much of a sissy to kill, but she had the anger. And the medical knowledge. Gary's wife had sold Charlotte/Charles story in exchange for Haylee's silence about Gary. What if Haylee had called Charles for an interview? They had planned to meet at the Belvedere Club. Haylee wanted photos to compare with the club's photos of Charlotte, but Charles and Rebecca showed up instead. Yes, it was possible.

I needed to leave.

I picked up my handbag just as Rebecca reentered the room. She snapped the cell phone shut like castanets and slipped it in her pants' pocket. In her right hand, she gripped a black handled kitchen knife, roughly the size of the one used to kill Haylee.

Oh, boy.

Before my flight reaction kicked in, she was across the room and around the sofa. I dropped the handbag and grasped a nursing magazine, holding it before me like a shield. She lashed out.

The blade came within inches of my arm.

Again, she drove the knife forward and I reacted with the flat of the magazine. The blade ripped through the pages like a scalpel through soft skin.

Dropping the magazine, I straddled the coffee table and lunged for the door, but the point of the knife cut into my calf. I snapped an arm back across her bleached strands, but she managed to side-step me, blocking my exit. Breathing heavily, she poised in a semi-squat between me and the doorway, the knife raised.

Facing each other, we both tried to catch our breath. My lungs, arteries, and veins felt exposed like a medical study chart. All I could do was wish for my gun, the one Haylee had taken away months ago. My eyes darted about, keeping Rebecca in sight while simultaneously looking for some type of weapon. I thought about grabbing a sofa cushion and charging her, but before I worked it out in my mind she lunged forward. I jumped to the side. She lurched right, swinging the blade.

The room was windowless with only one exit. I would have to go through her. I grabbed the overstuffed cushion and ran straight for her. She hadn't expected it, but she wasn't fazed. She lashed out, knocking me to the side. My injured leg swung into the dollhouse and I cried out. Something behind me crashed to the ground and shattered.

"Bitch."

I charged again. "Fish Monger."

The blade ripped into the fabric with a tearing sound. I was forced to let go if I wanted to get around her. When I did, she leaped onto a chair, yanking the knife from the cushion and striking outward. I kicked the chair over, but she leaped off before it hit the ground. For an Image Queen, she was surprisingly agile, not to mention quick. I got as far as the doorway when the blade nicked my right shoulder. I shot left only to block myself again in the kitchen, Rebecca on my heels.

The kitchen was colder or else, I was going into shock. My leg ached, my shoulder, barely, but blood was soaking my blouse at an alarming rate. Still, I had a ways to go before I gave up the fight.

There was a rear door, but not enough distance between me and Rebecca to reach it. I grabbed the edge of a center island and used it to whip myself around. My gaze registered every item on the countertop. Hoping to slow her down, I grabbed everything within reach and threw it at her. A potted rubber plant. A bottle of olive oil. I managed to get the island between us and once again, we faced off.

"Two women are dead."

She rushed left. "What's a third?"

I lunged to my left. "The police know about Charles. It's only a matter of time."

"Time enough."

So much for logic. "Killing me won't hide anything." I glanced over her shoulder looking for a knife rack, but she used the moment to rush me. I shifted left again, circling the island, but losing my bearings for a moment. A little farther to my left and I could dash up the corridor and back to the entranceway. She must have read my thoughts because she rushed me again and as I lunged left, I went for it. However slim, it was my only chance.

My shoes slid across the tile. Ahead, the entrance door loomed, twelve maybe fifteen feet, but Rebecca's hand locked onto a chunk of my hair and drew me backwards. She shoved me against the wall with a thump. Damn, she was strong. I had to rethink this yoga stuff.

The blade pressed my throat and I realized that I was about to receive the same slash that had killed Haylee and Emily. I thrust my knee up, shoving her backwards, but not enough. She jabbed the blade downward, slicing through muscle and tissue as it entered my chest.

An electric wave shot down my spine, momentarily paralyzing me. I grabbed for the black handle, held in my flesh, and we both struggled. She was trying to pull it out, while I was trying to hold it in place. I sensed she'd aimed too high and missed my lung, but with her knowledge of the body, she might well have opened an artery or vein. I couldn't take that chance. She wasn't getting away with another murder.

She leaned forward, her mouth open to bite into my hands, but she froze. Her eyes strained open. A choking noise escaped her lips. Her grip slipped as she was ripped away from me. Charles, wigless but in full makeup, shoved her against the opposite wall. I slid down to my knees, breathing deeply. I had to quit smoking.

His voice boomed. "Not again."

In contrast, her words hit notes so high I expected a pack of dogs to come running. "Look at you, you freak. This is your fault. We'll lose everything. You couldn't stop, you promised."

"No more killing. It's not worth it. Nothing's worth it."

Rebecca stopped struggling against him. She was crying, her face covered by her hands. "We'll lose everything." Her voice was resigned and I sensed more than saw Charles release her. I tensed as he turned towards me and bent.

"It's okay," he said. "She's upset, she didn't mean to hurt you."

"Huh."

I'm not sure what happened next, Rebecca moved so fast. She jumped Charles and he leaped up, throwing her against the wall. A painting crashed to the floor, the frame breaking into pieces.

Rebecca clung to Charles's back. Her arms wrapped his neck, squeezing as he choked off his words. He tore at her arms. His face reddened. His mascara eyes bulged as his breath faded. He needed help, but as soon as I pushed myself up, lightning pain exploded through my left side, and my legs buckled.

The front door burst open, the tiles echoing footsteps. Burly silhouettes rushed us, making me think a flight of angels. At that point, I was pretty sure I was dying.

Gasping in air, Charles's face hit the tile beside me. We locked eyes for half a second before Rebecca's thin leg kicked out, missing its target.

Dusty's voice filled my ear. "Don't move, Slugger. I'm calling for an ambulance. Hang on."

Rebecca screamed obscenities, her voice piercing as she struggled against two uniformed police officers.

I was still clutching the knife handle, the blade asleep in my flesh. "I may have found the murder weapon," I said before a coughing fit overtook me. Each contraction sent pain shooting down my arm.

The Hospital

Dusty rode with me in the ambulance for the three and a half minutes it took to reach the emergency room. He stayed close while a barrage of medical personnel poked and prodded my chest and took x-rays. No one seemed to notice my calf was sliced open.

An hour or so later, I had a diagnosis. The blade hadn't reached my lung, but the struggle with the knife had badly wrecked my pectoralis major. The doctor, a Filipino woman with flawless skin and a gentle touch, explained the minor surgery where they would remove the knife and sew up the muscle. She told me I wouldn't be playing tennis for awhile. I didn't bother to ask if tennis was anything like stickball—I hadn't played stickball in years.

* * *

I awoke in a large room filled with several occupied beds. Grunts and moans kept the two nurses running from patient to patient. So far no one had noticed me. At my side, Dusty sat in a plastic chair, scribbling onto a legal pad.

A drip was plugged in at my elbow and it pulled when I tried to move. "Ouch, ouch."

Dusty stood. "You're awake."

"How long was I out?"

He checked his watch. "Not long. The surgery was quick. How do you feel?"

"Like I need better drugs. Is everything finished?"

He nodded. "Even your leg—six stitches. Eight in your shoulder and who knows how many there." He pointed to the large white bandage covering my chest.

"Here, take a look at this." He bent over and came up

holding a plastic bag with a burnt piece of something that looked vaguely familiar. "Recognize it?"

"Fifi?"

He laughed. "Fifi's back at the boat, waiting to be fed."

"Ouch." I drew the bag closer, eyeing the burnt edging and the dense color with a billowing of beige. "Where have I seen this before?"

He refused to offer any clues.

I closed my eyes and reconstructed the beige form in my mind. It was a drape of cloth, or more exact, a painted illusion of draped cloth. "The angel. Haylee's notebook. You found it! Ouch."

"Stay still. It's a piece anyway. Can you testify in court that this was the cover of Haylee's notebook?"

He pulled the bag away. "How did you figure it out? There's not much there."

Again he disappeared below my view, returning with a thick book opened to an angel sitting on a rock. "*Stevenson Memorial*, by Abbott Thayer." He held the plastic bag next to the painting and it was easy to see the notebook cover was a reproduction.

"Speaking of angels, what time is it? I have a plane to catch. Ouch." I tried to sit up, but the needle in my arm pinched. "Is this thing still necessary?" I started to remove the tape on the needle.

"Stop." Dusty dropped the book and bag into his chair and slapped my hand away from the tape. "It's antibiotics. Leave it alone."

"I prefer morphine. Seriously, I'm good. I don't need it anymore."

A nurse heard us arguing and rushed over to the bed. "You're disturbing the other patients. Can I do something?"

"Yes, I have a plane to catch." I ripped the medical tape free, revealing an area starting to blue. "Ouch. Can you get this thing out of me?"

Frowning, the nurse turned to look at Dusty, who had backed away from the bed and was turning pale.

He raised his hands in surrender and the nurse looked back at me. "Please, leave that alone. You're not a doctor."

She taped the needle with fresh tape. "I'll be right back," she said.

When she returned, the pretty Filipino doctor who had taken me into surgery was with her. The doctor didn't touch me, but asked how I was doing. I explained that I had a plane to catch at midnight and if she could just give me some pain meds, I should get moving.

She checked the bandage on my chest. "Not today."

"This isn't a choice kind of thing. It's a 'do or die' thing. I can lie here an hour or maybe two, but I need to be at SFO by eleven p.m. so shouldn't I get up and start moving around?"

"There's a high chance of infection. Cabin pressure, re-circulated air—you can't travel today, maybe tomorrow."

I was already feeling ragged out just from arguing. "Dusty, talk to her. I can't miss Haylee's wake. I can't, I can't, I can't."

"I understand you aren't to have pain medication, but I can knock you out if I have to." With that, the doctor took something from the nurse before marching away like a drill sergeant.

"Dusty. I'm not a prisoner. They can't keep me here. Tell them…I don't know what. Tell them I don't have insurance. That should get me released."

"The hospital called your office. They know you do. Calm down and don't try to rip anything else out. Let me talk to the doctor, maybe I can find a solution." He patted the top of my head like I was Fifi. "Where's that wake again?"

"Boston. I have to get to Logan."

"I'll be back. Promise you'll rest until then."

"If I'm on that flight, I'll be okay, otherwise, bedpans are going to fly." I closed my eyes, sinking into the pillow. I would wait—for now—but I was *going* to Haylee's wake one way or another.

The angel painting had surprised me, humbled me a bit, too. Dusty's investigation had gone deeper than what he'd shared with me. He had hidden that book of paintings while he'd been searching for Haylee's notebook. I wondered what else he'd hidden from me.

And here I'd thought I'd been manipulating him into running my investigation. It'd never once occurred to me that he was working his own angles at the same time, but he was because he was a professional. Thank God. Otherwise, I might have been Rebecca Warren's third victim.

My opinion of Dusty had softened since our initial meeting, but never more than it had today. Except for my inflated ego, we weren't all that different. For all his chanting, silly sandals, and Buddha idols, he, like me, was simply another lonely soul, trying to make a difference and without compromise. Haylee would have liked him.

It might be that I was going to miss the big guy when I returned to…? Where? The question had been bouncing around beneath my other thoughts for some time, but with everything else solved, I needed to focus on finding an answer. Where would I go after Haylee's funeral? Washington—a town and job that no longer interested me? Or would I play it safe and holdup in Boston where I had a backup network of Haylee's family and my few siblings that might still be speaking to me?

It was too much to think about. My eyelids grew heavy, my heart heavier.

* * *

When Dusty returned, I was dressed in hospital scrubs and sitting on the edge of the bed. The nurse was attaching some sort of sling around my neck. Dusty wasn't alone. Charles Warren and a Marin County deputy were with him. Charles's head was wrapped in white gauze. He rushed ahead of the others until he reached my bedside.

"Oh dear, look at you. Does it hurt?"

Mascara chunks clung to his lashes, but the rest of the makeup had been washed away. I now knew it wasn't his fault, but as I looked into his questioning eyes, I wondered how to make him understand that the loss of Haylee cut deeper than any blade ever could. It was the kind of pain that would never heal.

"What happened to your head?" I asked instead.

He fingered the bandage. "Four stitches and a slight concussion. Hurts like crazy."

Dusty stepped up behind Charles. "He wanted to see you before heading back to the department. He's got a statement to make although we've got a full confession."

Charles took my hand. "I can't believe Rebecca did this." He choked. "There's so much I don't understand." He choked again and his eyes watered. "I'm so, so sorry. I don't know what to do to make this right."

Dusty nodded to the deputy who led Charles away. As I watched him go, I thought about his double lifestyle. His feminine side hated his wife; his masculine side depended on her. Was that enough to turn someone into a killer?

Dusty sat. "So how does this fit your Pulitzer angle?"

I'd been thinking about that. "It doesn't. That's why Haylee ended up dead. Charles—the double life, both in the public eye, the wealthy Belvedere Club, the government contracts—Charles was the Pulitzer, sex and money. Probably Haylee had called me to photograph him as both himself and Charlotte, but she hadn't factored in Rebecca. It's the wildcard you have to look out for."

Dusty looked pensive. After a few moments, he nodded.

"I spoke with your doctor, your travel plans have been arranged."

"Great. Before the flight, do I get something for the pain? I assume it's only going to get worse."

"Sorry. I told her about your alcohol problem. She's prescribing Tylenol."

What! "Thanks for nothing. My problem, as you said, is with the drink, not drugs. I want the good stuff. Now. Before I get on some bumpy runway."

"If you went to a twelve step program, you'd know one is as good as another. Come on, you need to sign some papers and we need to get you to the airport. Your bags and that white ball of fluff are in my car."

"With the windows down or up?"

He grinned as he helped me into the wheelchair. "You better hurry."

At the front desk I signed both the insurance forms and the release forms with my doctor looking on. She was not happy. I thanked her and shook her hand, but she had a few more instructions.

"If you start to feel feverish, or if this area becomes tender to the touch, you get to an emergency room immediately. Otherwise, the stitches in your leg and shoulder need to be removed in about seven days. These here," she pointed to the bandaged area. "The exterior ones also need to be removed in about ten days, the interior ones will dissolve, but as it starts healing you may want to consult a plastic surgeon for cosmetic reasons. We did a good job and there weren't any complications. Scarring should be minimal."

Dusty pushed my wheelchair to the loading zone where his car was parked. Fifi slept curled up on a towel in the backseat. Both front windows were cracked open.

"You big softy. Where's my rental car?"

"One of my deputies returned it to the local lot. Terrance

took care of the charges. He said he expected you to call in the story before the end of the day. I recharged your cellular."

It was early. The sun, although low, was hours from setting. When I was strapped in, I checked the dashboard clock—five-thirty. "Did you get me on an earlier flight?"

"Something like that."

When we reached 101, Dusty took the north ramp. San Francisco International was south. It was time for me to stop asking questions and trust him, however difficult that might be. Sore and tired, I was dreading the cross-country flight pent up in an economy seat.

I closed my eyes and thought about the Belvedere Club and its ladies. Since there weren't any female family members old enough to take Charlotte/Charles's place, was this the end of the century old club or would they go on pretending with Charlotte as acting president until Charles's daughter was old enough to take the reign?

A short time later, Dusty nudged me awake. "You can sleep on the plane."

I glanced out the window. A row of small private planes lined the tarmac. "Where are we?"

"Warren wanted to help. Securitec owns three business jets. Also, the Cessnas don't fly as high as a commercial plane, the pressurization isn't as harsh. You'll be more comfortable and your doctor signed off on it. If you need assistance, the pilot can land at any local airport. You'll be fine."

"What did you do? Threaten him with conspiracy?"

"Nothing. I swear." He parked next to an aluminum hangar with Securitec's logo painted over the door. "After Peters' death Charles suspected his wife, although he didn't want to believe it. Rebecca thought Peters had given up the secret to Haylee."

"She didn't. I'm pretty sure it was Lenora Larkin."

"I figured as much. Charles still can't believe Rebecca killed to hide his secret. He didn't think she cared for him that much. Personally, I think she cares about his money and her social circles, but what do I know? He's cooperating. He's at the courthouse while the Ross, Belvedere, Santa Rosa police forces fight us over jurisdiction."

"He's a pretty decent guy, cross-dresser and all."

Dusty caressed his bare scalp. "Guess he is. Come on, they're waiting for you." He tugged Fifi out by her leash and linked the leash around his wrist while removing my camera bag, knapsack, and overcoat. "Here. Boston's expecting a cold front," he said, handing me the overcoat.

The Cessna's pilot and copilot waited in front of the hangar. The copilot relieved Dusty of my bags.

We stood facing each other. My stomach tensed and tears filled my eyes. I couldn't think of a thing to say. I hadn't expected leaving would be this hard.

Looking as uncomfortable as I felt, Dusty passed me Fifi's leash. "So, this is good-bye." He touched his heart and pressed his palms together in prayer position and bowed his head. "Namaste."

Oh, please.

With my good hand, I touched his forehead with my first two fingers. "May you be in heaven a half hour before the Devil knows you're dead," I said and winked.

His laughter trailed me into the plane.

The End
©2012

About the Author

Nicola Trwst has a gypsy heart. She currently resides in California, but has lived in Virginia, Georgia, France, and Canada. She loves languages and speaks several, including Pig Latin. Due to an overactive imagination, her stories thread many genres such as mystery, thriller, paranormal, and contemporary. Her short stories have appeared in several anthologies.

Discover more of Nicola's work at **www.nicolatrwst.com**

Also by Nicola Trwst
Bayou Nights (2013)

Briana Kaleigh Mysteries
The Belvedere Club (2012)
Bolinas Bongo (2013)

Continue reading for the opening of the next Briana Kaleigh Mystery, *Bolinas Bongo*

Bolinas Bongo

The Move

This cross-country move to California was supposed to be my epic second act in the tragedy called *My Life*, but this apartment looked more like a toxic wasteland than a promising new future.

The walls were pumpkin orange, the baseboards a dark yellow-brown. The forest green rug, once plush, was trampled as flat as a football field. A sofa covered in psychedelic fabric that had seen better days was pushed against the far wall. A blue and white print of a rowboat hung askew above it. White vertical blinds, at least they had been white about fifty years ago, covered a picture window that faced west.

"It's sorta dark," I said.

Dusty—my latest buddy and Marin County Sheriff's Detective—bounded to the window like a six-foot-two, two-hundred-pound five-year-old. "Look, Briana." He yanked the blinds open. "You'll get plenty of light in the afternoons. Come through here and look at the bedrooms."

I followed him to a corridor that split left and right. He went into the room at the right, I headed left. The empty bedroom was pale blue and smelled like cat piss.

Dusty pulled up behind me, excitement radiating off him in waves. "This is the guestroom. You can use it as an office or rent it out for some extra cash. Come see your bedroom."

The larger bedroom was also pale blue, a respite from the multicolored main room. A mattress/box spring set was shoved into one corner, the mattress stained and sunken in the middle.

Longfellow once wrote: *Into each life a little rain must fall*. My poor, pitiful life had been stuck under a deluge for far too long.

I'd quit my D.C. job at the *District Dispatch*, or maybe I was fired; through all the shouting it was unclear who had the upper hand, me or my ex-editor, Terrance. I sold all my earthly belongings: a Honda Civic, a Salvation Army sofa, a large-screen T.V., and an air mattress. And I flew across the U.S. to start over with the only friend I had left in the world.

Friend might be a strong definition for my relationship with Dusty. We'd met a little more than two months before when I'd wormed my way into his murder investigation of my best friend, Haylee's, death. That trip to California had just about been the end of me, emotionally and physically. I still had awful nightmares, and, from time to time, I heard Haylee's voice speaking to me. One of the reasons for this cross-country move was to remove the familiar from my sight and, hopefully from my hearing.

"Not bad for two thousand a month," Dusty said, rubbing his hands together. "It's a steal in Marin, believe me. The landlord is also throwing in the heating."

"How cold does it get?"

"It's June. In another month it'll be pretty cold."

Did that make sense?

I walked back into the main room and might have burst into tears except that I'd been raised with six brothers and learned pretty early on that tears from a female reduced most men to blithering idiots. Dusty didn't deserve that. Not yet.

I headed to the narrow kitchen. The linoleum floor was a green and grayish white checkerboard. "I thought you said it was furnished."

Dusty shoved past me to open a cabinet. The shelves were full of chipped plates and fogged glasses. "See! All your cooking needs."

What I saw was the fat cockroach, slinking across the stovetop. Two thousand a month, furnished, and heated had sounded too good to be true. Now I knew it was, but I was unemployed and my savings were meager. At the moment, I couldn't afford better, especially here. Marin County has the fifth largest income per capita in the country. It makes the middleclass neighborhood where I grew up in Boston look like a ghetto.

Dusty continued, unfazed by my lack of interest. "There's the sofa and the bed…you said you had sheets, and we'll get you a table and chairs from my friend Bob, who recycles."

He was so energized, so thrilled at his precious find that I couldn't break his heart by telling him that I'd have to be dead and four days buried before I'd lie on that bed.

Before leaving my East Coast life, I'd gone to Boston to say goodbye to the four of my six brothers who were still speaking to me and to visit my adopted family, the Macklins. The Macklins were Haylee's parents, and no matter how hard the visit was, I owed it to Haylee to look out for them.

"Yer know, they call dat place Sodom and Gomorrah," Mrs. Macklin had said in her heavy Irish brogue. "Waaat will yer do in de land of sin? They'll eat a grand lassy loike ye for breakfast."

Lassie? I was thirty-two.

"Detective Arkansas has some contacts in San Francisco. He'll help me get a few investigative stories written that, hopefully, I can sell freelance. Otherwise, I always have my camera."

Mrs. Macklin crossed herself with the sign of the Trinity. "De one with idols on 'is desk?"

"Buddha."

"That's waaat oi said, idols."

She, like I, had distrusted Detective Arkansas—Dusty—from the first meeting. The size of a bear, Dusty was a

Buddhist monk in the making. He shaved his head before a full moon, chanted, did yoga, and kept Buddha statues all over his office. But the big fellow had a way of growing on a person. Okay, that's not really true. He'd grown on me, but most of his fellow officers considered him too weird for words.

Afraid of catching botulism or picking up some flesh-eating bacteria in the apartment, I walked back to my three large suitcases and flipped one on its side. I sat on top. "I'll need to install a cable connection for my computer."

Dusty dropped down on the sofa and the cushions on each side rose up around him. "All you need is wi-fi. The guy next door has a router and it's not password protected."

Did a sheriff's detective just tell me to steal bandwidth from my neighbor?

Dusty's cell phone chirped. He pulled it from his shirt pocket and looked at the faceplate. "I have to take it. I'm on call."

I stood and peered out the front window. My rent-a-wreck was the only car in the asphalt parking lot. A green Ford Focus with a cellulite-pocked body and a black hood. Rent-a-wreck was too kind. Rent-a-disaster. Rent-a-joke. But at ten dollars a day, the price was right.

"Fish and Game," Dusty said, shoving his cell back in his pocket. "There's been a shark attack out in Bolinas. I have to go."

"I'll go with you."

"You just arrived. Don't you want to settle in?"

I watched the sun-splashed dust particles rise from the sofa as Dusty stood. "I'm more interested in earning some cash," I said. "Maybe this is the story that'll introduce me to the local market."

He shrugged. "Suit yourself. It won't be pretty." He paused, running his eyes down my tan Tahari pants.

"Besides, shark attacks are way too common. Sort of like jumpers. Neither story will draw much interest."

I figured his reluctance had something to do with my mini freak-out over Haylee's death. That was personal, this wasn't. I grabbed my camera bag. "Maybe I can sell it as a human interest piece."

He scrunched up his nose. "Do you, at least, have sandals or tennis shoes?" He asked, looking at my ankle boots. "Sand will be involved."

I dumped out one suitcase on the rug and grabbed my running shoes as Dusty hovered in the doorway. "I'll change in the car."

I locked the apartment and followed Dusty down the stairs and up the road to where his black Sentra was parked in Lowrie's parking lot. Since his divorce, he'd been living on a boat in Lowrie's Yacht Harbor. Another way to live within your means in Marin County.

After I switched shoes and we settled in for the drive across sunny San Rafael, I thought about the Golden Gate Bridge, which was farther south and majestically linked Marin County to San Francisco. Dusty's earlier remark about jumpers referred to the dozens of people each year who turn up from all over the country to fling themselves off the famous landmark. The jumpers hit the water at about seventy-five mph. Like hitting a cement sidewalk. Most die on impact. Not fun.

I'd lost my mother to childbirth, my baby girl to SIDS, and my best friend to a psychopath. No one knew better than I the weight of sorrow, but I'd never once considered suicide as a solution. For a while, I'd lost myself inside a bottle of Irish whiskey, which some considered a sideways attempt to end it all. I don't think I'm that complicated. If I'd wanted to off myself, I'd have offed myself.

No matter how bad things got (and some say I was comatose after I lost my daughter), there was always a pinprick of something, call it hope—but that seems too strong an emotion; call it faith—but I'm not sure what I believe anymore; or call it simply a wish. A minuscule golden nugget at the back of my mind that made me know I'd survive.

Just as my thoughts had crossed to the dark side, so had the sun. We were speeding down a narrow incline, driving through a thick gray cloud. "What's going on? I'm getting cold."

"Coastal fog," Dusty said, and reached across the console to switch on the heater. His windbreaker crackled. "Wait till next month when all this moves inland."

"That's why I'll need heat in July?"

He nodded. "Welcome to California."